BY ERNEST HEMINGWAY

HEMINGWAY LIBRARY EDITIONS
A Farewell to Arms

NOVELS
The Torrents of Spring
The Sun Also Rises
A Farewell to Arms
To Have and Have Not
For Whom the Bell Tolls
Across the River and into the Trees
The Old Man and the Sea
Islands in the Stream
The Garden of Eden
True at First Light

STORIES
In Our Time
Men Without Women
Winner Take Nothing
The Fifth Column and Four Stories of the Spanish Civil War
The Short Stories of Ernest Hemingway
The Snows of Kilimanjaro and Other Stories
The Nick Adams Stories
The Complete Short Stories of Ernest Hemingway

NONFICTION
Death in the Afternoon
Green Hills of Africa
Selected Letters 1917–1961
On Writing
A Moveable Feast
The Dangerous Summer
Dateline: Toronto
By-Line: Ernest Hemingway
A Moveable Feast: The Restored Edition

ANTHOLOGIES
Hemingway on Fishing
Hemingway on Hunting
Hemingway on War

HEMINGWAY ON FISHING

ERNEST HEMINGWAY

Edited and with an Introduction by
NICK LYONS

Foreword by Jack Hemingway

SCRIBNER
New York   London   Toronto   Sydney

This edition is for
Tony

Who goes out far, but never too far

SCRIBNER

1230 Avenue of the Americas
New York, NY 10020

First Scribner trade paperback edition 2004
This compilation first published in 2000 by The Lyons Press

SCRIBNER and design are trademarks of Macmillan Library Reference USA, Inc.,
used under license by Simon & Schuster, the publisher of this work.

For information about special discounts for bulk purchases,
please contact Simon & Schuster Special Sales:
1-800-456-6798 or business@simonandschuster.com

Manufactured in the United States of America

11   13   15   17   19   20   18   16   14   12

The Library of Congress Control Number: 00060872

ISBN-13: 978-1-58574-144-1
ISBN-10:   1-58574-144-2
ISBN-13: 978-0-7432-1918-1 (Pbk)
ISBN-10:   0-7432-1918-X (Pbk)

"What did I know best that I had not written about and lost? What did I know about truly and care for the most? There was no choice at all."
—*A Moveable Feast,*
about starting to write
"Big Two-Hearted River"

"To me heaven would be a bull ring with me holding two barrera seats and a trout stream outside that no one else was allowed to fish in. . . ."
—Letter to F. Scott Fitzgerald
Burguete, Spain, July 1, 1925

"The Gulf Stream is alive with fish."
—Letter to Maxwell Perkins
Key West, January 8, 1929

Contents

I

From up in Michigan to the Pyrenées

Table of Contents

II

Dispatches from Various Waters—The Soo to the Great Blue River

III

The Sea—Respite and Ultimate Challenge

A Brief Fisherman's Chronology

1899 July 21. Born in Oak Park, Illinois.

1900 Family buys "Windemere" on Walloon Lake, near Petoskey, Michigan, and EH begins to spend summers there for his entire childhood. Here EH learns to fish and shoot, chiefly under the influence of his father, Dr. Clarence Hemingway. The family still owns the property.

1903 Joins a local nature-study group started by his father, the Agassiz Club.

1916 June 10–21. Takes a steamer from Chicago to Onekama, Michigan, with Lewis Clarahan, and hikes to Petoskey— camping, fishing the Bear, the Manistee, the Boardman. There are good accounts of this in both Baker's biography and Johnson's articles (see Bibliography).

1919 September. Trip to Fox River, near Seney, on Michigan's Upper Peninsula, with Jock Pentecost and Al Walker. (See letter to Howell Jenkins dated September 15, 1919.)

1924 First trip to Irati River in Pyrenées, with Hadley Hemingway, the Birds, and the McAlmons. Writes "Big Two-Hearted River" in Paris.

1925   Returns to Irati River, now ruined by loggers. EH writes: "Fish killed, pools destroyed, dams broken."

1928   First visit to Key West, Florida. EH fishes on wharves and bridges, then boats, for a great variety of saltwater fish.

1930   First visit to Nordquist Ranch in Wyoming. Fishes Clark's Fork of the Yellowstone with great pleasure. Returns frequently until 1939.

1932   May. Fishes for marlin for first time. First visit to Cuba.

1933   Arnold Gingrich invites EH to write personal essays for *Esquire*.

1934   Buys the *Pilar* for $7,500, with money advanced by Gingrich; boat is diesel-powered 38-footer, from Wheeler Shipyard in Brooklyn, delivered FOB Miami. It has outriggers and can fish four rods.

1935   April. First trip to Bimini. Sees tuna and marlin attacked by sharks. Shoots himself in both legs with Colt pistol while firing at a shark. In May, EH catches first two tuna—350, 400 pounds—caught off Bimini.

1936   "On the Blue Water"—*Esquire* article includes story of a large fish caught by a commercial fisherman after a struggle lasting two days and nights, only to have the fish destroyed by sharks because it was too big to get into the boat.

1939   First visit to Sun Valley. Michael Lerner founds International Game Fish Association.

1940   December 28. EH buys La Finca Vigia, near Havana, Cuba.

1952   Publication of the novella *The Old Man and the Sea*, first in *Life* magazine, then as a book. Wins Pulitzer Prize.

1955   Wins Nobel Prize. In his acceptance speech, in absentia, he says: "It is because we have had such great writers in the past that a writer is driven out past where he can go, out to where no one can help him."

1955   August. Fishing out of Cojimar, Cuba, for marlin—to be used in footage for the movie of *The Old Man and the Sea*.

1956   Fishes for a month in Capo Blanco, Peru, for marlin footage for the movie.

1961   Health deteriorates and, on July 2, death in Idaho.

Foreword

In our family not only fly fishing but all sporting forms of fishing were a sort of religion. Being the oldest of Ernest Hemingway's three sons, I was the first to be converted to the fly rod and later to the fly. My father's conversion to the fly did not take place early. "Big Two-Hearted River" more than made that point, as did "The Last Good Country" and the trout fishing on the Irati in *The Sun Also Rises*. I remember that when we went to the L Bar T Ranch near Cook City in 1929 there was a wide selection of Hardy tackle and later, in Key West, there was a trunkful which I remember raiding. I felt less guilty about that when the whole trunk was lost by Railway Express on the way to Sun Valley in 1940.

The streams revisited in my father's mind in "Now I Lay Me," as a defense against the frightening prospect of possible death while asleep, bring back to me my years of depression as an unsuccessful young businessman with a heavy load of debt as well as my six months as a prisoner of war; during those times my only escape was imagining and reconstructing trout streams. I now have trouble remembering whether some of those rivers were real or just fantasies that were simply morbid creations of my imagination.

What is obvious, and what Nick Lyons has properly pointed out, is that fishing always was an important part of Papa's life and that, like all of his interests, he had a passionate desire to know as much as possible about it. He also had a need to share the pleasure fishing gave him. This made him a good teacher. I always felt his close friends and his wives were the prime beneficiaries of this trait.

While his fascination with the sea and with saltwater fishing started during his days as a reporter, Key West was where he first truly caught the bug. There are pictures of him fishing off the bridges on the old overseas highway. His friendships with Charles Thompson and the prototypical Key West conch, Captain Bra Saunders, saw him graduating to boat fishing for tarpon—the quarry of choice; he usually fished for them at night, using mullet for bait. There are fine pictures of him and John Dos Passos with tarpon caught that way and with other friends including Mike Strater and Waldo Peirce, both painters.

Their forays kept stretching farther afield and sailfish then became their favorite prey, along with dolphin and whatever good eating fish were caught trolling on the eighteen-mile ride out to Sand Key light; there the northern edge of the Gulf Stream offered up the best chances for billfish, and there Mike Strater gave Papa his first experience of watching a big marlin taken by sharks. Being a good host, he let Mike take the rod when the big fish struck. That fight was too long for Mike and at the end he pumped in a head and shoulders that weighed over five hundred pounds. The rest had been taken by sharks.

After he acquired his own boat, the *Pilar*, and no longer depended on Josie Russell's *Anita*, he started making the run to Havana for the white marlin run in April and May and began spending a month to six weeks in Bimini. In the process he became a good navigator and a boatman, and in Bimini he became one of the first fishermen to land a big bluefin tuna that was unscarred by sharks. His friendship with Mike Lerner and with some of the professional guides like Tommy Gifford added to his stature and expertise and led to the beginnings of the IGFA.

Is it any wonder that fishing continued to be an element of his fiction? How men fished as well as how they behaved under pressure of all kinds became a part of the "Hemingway code," as it was called by early critics. His feelings about hunting big game and bird shooting were similar to those he had for fishing; they called for a thorough knowledge of the prey as well as sympathy and even love for it. *The Old Man and the Sea*, his most widely read work, had all these elements as well as a triumph of the human spirit under tragic circumstances.

This selection of stories and excerpts is important because not only are they splendid reading, but they also illustrate how important fishing was in my father's life and in his literature—just as it has been in my own on a lesser scale.

—Jack Hemingway
Sun Valley, Idaho
May 2000

Acknowledgments

My warm thanks to Lamar Underwood and Howell Raines for a number of excellent suggestions on which pieces to include in this volume; to Robert M. Myers for additional suggestions, and for sending me a copy of the unusual memoir by Harald Greig; to Mark Weinstein for helpful typing and checking; to John H. N. Hemingway, fellow fly fisherman, for his warm Foreword and for answering various queries about his father's fishing life; to Michael Katakis, whose idea this book originally was and who facilitated in a number of ways its creation—and to John, Patrick, and Gregory Hemingway, whom he represents; to Charles Scribner, for wise and helpful counsel, and for helping to un-tangle various complicated rights questions; and to my editor Brando Skyhorse, for a whole variety of contributions to this book, including original research.

Introduction

1

"What did I know best that I had not written about and lost?" Hemingway asks in *A Moveable Feast*, as he recalls sitting in a corner of the Closerie des Lilas on the rue Notre-Dame-des-Champs in 1924 and beginning to write "Big Two-Hearted River." It was to be his longest story until then—some one hundred pages of handwritten manuscript. And the subject? "There was no choice at all."

There is a wonderful photograph of Hemingway, already a fisherman, with a broad-brimmed straw hat and a huge cane pole; it was taken on Horton's Creek, near Charlevoix, Michigan, when he was five years old. The creel over his shoulder looks large enough to carry one hundred brook trout. He fished first with his father, Dr. Clarence Hemingway, a keen sportsman, and with friends like Howell Jenkins, Lewis Clarahan, John Pentecost, Bill Smith, Al Walker, and others, on rivers and in lakes in northern Michigan, near the family's summer home on Walloon Lake, near Petoskey. There are photographs of him with pike, bass, and perch, but he seems from early on to have preferred moving water and trout. And always, as Carlos Baker notes in *Ernest Hemingway: A Life Story*, he "shared his father's determination to do things 'properly'"—a phrase and concept he carried with him into his love of hunting, his passion for bullfighting, his big-game fishing, and his fierce will to be a great writer.

In June of 1916, he took a steamer from Chicago to Onekama, Michigan, and trekked with Lewis Clarahan for ten days to Petoskey, keeping a detailed diary. They fished Bear Creek, the Manistee, the Boardman, and the Rapid, and the diary is early evidence of the care he devoted first to planning the trip, to recording what he saw, and to his skill at camping and fishing. Closer to Walloon Lake he had long fished little creeks like Schultz's and Horton's, often by lowering bait into the tangles of deadfalls and hoisting fish abruptly out onto the shore, and later the Black, the Sturgeon, and the Pigeon in the Pine Barrens southeast of Petoskey, usually with worms or grasshoppers, though occasionally with a fly. The McGinty was the first fly he had confidence in, and he never progressed as a fly fisherman much beyond wet-fly fishing. His son Jack says, in *Misadventures of a Fly Fisherman*, that his father liked best to fish a "two- or three-fly wet-fly rig through the riffles"— using a McGinty, a Coch-y-Bondhu, and a Woodcock Green and Yellow for the tail fly. Ninety percent of his fly fishing was done across and downstream with this team of flies, which sometimes included a Yellow Sally or a Royal Coachman. For a writer so beloved by fly fishermen, he shows little interest in this brand of fishing, makes a sharp comment about fly fishermen in "Big Two-Hearted River," and there's little evidence throughout his life that he released fish except if they were too small or he'd taken enough to eat; he claimed he hated to be photographed but there are thousands of photographs of him with gigantic dead fish.

Perhaps Hemingway found the esoterica of fly fishing—its fly-line sizes, Latin classifications of insects, and dozens of fly patterns and styles even then—to be too much like jargon. There is little in his language, in any of his writing about fishing, that is not self-explanatory, that cannot be read with full understanding by the alert general reader. We feel, in all of Hemingway's writing about fishing, that he has special knowledge, true authority—but we never feel he is writing in ways that exclude those without such special knowledge.

When Hemingway had finished writing for the day at the Closerie des Lilas, he "did not want to leave the river" and could still "see the trout in the pool, its surface pushing and swelling smooth against the resistance of the log-driven piles of the bridge." I have stood on that railroad bridge, just west of Seney, and though in the late 1990s I could not see one trout and the bottom had silted in, it is still a lovely piece of water and Hemingway caught it, and its tawny color, exactly right.

Hemingway's passion for fishing, the way it intertwines with his life as a writer and finally culminates in the novella *The Old Man and the Sea*, is the simple focus of this collection. The pilgrimage of his life is recorded in his stories and articles: from the solitary Nick to the public Papa, photographed with his big kills, from the stillness of trout fishing in northern Michigan, with its healing powers, to the unalloyed excitement and challenge of big-game fishing, where one is alone in other ways, locked in what approaches a life-and-death struggle. From the beginning, he loved sport, grew expert at the various aspects of the brand of fishing he chose to pursue, and always found a way to use it deftly in his writing. But beyond that, fishing, which kept him wedded to the natural world, was an important enough part of his life to affect all of his writing, and understanding its importance helps us understand a lot about the man and a lot about all of his writing, always his most stringent commitment.

Early photographs and letters, his 1916 diary of the trip to Walloon Lake, and then his first reportage for the *Toronto Star*, show that he fished regularly and with skill and success. Fishing was a source of sheer fun and adventure, a respite from the increasing complexity of his life, and a place to test his skills and to heal. Even early short stories like "Indian Camp"—still one of my favorites—. show how the details and language of fishing filtered naturally into his stories: the father sewing up the Indian woman, after performing a cesarian operation with a jackknife, with fishing gut, and the bass jumping at the end.

In "Big Two-Hearted River" he finds a connection between writing and fishing that was both new and remarkable, and here we can actually see how he transformed experience into art.

Hemingway had fished a river called the Fox, near the town of Seney on Michigan's Upper Peninsula, with his friends Al Walker and Jock Pentecost, in September 1919, after he had returned from Red Cross ambulance service in Italy during the First World War. He had been wounded by a mortar shell and machine-gun fire, and had been hospitalized in Milan with hundreds of pieces of shrapnel in his lower body. The trip he took with his friends, reported in a letter to Howell Jenkins, was scarcely the brooding, meditative, mysterious journey he describes in his story, but rather one filled with the excitement and high jinks of young men off in the woods, catching and boasting about having taken more than two hundred wild brook trout—some up to 2-1/2 pounds—camping out, shooting at deer with a .22. When he began to write "Big Two-Hearted River" in Paris, he started: "We got off the train at Seney." "Jock" and "Al" are characters in that first, tentative beginning, and "They all three" stand and look at the burned-out town of Seney; Al says: "This was the toughest town in Michigan." Then he changed the opening to "They got off the train at Seney"; and then, after three pages, he abandoned the story. Only when he begins, "The train went on up the track out of sight" and eliminates his two friends does the actual event begin to fade, in deference to the fictional event. He is already there; generalities like "toughest" are replaced by details like the "thirteen saloons that had once lined the streets of Seney"; details extraneous to the theme of the story (about the burned-out town, for example) are trimmed; and the country and his fishing and his inner life become the true center of the story.

The sight of the trout, clearly after some period of time away from trout rivers, leads him to feel "all the old feeling." He relishes the long and demanding trip upriver; and as he carefully and "properly" makes his camp, cooks his food, and the next day begins to fish, the underlying, unspoken tension is that he is, with deliberation, reconstructing a life. Each gesture—from rigging his tackle, collecting grasshoppers, putting them on the hook to catching and putting a few fish into his canvas fish sack—is performed with the same ritual care. We know nothing other than his actions about what might have precipitated this deliberateness. We know that he does not want to "rush" his sensations. We know he wants to master his feelings. Much later, in "The Art of the Short Story," Hemingway said that he had made up the entire story, that "there were many Indians in the story, just as the war was in the story, and none of the Indians nor the war appeared." The real trip has vanished.

Such writing depends first upon a capacity to "get the feeling of the actual life across," as he wrote to his father just before the story was to appear in *The Transatlantic Review*, "not to just depict life—or criticize it—but to actually make it alive. So that when you have read something by me you actually experience the thing." This is of course what happens most distinctly in "Big Two-Hearted River." We are very much there with the young man, participating in the fishing trip that is so much more than a fishing trip. The story has the feel of the river; it registers the young man's affection for the pursuit of trout; it represents by indirection a disciplined search for control by Nick, a control that he cannot yet extend to fishing in the swamp. Throughout, he uses images and events that ascend into metaphor. The sharks that devour Santiago's great marlin are real sharks and they suggest a hundred forces in a life that might attack and destroy one's accomplishments; the burned-out town of Seney suggests burned-out emotions; and the swamp, which I've seen, is still a very real danger. He will save that for another day.

The story is seminal to any understanding of Hemingway, both as a fisherman and as an artist. In it he finds a sure way to use the special, even expert, knowledge he has acquired about angling, which he will carry to *Islands in the Stream* and *The Old Man and the Sea*, and into his fiction about bullfighting and hunting. He learns, as he writes to Gertrude Stein, to "do" the country like Cézanne—as if seeing it for the first time, inventing tree and shadow, without sentimentality or rhetoric or "tricks" that will "go bad afterward," not mannered, not describing but reducing the imagery to an elemental world that we can enter and cannot leave, all of its forms pointing to one effect, direct, spare, elusive, as clear and mysterious as a spring creek, as clear today as it was in 1925—and just as rare.

2

Hemingway found saltwater fishing in 1928 when John Dos Passos introduced him to Key West and he soon moved there with his second wife, Pauline Pfeiffer. They bought the house at 907 Whitehead Street that is now a Hemingway museum, in 1931.

While in Europe, in the 1920s, he had fished for trout in the Black Forest and the Pyrenées and had written articles about the good places he had found; he shared his enthusiasm with his father—fishing remained their firmest connection—and he also shared his disappointment that the Irati, which he had fished with such pleasure in 1924, had been ruined by logging and the electric companies. But except for occasional trips to Wyoming, Montana, and Idaho, his primary fishing thereafter was all in salt water.

At first he fished mostly from the piers and bridges, catching that great grab bag of strong fish from the ocean that dwarfed in size the trout he'd been used to taking—grouper, jacks, snapper, and tarpon. Even later, after he had become fascinated by boats and bigger game, Kip Farrington reports: "Ernest was as happy with the catching of a five-pound fish as with catching a 400-pounder, and many times he would go bottom fishing in the evenings and bone-fishing after a long day in the Gulf Stream . . ." He even ends one of his Cuban Letters for *Esquire* magazine with these words: "I would like to go back to fishing for fun and take a day off and go snapper fishing over by the concrete ship."

But boats gave him a much broader world, a much larger playing field with discrete challenges, a place to test brawn and courage and endurance. He fished in the Marquesas and the Dry Tortugas, and now he grew to love to troll, especially rigged baits, for king-fish, wahoo, barracuda, and eventually sailfish, tuna, and marlin. He had a will to master, to win, and since he was a natural competitor—a boxer, hunter, lover of fighting cocks, and competition of all sorts—and since he loved both the physical risk and the life-and-death struggle, it was natural that he gravitated more toward big-game fishing and found in it an ultimate challenge. A fight with a truly big fish was a test of self. *"Il faut (d'abord) durer"* he liked to say, about life and a fight with some mammoth fish—one must, above all, endure.

After he bought the *Pilar* in 1935, in his fascination with the Gulf Stream and its great denizens, Hemingway studied sharks and marlin with the care and zeal of a naturalist. Beginning in 1928, he often fished with Carlos Gutierrez, a commercial fisherman from Cojimar, the small picturesque town ten miles east of Havana—and the home of Santiago, his central figure in *The Old Man and the Sea*. And he invited Charles M. B. Cadwalader, Director of the Academy of Natural Sciences in Philadelphia, and Henry Fowler, Chief Ichthyologist at the Academy, to study marlin with him. Together they caught, measured, and dissected fish, and Hemingway kept extensive day-log journals, amounting to many hundreds of pages, about what they learned. He also fished with Dr. Perry W. Gilbert, a shark expert and head of the Mote Laboratory in Sarasota, Florida. In the journals, he records the people on board, barometer readings, the amount of gas put in, the cost of the gas, the number of commercially caught marlin in the market (and their sizes), the time out, and the weather; there are detailed notations on what fish they caught, how, at what time, their sizes, time of capture, weather conditions, information about what sharks they saw, seeds for later writing, and what they had for dinner. He took careful notes on sharks and cataloged the principal kinds found in Cuban waters, their size range, and whether or not they were man-eaters, and if they would respond to shark repellents.

He had lost most of his first tuna and marlin to sharks off Bimini and devised two methods of dealing with them. He told Kip Farrington that it was necessary to bring fish in quickly, before sharks could locate them, and that for this you must "convince" all big fish, and to do this you must be willing to suffer. And he began to carry a Thompson submachine gun on board the *Pilar,* which he used with glee to kill sharks. Aggressive fishing became his hallmark.

Within six years of the time he began to fish for big game in the Gulf Stream, out of Key West, then Bimini, then Havana, he was viewed by many of the best big-game fishermen in the world—Farrington, Michael Lerner, Van Campen Heilner—as their peer and as a great innovator. He was asked to write the marlin section for Eugene V. Connett's *American Big Game Fishing* and the chapter on Cuban fishing for *Game Fish of the World,* as well as more fugitive but highly authoritative articles for *Esquire* and *Look.* He took a keen interest in the technology and ethics of big-game sport fishing and served on the governing board of the International Game Fish Association, founded by Michael Lerner in 1940. In his introduction to Kip Farrington's book *Atlantic Game Fishing,* he wrote that "The development of big-game angling was retarded for many years by inadequate tackle," but is now "in danger of being completely ruined as a sport through development of too efficient tackle." It was the balance, of course, that kept the challenge worth taking on.

Dozens of people fished with Hemingway in those years—Dos Passos, his editor Maxwell Perkins, Arnold Gingrich (who wrote a sharp, amusing chapter in *The Well-Tempered Angler* called "Horsing Them in with Hemingway"), Ben Finney, Grant and Jane Mason, the painters Waldo Peirce and Mike Strater, H. L. Woodward, a local contemporary Charles Thompson, and a host of others. Their opinions of him vary sharply, from overt adulation, even hagiography, to appreciation and affection, to claims that he was immensely exciting, a bully, a show-off, and a bad loser, and (in Gingrich's words) "more fun to fish with when there were fewer people aboard for him to show off for." No one disputes his prowess as a fisherman—or a writer.

Writing was always foremost in his mind, and only a bit of it, of course, was actually about fishing. For a while he entertained the idea of doing a book of "Sportsman's Sketches," deriving roughly from Turgenev's—and there is a manuscript of some fourteen typewritten pages in which he makes a start on such a project. His day-log journals were often the first step in a journey that leads to his journalistic articles or less successful books like *To Have and Have Not*, or to *Islands in the Stream* and *The Old Man and the Sea*. Sometimes, when working on a major novel, he would back out of commitments to fish. In 1939 Thomas Shevlin invited him to fish on the U.S. Tuna Team in Nova Scotia. Hemingway had accepted but on April 4 he wrote Shevlin: "Any guy who says he will do a thing and then rats out is a shit . . . I can't be a sportsman and write a novel at the same time. If I blow up on it (but I can't you see. That's the one thing you can't envisage. It's like quitting on a fish) I will wire you and fly over . . ." He writes to Marjorie Kinnan Rawlings that sport is for the times "in between" writing, "when you can't do it."

With occasional trips to Wyoming and then Sun Valley, where he hunted and fished for trout, Hemingway remained a passionate big-game fisherman until his late fifties. He was even asked to fish for a month in Capo Blanca, Peru, to capture a huge black marlin for the film of *The Old Man and the Sea*. He did not finally catch the fish they needed, found the entire trip upsetting, and thought Spencer Tracy a "very fat, rich, and old" Santiago.

3

A. E. Hotchner says that Hemingway once told him, concerning psychoanalysis, that he spent a hell of a lot of time killing animals and fish so he wouldn't kill himself. If he said it, and was reasonably sober and not posturing, it's one of those throwaway lines, true only north by northwest, feeding the stereotype.

Clearly Hemingway loved the visceral experience of fishing, from planning a trip, a campaign, an expedition, to arranging his gear and equipment, to the chase itself and the natural world in which it took place. He was fascinated with the technology and mechanics of fishing—from collecting and rigging bait for trout fishing to the advanced rods and reels he used for marlin. He loved to sit lazily on a dock and to troll for big game, and he loved the ache in his arms and the satisfaction of a thing well done. The naturalist in him loved the need to understand a mysterious quarry and its watery world. He loved, in his words, the "great pleasure of being on the sea, in the unknown wild suddenness of a great fish." This was man's play, fishing, and he enjoyed it for the sheer love of the game and he clearly loved it for the competition, against others, against oneself, against the fish. He loved the respite it brought from the weight of writing and the complexity of human relations. I sometimes think he fished because he loved to write about it—and he wrote about it superbly well.

In June 1961, less than a month before he shot himself, Hemingway wrote to his publisher, Charles Scribner, Jr., from the Mayo Clinic in Rochester, Minnesota, to thank him for a mimeographed guide to the waters of the Yellowstone area by H. G. Wellington. He asked that a copy be sent to Jack, "who is about as advanced a fisherman as Herbert Wellington"; he had started Jack on those waters years earlier and was obviously proud of his son's abiding interest in fishing. A few days later, he noted in a letter to young Frederick G. Saviers that he "saw some good bass jump in the river"; he'd never known anything about the upper Mississippi and found it beautiful country.

And then, his body torn with pain and his brain out of whack, unable to fish or hunt, or especially to write, he went to Sun Valley and ended matters.

4

There are three kinds of writing in the main sections of this book—short stories, sections from larger works (both fiction and nonfiction), and journalism.

I have begun with the most successful of Hemingway's stories centered on fishing, "Big Two-Hearted River," because it contains within it all of the elements of his love for fishing and the best of his prose. That its real subject lies somewhere within Nick's psyche, and that finally it is not a "fishing story" at all, only suggests something of why it has had such broad appeal.

A good number of the Nick Adams stories have references to fishing and some have whole sections devoted to it, but I have only chosen "The End of Something," and an excerpt from the rambling "The Last Good Country," and the haunting story "Now I Lay Me." None of these are "fishing stories" either but they use fishing well. All occur, chronologically, before "Big Two-Hearted River," and "Now I Lay Me"—the strongest of the others—shows how Nick, wounded and unable to sleep for fear of dying, creates a stay against his fears by fishing in his half-dreams rivers he had fished in his youth and knew well.

The section on fishing in the Seine provides a brief change of pace between the heavy undercurrents of the two dark stories to the bright trip to the Irati in *The Sun Also Rises*. The chapters from the novel suffer, of course, by being separated from the action in Pamplona and thereafter—for they are the simple foil against which the tense events of the fiesta are held, and here they have nothing upon which to reflect. That trip, though, moving from the oppressive heat and discomfort of Pamplona to the quiet, cool, and pastoral setting of Burguete, becomes almost a set piece—lyrical, full of amiable fun, showing the happy respite trout fishing could become in Hemingway's scheme.

The opening of the third section, the beginning of that strange book *The Garden of Eden*, also stands in sharp contrast to the increasingly complex gender explorations of the book itself. A big sea bass is caught is all, and then it is eaten, and it is simple fun for the couple whose life together soon begins to unravel.

In the second section I have collected a representative group of articles and essays on fishing, from his early dispatches for the *Toronto Star* through his Cuban Letters for *Esquire* and on to several late articles for *Holiday* and *Look*. I have had to make a few hard choices here. I preferred "Marlin off the Morro," a Cuban Letter, to the fuller, expanded version of the piece, "Marlin off Cuba," from Eugene V. Connett's *American Game Fishing*, chiefly because (for this book) it seemed more direct, more intimate, more spontaneous. I have not included several introductions he wrote, to S. Kip Farrington's *Atlantic Game Fishing* (though this shows his commitment to ethics and technology in big-game fishing), Van Campen Heilner's *Salt Water Fishing*, and Charles Ritz's *A Fly Fisher's Life*. Though there is some repetition in this section, it shows what a fine and interesting journalist Hemingway could be, how solid a researcher, with an increasing fascination for every aspect of life on the Gulf Stream. It also shows, along with some of his letters and journals, how important this kind of writing could be to his major work, in particular the story and kind of knowledge required for *The Old Man and the Sea*.

The final section begins with the sea-bass incident and rushes into the boy David's great and extended fight in *Islands in the Stream*, and then on to the elemental *The Old Man and the Sea*. I debated including the interesting section in *To Have and Have Not* centered on Johnson's fishing out of Morgan's boat, and the loss of Morgan's rig, but it just did not seem to add much to a book that was becoming quite full.

Introduction

I did not feel comfortable excerpting the tight novella; surely this story ought to be read in its entirety. I can only hope that the section here will send readers to the story itself, still Hemingway's most popular book.

This is a full book, and one that I think shows—for fishermen and general readers—the full range of Hemingway's passion for fishing, and the immense skill with which he wrote about this sport he loved all of his life.

—Nick Lyons
New York City
June 2000

I

From up in Michigan to the Pyrenées

Big Two-Hearted River

Part I

The train went on up the track out of sight, around one of the hills of burnt timber. Nick sat down on the bundle of canvas and bedding the baggage man had pitched out of the door of the baggage car. There was no town, nothing but the rails and the burned-over country. The thirteen saloons that had lined the one street of Seney had not left a trace. The foundations of the Mansion House hotel stuck up above the ground. The stone was chipped and split by the fire. It was all that was left of the town of Seney. Even the surface had been burned off the ground.

Nick looked at the burned-over stretch of hillside, where he had expected to find the scattered houses of the town and then walked down the railroad track to the bridge over the river. The river was there. It swirled against the log spiles of the bridge. Nick looked down into the clear, brown water, colored from the pebbly bottom, and watched the trout keeping themselves steady in the current with wavering fins. As he watched them they changed their positions by quick angles, only to hold steady in the fast water again. Nick watched them a long time.

He watched them holding themselves with their noses into the current, many trout in deep, fast moving water, slightly distorted as he watched far down through the glassy convex surface of the pool, its surface pushing and swelling smooth against the resistance of the log-driven piles of the bridge. At the bottom of the pool were the big trout. Nick did not see them at first. Then he saw them at the bottom of the pool, big trout looking to hold themselves on the gravel bottom in a varying mist of gravel and sand, raised in spurts by the current.

Nick looked down into the pool from the bridge. It was a hot day. A kingfisher flew up the stream. It was a long time since Nick had looked into a stream and seen trout. They were very satisfactory. As the shadow of the kingfisher moved up the stream, a big trout shot upstream in a long angle, only his shadow marking the angle, then lost his shadow as he came through the surface of the water, caught the sun, and then, as he went back into the stream under the surface, his shadow seemed to float down the stream with the current, unresisting, to his post under the bridge where he tightened facing up into the current.

Nick's heart tightened as the trout moved. He felt all the old feeling.

He turned and looked down the stream. It stretched away, pebbly-bottomed with shallows and big boulders and a deep pool as it curved away around the foot of a bluff.

Nick walked back up the ties to where his pack lay in the cinders beside the railway track. He was happy. He adjusted the pack harness around the bundle, pulling straps tight, slung the pack on his back, got his arms through the shoulder straps and took some of the pull off his shoulders by leaning his forehead against the wide band of the tump-line. Still, it was too heavy. It was much too heavy. He had his leather rod-case in his hand and leaning forward to keep the weight of the pack high on his shoulders he walked along the road that paralleled the railway track, leaving the burned town behind in the heat, and then turned off around a hill with a high, fire-scarred hill on either side onto a road that went back into the country. He walked along the road feeling the ache from the pull of the heavy pack. The road climbed steadily. It was hard work walking up-hill. His muscles ached and the day was hot, but Nick felt happy. He felt he had left everything behind, the need for thinking, the need to write, other needs. It was all back of him.

From the time he had gotten down off the train and the baggage man had thrown his pack out of the open car door things had been different. Seney was burned, the country was burned over and changed, but it did not matter. It could not all be burned. He knew that. He hiked along the road, sweating in the sun, climbing to cross the range of hills that separate the railway from the pine plains.

The road ran on, dipping occasionally, but always climbing. Nick went on up. Finally the road after going parallel to the burnt hillside reached the top. Nick leaned back against a stump and slipped out of the pack harness. Ahead of him, as far as he could see, was the pine plain. The burned country stopped off at the left with the range of hills. On ahead islands of dark pine trees rose out of the plain. Far off to the left was the line of the river. Nick followed it with his eye and caught glints of the water in the sun.

There was nothing but the pine plain ahead of him, until the far blue hills that marked the Lake Superior height of land. He could hardly see them, faint and far away in the heat-light over the plain. If he looked too steadily they were gone. But if he only half-looked they were there, the far-off hills of the height of land.

Nick sat down against the charred stump and smoked a cigarette. His pack balanced on the top of the stump, harness holding ready, a hollow molded in it from his back. Nick sat smoking, looking out over the country. He did not need to get his map out. He knew where he was from the position of the river.

As he smoked, his legs stretched out in front of him, he noticed a grasshopper walk along the ground and up onto his woolen sock. The grasshopper was black. As he had walked along the road, climbing, he had started many grasshoppers from the dust. They were all black. They were not the big grasshoppers with yellow and black or red and black wings whirring out from their black wing sheathing as they fly up. These were just ordinary hoppers, but all a sooty black in color. Nick had wondered about them as he walked, without really thinking about them. Now, as he watched the black hopper that was nibbling at the wool of his sock with its fourway lip, he realized that they had all turned black from living in the burned-over land. He realized that the fire must have come the year before, but the grasshoppers were all black now. He wondered how long they would stay that way.

Carefully he reached his hand down and took hold of the hopper by the wings. He turned him up, all his legs walking in the air, and looked at his jointed belly. Yes, it was black too, iridescent where the back and head were dusty.

"Go on, hopper," Nick said, speaking out loud for the first time. "Fly away somewhere."

He tossed the grasshopper up into the air and watched him sail away to a charcoal stump across the road.

Nick stood up. He leaned his back against the weight of his pack where it rested upright on the stump and got his arms through the shoulder straps. He stood with the pack on his back on the brow of the hill looking out across the country, toward the distant river and then struck down the hillside away from the road. Underfoot the ground was good walking. Two hundred yards down the hillside the fire line stopped. Then it was sweet fern, growing ankle high, to walk through, and clumps of jack pines; a long undulating country with frequent rises and descents, sandy underfoot and the country alive again.

Nick kept his direction by the sun. He knew where he wanted to strike the river and he kept on through the pine plain, mounting small rises to see other rises ahead of him and sometimes from the top of a rise a great solid island of pines off to his right or his left. He broke off some sprigs of the heathery sweet fern, and put them under his pack straps. The chafing crushed it and he smelled it as he walked.

He was tired and very hot, walking across the uneven, shadeless pine plain. At any time he knew he could strike the river by turning off to his left. It could not be more than a mile away. But he kept on toward the north to hit the river as far upstream as he could go in one day's walking.

For some time as he walked Nick had been in sight of one of the big islands of pine standing out above the rolling high ground he was crossing. He dipped down and then as he came slowly up to the crest of the bridge he turned and made toward the pine trees.

There was no underbrush in the island of pine trees. The trunks of the trees went straight up or slanted toward each other. The trunks were straight and brown without branches. The branches were high above. Some interlocked to make a solid shadow on the brown forest floor. Around the grove of trees was a bare space. It was brown and soft underfoot as Nick walked on it. This was the overlapping of the pine needle floor, extending out beyond the width of the high branches. The trees had grown tall and the branches moved high, leaving in the sun this bare space they had once covered with shadow. Sharp at the edge of this extension of the forest floor commenced the sweet fern.

Nick slipped off his pack and lay down in the shade. He lay on his back and looked up into the pine trees. His neck and back and the small of his back rested as he stretched. The earth felt good against his back. He looked up at the sky, through the branches, and then shut his eyes. He opened them and looked up again. There was a wind high up in the branches. He shut this eyes again and went to sleep.

Nick woke stiff and cramped. The sun was nearly down. His pack was heavy and the straps painful as he lifted it on. He leaned over with the pack on and picked up the leather rod-case and started out from the pine trees across the sweet fern swale, toward the river. He knew it could not be more than a mile.

He came down a hillside covered with stumps into a meadow. At the edge of the meadow flowed the river. Nick was glad to get to the river. He walked upstream through the meadow. His trousers were soaked with the dew as he walked. After the hot day, the dew had come quickly and heavily. The river made no sound. It was too fast and smooth. At the edge of the meadow, before he mounted to a piece of high ground to make camp, Nick looked down the river at the trout rising. They were rising to insects come from the swamp on the other side of the stream when the sun went down. The trout jumped out of water to take them. While Nick walked through the little stretch of meadow alongside the stream, trout had jumped high out of water. Now as he looked down the river, the insects must be settling on the surface, for the trout were feeding steadily all down the stream. As far down the long stretch as he could see, the trout were rising, making circles all down the surface of the water, as though it were starting to rain.

The ground rose, wooded and sandy, to overlook the meadow, the stretch of river and the swamp. Nick dropped his pack and rod-case and looked for a level piece of ground. He was very hungry and he wanted to make his camp before he cooked. Between two jack pines, the ground was quite level. He took the ax out of the pack and chopped out two projecting roots. That leveled a piece of ground large enough to sleep on. He smoothed out the sandy soil with his hand and pulled all the sweet fern bushes by their roots. His hands smelled good from the sweet fern. He smoothed the uprooted earth. He did not want anything making lumps under the blankets. When he had the ground smooth, he spread his three blankets. One he folded double, next to the ground. The other two he spread on top.

With the ax he slit off a bright slab of pine from one of the stumps and split it into pegs for the tent. He wanted them long and solid to hold in the ground. With the tent unpacked and spread on the ground, the pack, leaning against a jackpine, looked much smaller. Nick tied the rope that served the tent for a ridge-pole to the trunk of one of the pine trees and pulled the tent up off the ground with the other end of the rope and tied it to the other pine. The tent hung on the rope like a canvas blanket on a clothesline. Nick poked a pole he had cut up under the back peak of the canvas and then made it a tent by pegging out the sides. He pegged the sides out taut and drove the pegs deep, hitting them down into the ground with the flat of the ax until the rope loops were buried and the canvas was drum tight.

Across the open mouth of the tent Nick fixed cheesecloth to keep out mosquitoes. He crawled inside under the mosquito bar with various things from the pack to put at the head of the bed under the slant of the canvas. Inside the tent the light came through the brown canvas. It smelled pleasantly of canvas. Already there was something mysterious and homelike. Nick was happy as he crawled inside the tent. He had not been unhappy all day. This was different though. Now things were done. There had been this to do. Now it was done. It had been a hard trip. He was very tired. That was done. He had made his camp. He was settled. Nothing could touch him. It was a good place to camp. He was there, in the good place. He was in his home where he had made it. Now he was hungry.

He came out, crawling under the cheesecloth. It was quite dark outside. It was lighter in the tent.

Nick went over the pack and found, with his fingers, a long nail in a paper sack of nails, in the bottom of the pack. He drove it into the pine tree, holding it close and hitting it gently with the flat of the ax. He hung the pack up on the nail. All his supplies were in the pack. They were off the ground and sheltered now.

Nick was hungry. He did not believe he had ever been hungrier. He opened and emptied a can of pork and beans and a can of spaghetti into the frying pan.

"I've got a right to eat this kind of stuff, if I'm willing to carry it," Nick said. His voice sounded strange in the darkening woods. He did not speak again.

He started a fire with some chunks of pine he got with the ax from a stump. Over the fire he stuck a wire grill, pushing the four legs down into the ground with his boot. Nick put the frying pan on the grill over the flames. He was hungrier. The beans and spaghetti warmed. Nick stirred them and mixed them together. They began to bubble, making little bubbles that rose with difficulty to the surface. There was a good smell. Nick got out a bottle of tomato catchup and cut four slices of bread. The little bubbles were coming faster now. Nick sat down beside the fire and lifted the frying pan off. He poured about half the contents out into the tin plate. It spread slowly on the plate. Nick knew it was too hot. He poured on some tomato catchup. He knew the beans and spaghetti were still too hot. He looked at the fire, then at the tent, he was not going to spoil it all by burning his tongue. For years he had never enjoyed fried bananas because he had never been able to wait for them to cool. His tongue was very sensitive. He was very hungry. Across the river in the swamp, in the almost dark, he saw a mist rising. He looked at the tent once more. All right. He took a full spoonful from the plate.

"Chrise," Nick said, "Geezus, Chrise," he said happily.

He ate the whole plateful before he remembered the bread. Nick finished the second plateful with the bread, mopping the plate shiny. He had not eaten since a cup of coffee and a ham sandwich in the station restaurant at St. Ignace. It had been a very fine experience. He had been that hungry before, but had not been able to satisfy it. He could have made camp hours before if he had wanted to. There were plenty of good places to camp on the river. But this was good.

Nick tucked two big chips of pine under the grill. The fire flared up. He had forgotten to get water for the coffee. Out of the pack he got a folding canvas bucket and walked down the hill, across the edge of the meadow, to the stream. The other bank was in the white mist. The grass was wet and cold as he knelt on the bank and dipped the canvas bucket into the stream. It bellied and pulled hard in the current. The water was ice cold. Nick rinsed the bucket and carried it full up to the camp. Up away from the stream it was not so cold.

Nick drove another big nail and hung up the bucket full of water. He dipped the coffee pot half full, put some more chips under the grill onto the fire and put the pot on. He could not remember which way he made coffee. He could remember an argument about it with Hopkins, but not which side he had taken. He decided to bring it to a boil. He remembered now that was Hopkins's way. He had once argued about everything with Hopkins. While he waited for the coffee to boil, he opened a small can of apricots. He liked to open cans. He emptied the can of apricots out into a tin cup. While he watched the coffee on the fire, he drank the juice syrup of the apricots, carefully at first to keep from spilling, then meditatively, sucking the apricots down. They were better than fresh apricots.

The coffee boiled as he watched. The lid came up and coffee and grounds ran down the side of the pot. Nick took it off the grill. It was a triumph for Hopkins. He put sugar in the empty apricot cup and poured some of the coffee out to cool. It was too hot to pour and he used his hat to hold the handle of the coffee pot. He would not let it steep in the pot at all. Not the first cup. It should be straight Hopkins all the way. Hop deserved that. He was a very serious coffee drinker. He was the most serious man Nick had ever known. Not heavy, serious. That was a long time ago. Hopkins spoke without moving his lips. He had played polo. He made millions of dollars in Texas. He had borrowed carfare to go to Chicago, when the wire came that his first big well had come in. He could have wired for money. That would have been too slow. They called Hop's girl the Blonde Venus. Hop did not mind because she was not his real girl. Hopkins said very confidently that none of them would make fun of his real girl. He was right. Hopkins went away when the telegram came. That was on the Black River. It took eight days for the telegram to reach him. Hopkins gave away his .22 caliber Colt automatic pistol to Nick. He gave his camera to Bill. It was to remember him always by. They were all going fishing again next summer. The Hop Head was rich. He would get a yacht and they would all cruise along the north shore of Lake Superior. He was excited but serious. They said good-bye and all felt bad. It broke up the trip. They never saw Hopkins again. That was a long time ago on the Black River.

Nick drank the coffee, the coffee according to Hopkins. The coffee was bitter. Nick laughed. It made a good ending to the story. His mind was starting to work. He knew he could choke it because he was tired enough. He spilled the coffee out of the pot and shook the grounds loose into the fire. He lit a cigarette and went inside the tent. He took off his shoes and trousers, sitting on the blankets, rolled the shoes up inside the trousers for a pillow and got in between the blankets.

Out through the front of the tent he watched the glow of the fire, when the night wind blew on it. It was a quiet night. The swamp was perfectly quiet. Nick stretched under the blanket comfortably. A mosquito hummed close to his ear. Nick sat up and lit a match. The mosquito was on the canvas, over his head. Nick moved the match quickly up to it. The mosquito made a satisfactory hiss in the flame. The match went out. Nick lay down again under the blanket. He turned on his side and shut his eyes. He was sleepy. He felt sleep coming. He curled up under the blanket and went to sleep.

Big Two-Hearted River

Part II

In the morning the sun was up and the tent was starting to get hot. Nick crawled out under the mosquito netting stretched across the mouth of the tent, to look at the morning. The grass was wet on his hands as he came out. He held his trousers and his shoes in his hands. The sun was just up over the hill. There was the meadow, the river and the swamp. There were birch trees in the green of the swamp on the other side of the river.

The river was clear and smoothly fast in the early morning. Down about two hundred yards were three logs all the way across the stream. They made the water smooth and deep above them. As Nick watched, a mink crossed the river on the logs and went into the swamp. Nick was excited. He was excited by the early morning and the river. He was really too hurried to eat breakfast, but he knew he must. He built a little fire and put on the coffee pot.

While the water was heating in the pot he took an empty bottle and went down over the edge of the high ground to the meadow. The meadow was wet with dew and Nick wanted to catch grasshoppers for bait before the sun dried the grass. He found plenty of good grasshoppers. They were at the base of the grass stems. Sometimes they clung to a grass stem. They were cold and wet with the dew, and could not jump until the sun warmed them. Nick picked them up, taking only the medium-sized brown ones, and put them into the bottle. He turned over a log and just under the shelter of the edge were several hundred hoppers. It was a grasshopper lodging house. Nick put about fifty of the medium browns into the bottle. While he was picking up the hoppers the others warmed in the sun and commenced to hop away. They flew when they hopped. At first they made one flight and stayed stiff when they landed, as though they were dead.

Nick knew that by the time he was through with breakfast they would be as lively as ever. Without dew in the grass it would take him all day to catch a bottle full of good grasshoppers and he would have to crush many of them, slamming at them with his hat. He washed his hands at the stream. He was excited to be near it. Then he walked up to the tent. The hoppers were already jumping stiffly in the grass. In the bottle, warmed by the sun, they were jumping in a mass. Nick put in a pine stick as a cork. It plugged the mouth of the bottle enough, so the hoppers could not get out and left plenty of air passage.

He had rolled the log back and knew he could get grasshoppers there every morning.

Nick laid the bottle full of jumping grasshoppers against a pine trunk. Rapidly he mixed some buckwheat flour with water and stirred it smooth, one cup of flour, one cup of water. He put a handful of coffee in the pot and dipped a lump of grease out of a can and slid it sputtering across the hot skillet. On the smoking skillet he poured smoothly the buckwheat batter. It spread like lava, the grease spitting sharply. Around the edges the buckwheat cake began to firm, then brown, then crisp. The surface was bubbling slowly to porousness. Nick pushed under the browned under surface with a fresh pine chip. He shook the skillet sideways and the cake was loose on the surface. I won't try and flop it, he thought. He slid the chip of clean wood all the way under the cake, and flopped it over onto its face. It sputtered in the pan.

When it was cooked Nick regreased the skillet. He used all the batter. It made another big flapjack and one smaller one.

Nick ate a big flapjack and a smaller one, covered with apple butter. He put apple butter on the third cake, folded it over twice, wrapped it in oiled paper and put it in his shirt pocket. He put the apple butter jar back in the pack and cut bread for two sandwiches.

In the pack he found a big onion. He sliced it in two and peeled the silky outer skin. Then he cut one half into slices and made onion sandwiches. He wrapped them in oiled paper and buttoned them in the other pocket of his khaki shirt. He turned the skillet upside down on the grill, drank the coffee, sweetened and yellow brown with the condensed milk in it, and tidied up the camp. It was a good camp.

Nick took his fly rod out of the leather rod-case, jointed it, and shoved the rod-case back into the tent. He put on the reel and threaded the line through the guides. He had to hold it from hand to hand, as he threaded it, or it would slip back through its own weight. It was a heavy, double tapered fly line. Nick had paid eight dollars for it a long time ago. It was made heavy to lift back in the air and come forward flat and heavy and straight to make it possible to cast a fly which has no weight. Nick opened the aluminum leader box. The leaders were coiled between the damp flannel pads. Nick had wet the pads at the water cooler on the train up to St. Ignace. In the damp pads the gut leaders had softened and Nick unrolled one and tied it by a loop at the end to the heavy fly line. He fastened a hook on the end of the leader. It was a small hook; very thin and springy.

Nick took it from his hook book, sitting with the rod across his lap. He tested the knot and the spring of the rod by pulling the line taut. It was a good feeling. He was careful not to let the hook bite into his finger.

He started down to the stream, hooking his rod, the bottle of grasshoppers hung from his neck by a thong tied in half hitches around the neck of the bottle. His landing net hung by a hook from his belt. Over his shoulder was a long flour sack tied at each corner into an ear. The cord went over his shoulder. The sack flapped against his legs.

Nick felt awkward and professionally happy with all his equipment hanging from him. The grasshopper bottle swung against his chest. In his shirt the breast pockets bulged against him with the lunch and his fly book.

He stepped into the stream. It was a shock. His trousers clung tight to his legs. His shoes felt the gravel. The water was a rising cold shock.

Rushing, the current sucked against his legs. Where he stepped in, the water was over his knees. He waded with the current. The gravel slid under his shoes. He looked down at the swirl of water below each leg and tipped up the bottle to get a grasshopper.

The first grasshopper gave a jump in the neck of the bottle and went out into the water. He was sucked under in the whirl by Nick's right leg and came to the surface a little way down stream. He floated rapidly, kicking. In a quick circle, breaking the smooth surface of the water, he disappeared. A trout had taken him.

Another hopper poked his face out of the bottle. His antennae wavered. He was getting his front legs out of the bottle to jump. Nick took him by the head and held him while he threaded the slim hook under his chin, down through his thorax and into the last segments of his abdomen. The grasshopper took hold of the hook with his front feet, spitting tobacco juice on it. Nick dropped him into the water.

Holding the rod in his right hand he let out line against the pull of the grasshopper in the current. He stripped off line from the reel with his left hand and let it run free. He could see the hopper in the little waves of the current. It went out of sight.

There was a tug on the line. Nick pulled against the taut line. It was his first strike. Holding the now living rod across the current, he brought in the line with his left hand. The rod bent in jerks, the trout pumping against the current. Nick knew it was a small one. He lifted the rod straight up in the air. It bowed with the pull.

He saw the trout in the water jerking with his head and body against the shifting tangent of the line in the stream.

Nick took the line in his left hand and pulled the trout, thumping tiredly against the current, to the surface. His back was mottled the clear, water-over-gravel color, his side flashing in the sun. The rod under his right arm, Nick stopped, dipping his right hand into the current. He held the trout, never still, with his moist right hand, while he unhooked the barb from his mouth, then dropped him back into the stream.

He hung unsteadily in the current, then settled to the bottom beside a stone. Nick reached down his hand to touch him, his arm to the elbow under water. The trout was steady in the moving stream, resting on the gravel, beside a stone. As Nick's fingers touched him, touched his smooth, cool, underwater feeling he was gone, gone in a shadow across the bottom of the stream.

He's all right, Nick thought. He was only tired.

He had wet his hand before he touched the trout, so he would not disturb the delicate mucus that covered him. If a trout was touched with a dry hand, a white fungus attacked the unprotected spot. Years before when he had fished crowded streams, with fly fishermen ahead of him and behind him, Nick had again and again come on dead trout, furry with white fungus, drifted against a rock, or floating belly up in some pool. Nick did not like to fish with other men on the river. Unless they were of your party they spoiled it.

He wallowed down the stream, above his knees in the current, through the fifty yards of shallow water above the pile of logs that crossed the stream. He did not rebait his hook and held it in his hand as he waded. He was certain he could catch small trout in the shallows, but he did not want them. There would be no big trout in the shallows this time of day.

Now the water deepened up his thighs sharply and coldly. Ahead was the smooth dammed-back flood of water above the logs. The water was smooth and dark; on the left, the lower edge of the meadow; on the right the swamp.

Nick leaned back against the current and took a hopper from the bottle. He threaded the hopper on the hook and spat on him for good luck. Then he pulled several yards of line from the reel and tossed the hopper out ahead onto the fast, dark water. It floated down towards the logs, then the weight of the line pulled the bait under the surface. Nick held the rod in his right hand, letting line run out through his fingers.

There was a long tug. Nick struck and the rod came alive and dangerous, bent double, the line tightening, coming out of water, tightening, all in a heavy, dangerous, steady pull. Nick felt the moment when the leader would break if the strain increased and let the line go.

The reel ratcheted into a mechanical shriek as the line went out in a rush. Too fast. Nick could not check it, the line rushing out, the reel note rising as the line ran out.

With the core of the reel showing, his heart feeling stopped with the excitement, leaning back against the current that mounted icily his thighs, Nick thumbed the reel hard with his left hand. It was awkward getting his thumb inside the fly reel frame.

As he put on pressure the line tightened into sudden hardness and beyond the logs a huge trout went high out of water. As he jumped, Nick lowered the tip of the rod. But he felt, as he dropped the tip to ease the strain, the moment when the strain was too great; the hardness too tight. Of course, the leader had broken. There was no mistaking the feeling when all spring left the line and it became dry and hard. Then it went slack.

His mouth dry, his heart down, Nick reeled in. He had never seen so big a trout. There was a heaviness, a power not to be held, and then the bulk of him, as he jumped. He looked as broad as a salmon.

Nick's hand was shaky. He reeled in slowly. The thrill had been too much. He felt, vaguely, a little sick, as though it would be better to sit down.

The leader had broken where the hook was tied to it. Nick took it in his hand. He thought of the trout somewhere on the bottom, holding himself steady over the gravel, far down below the light under the logs, with the hook in his jaw. Nick knew the trout's teeth would cut through the snell of the hook. The hook would imbed itself in his jaw. He'd bet the trout was angry. Anything that size would be angry. That was a trout. He had been solidly hooked. Solid as a rock. He felt like a rock, too, before he started off. By God, he was a big one. By God, he was the biggest one I ever heard of.

Nick climbed out onto the meadow and stood, water running down his trousers and out of his shoes, his shoes squlchy. He went over and sat on the logs. He did not want to rush his sensations any.

He wriggled his toes in the water, in his shoes, and got out a cigarette from his breast pocket. He lit it and tossed the match into the fast water below the logs. A tiny trout rose at the match, as it swung around in the fast current. Nick laughed. He would finish the cigarette.

He sat on the logs, smoking, drying in the sun, the sun warm on his back, the river shallow ahead entering the woods, curving into the woods, shallows, light glittering, big water-smooth rocks, cedars along the bank and white birches, the logs warm in the sun, smooth to sit on, without bark, gray to the touch; slowly the feeling of disappointment left him. It went away slowly, the feeling of disappointment that came sharply after the thrill that made his shoulders ache. It was all right now. His rod lying out on the logs. Nick tied a new hook on the leader, pulling the gut tight until it grimped into itself in a hard knot.

He baited up, then picked up the rod and walked to the far end of the logs to get into the water, where it was not too deep. Under and beyond the logs was a deep pool. Nick walked around the shallow shelf near the swamp shore until he came out on the shallow bed of the stream.

On the left, where the meadow ended and the woods began, a great elm tree was uprooted. Gone over in a storm, it lay back into the woods, its roots clotted with dirt, grass growing in them, rising a solid bank beside the stream. The river cut to the edge of the uprooted tree. From where Nick stood he could see deep channels, like ruts, cut in the shallow bed of the stream by the flow of the current. Pebbly where he stood and pebbly and full of boulders beyond; where it curved near the tree roots, the bed of the stream was marly and between the ruts of deep water green weed fronds swung in the current.

Nick swung the rod back over his shoulder and forward, and the line, curving forward, laid the grasshopper down on one of the deep channels in the weeds. A trout struck and Nick hooked him.

Holding the rod far out toward the uprooted tree and sloshing backward in the current, Nick worked the trout, plunging, the rod bending alive, out of the danger of the weeds into the open river. Holding the rod, pumping alive against the current, Nick brought the trout in. He rushed, but always came, the spring of the rod yielding to the rushes, sometimes jerking under water, but always bringing him in. Nick eased downstream with the rushes. The rod above his head he led the trout over the net, then lifted.

The trout hung heavy in the net, mottled trout back and silver sides in the meshes. Nick unhooked him; heavy sides, good to hold, big undershot jaw, and slipped him, heaving and big sliding, into the long sack that hung from his shoulders in the water.

Nick spread the mouth of the sack against the current and it filled, heavy with water. He held it up, the bottom in the stream, and the water poured out through the sides. Inside at the bottom was the big trout, alive in the water.

Nick moved downstream. The sack out ahead of him sunk heavy in the water, pulling from his shoulders.

It was getting hot, the sun hot on the back of his neck.

Nick had one good trout. He did not care about getting many trout. Now the stream was shallow and wide. There were trees along both banks. The trees of the left bank made short shadows on the current in the forenoon sun. Nick knew there were trout in each shadow. In the afternoon, after the sun had crossed toward the hills, the trout would be in the cool shadows on the other side of the stream.

The very biggest ones would lie up close to the bank. You could always pick them up there on the Black. When the sun was down they all moved out into the current. Just when the sun made the water blinding in the glare before it went down, you were liable to strike a big trout anywhere in the current. It was almost impossible to fish then, the surface of the water was blinding as a mirror in the sun. Of course, you could fish upstream, but in a stream like the Black, or this, you had to wallow against the current and in a deep place, the water piled up on you. It was no fun to fish upstream with this much current.

Nick moved along through the shallow stretch watching the banks for deep holes. A beech tree grew close beside the river, so that the branches hung down into the water. The stream went back in under the leaves. There were always trout in a place like that.

Nick did not care about fishing that hole. He was sure he would get hooked in the branches.

It looked deep though. He dropped the grasshopper so the current took it under water, back in under the overhanging branch. The line pulled hard and Nick struck. The trout threshed heavily, half out of water in the leaves and branches. The line was caught. Nick pulled hard and the trout was off. He reeled in and holding the hook in his hand, walked down the stream.

Ahead, close to the left bank, was a big log. Nick saw it was hollow; pointing up river the current entered it smoothly, only a little ripple spread each side of the log. The water was deepening. The top of the hollow log was gray and dry. It was partly in the shadow.

Nick took the cork out of the grasshopper bottle and a hopper clung to it. He picked him off, hooked him and tossed him out. He held the rod far out so that the hopper on the water moved into the current flowing into the hollow log. Nick lowered the rod and the hopper floated in. There was a heavy strike. Nick swung the rod against the pull. It felt as though he were hooked into the log itself, except for the live feeling.

He tried to force the fish out into the current. It came, heavily.

The line went slack and Nick thought the trout was gone. Then he saw him, very near, in the current, shaking his head, trying to get the hook out. His mouth was clamped shut. He was fighting the hook in the clear flowing current.

Looping in the line with his left hand, Nick swung the rod to make the line taut and tried to lead the trout toward the net, but he was gone, out of sight, the line pumping. Nick fought him against the current, letting him thump in the water against the spring of the rod. He shifted the rod to his left hand, worked the trout upstream, holding his weight, fighting on the rod, and then let him down into the net. He lifted him clear of the water, a heavy half circle in the net, the net dripping, unhooked him and slid him into the sack.

He spread the mouth of the sack and looked down in at the two big trout alive in the water.

Through the deepening water, Nick waded over to the hollow log. He took the sack off, over his head, the trout flopping as it came out of water, and hung it so the trout were deep in the water. Then he pulled himself up on the log and sat, the water from his trouser and boots running down into the stream. He laid his rod down, moved along to the shady end of the log and took the sandwiches out of his pocket. He dipped the sandwiches in the cold water. The current carried away the crumbs. He ate the sandwiches and dipped his hat full of water to drink, the water running out through his hat just ahead of his drinking.

It was cool in the shade, sitting on the log. He took a cigarette out and struck a match to light it. The match sunk into the gray wood, making a tiny furrow. Nick leaned over the side of the log, found a hard place and lit the match. He sat smoking and watching the river.

Ahead the river narrowed and went into a swamp. The river became smooth and deep and the swamp looked solid with cedar trees, their trunks close together, their branches solid. It would not be possible to walk through a swamp like that. The branches grew so low. You would have to keep almost level with the ground to move at all. You could not crash through the branches. That must be why the animals that lived in swamps were built the way they were, Nick thought.

He wished he had brought something to read. He felt like reading. He did not feel like going on into the swamp. He looked down the river. A big cedar slanted all the way across the stream. Beyond that the river went into the swamp.

Nick did not want to go in there now. He felt a reaction against deep wading with the water deepening up under his armpits, to hook big trout in places impossible to land them. In the swamp the banks were bare, the big cedars came together overhead, the sun did not come through, except in patches; in the fast deep water, in the half light, the fishing would be tragic. In the swamp fishing was a tragic adventure. Nick did not want it. He did not want to go down the stream any further today.

He took out his knife, opened it and stuck it in the log. Then he pulled up the sack, reached into it and brought out one of the trout. Holding him near the tail, hard to hold, alive, in his hand, he whacked him against the log. The trout quivered, rigid. Nick laid him on the log in the shade and broke the neck of the other fish the same way. He laid them side by side on the log. They were fine trout.

Nick cleaned them, slitting them from the vent to the tip of the jaw. All the insides and the gills and tongue came out in one piece. They were both males; long gray-white strips of milt, smooth and clean. All the insides clean and compact, coming out all together. Nick tossed the offal ashore for the minks to find.

He washed the trout in the stream. When he held them back up in the water they looked like live fish. Their color was not gone yet. He washed his hands and dried them on the log. Then he laid the trout on the sack spread out on the log, rolled them up in it, tied the bundle and put it in the landing net. His knife was still standing, blade stuck in the log. He cleaned it on the wood and put it in his pocket.

Nick stood up on the log, holding his rod, the landing net hanging heavy, then stepped into the water and splashed ashore. He climbed the bank and cut up into the woods, toward the high ground. He was going back to camp. He looked back. The river just showed through the trees. There were plenty of days coming when he could fish the swamp.

The End of Something

In the old days Hortons Bay was a lumbering town. No one who lived in it was out of sound of the big saws in the mill by the lake. Then one year there were no more logs to make lumber. The lumber schooners came into the bay and were loaded with the cut of the mill that stood stacked in the yard. All the piles of lumber were carried away. The big mill building had all its machinery that was removable taken out and hoisted on board one of the schooners by the men who had worked in the mill. The schooner moved out of the bay toward the open lake carrying the two great saws, the travelling carriage that hurled the logs against the revolving, circular saws and all the rollers, wheels, belts and iron piled on a hull-deep load of lumber. Its open hold covered with canvas and lashed tight, the sails of the schooner filled and it moved out into the open lake, carrying with it everything that had made the mill a mill and Hortons Bay a town.

The one-story bunk houses, the eating-house, the company store, the mill offices, and the big mill itself stood deserted in the acres of sawdust that covered the swampy meadow by the shore of the bay.

Ten years later there was nothing of the mill left except the broken white limestone of its foundations showing through the swampy second growth as Nick and Marjorie rowed along the shore. They were trolling along the edge of the channel-bank where the bottom dropped off suddenly from sandy shallows to twelve feet of dark water. They were trolling on their way to the point to set night lines for rainbow trout.

"There's our old ruin, Nick," Marjorie said.

Nick, rowing, looked at the white stone in the green trees.

"There it is," he said.

"Can you remember when it was a mill?" Marjorie asked.

"I can just remember," Nick said.

"It seems more like a castle," Marjorie said.

Nick said nothing. They rowed on out of sight of the mill, following the shore line. Then Nick cut across the bay.

"They aren't striking," he said.

"No," Marjorie said. She was intent on the rod all the time they trolled, even when she talked. She loved to fish. She loved to fish with Nick.

Close beside the boat a big trout broke the surface of the water. Nick pulled hard on one oar so the boat would turn and the bait spinning far behind would pass where the trout was feeding. As the trout's back came up out of the water the minnows jumped wildly. They sprinkled the surface like a handful of shot thrown into the water. Another trout broke water, feeding on the other side of the boat.

"They're feeding," Marjorie said.

"But they won't strike," Nick said.

He rowed the boat around to troll past both the feeding fish, then headed it for the point. Marjorie did not reel in until the boat touched the shore.

They pulled the boat up the beach and Nick lifted out a pail of live perch. The perch swam in the water in the pail. Nick caught three of them with his hands and cut their heads off and skinned them while

Marjorie chased with her hands in the bucket, finally caught a perch, cut its head off and skinned it. Nick looked at her fish.

"You don't want to take the ventral fin out," he said. "It'll be all right for bait but it's better with the ventral fin in."

He hooked each of the skinned perch through the tail. There were two hooks attached to a leader on each rod. Then Marjorie rowed the boat out over the channel-bank, holding the line in her teeth, and looking toward Nick, who stood on the shore holding the rod and letting the line run out from the reel.

"That's about right," he called.

"Should I let it drop?" Marjorie called back, holding the line in her hand.

"Sure. Let it go." Marjorie dropped the line overboard and watched the baits go down through the water.

She came in with the boat and ran the second line out the same way. Each time Nick set a heavy slab of driftwood across the butt of the rod to hold it solid and propped it up at an angle with a small slab. He reeled in the slack line so the line ran taut out to where the bait rested on the sandy floor of the channel and set the click on the reel. When a trout, feeding on the bottom, took the bait it would run with it, taking line out of the reel in a rush and making the reel sing with the click on.

Marjorie rowed up the point a little way so she would not disturb the line. She pulled hard on the oars and the boat went way up the beach. Little waves came in with it. Marjorie stepped out of the boat and Nick pulled the boat high up the beach.

"What's the matter, Nick?" Marjorie asked.

"I don't know," Nick said, getting wood for a fire.

They made a fire with driftwood. Marjorie went to the boat and brought a blanket. The evening breeze blew the smoke toward the point, so Marjorie spread the blanket out between the fire and the lake.

Marjorie sat on the blanket with her back to the fire and waited for Nick. He came over and sat down beside her on the blanket. In back of them was the close second-growth timber of the point and in front was the bay with the mouth of Hortons Creek. It was not quite dark. The fire-light went as far as the water. They could both see the two steel rods at an angle over the dark water. The fire glinted on the reels.

Marjorie unpacked the basket of supper.

"I don't feel like eating," said Nick.

"Come on and eat, Nick."

"All right."

They ate without talking, and watched the two rods and the fire-light in the water.

"There's going to be a moon tonight," said Nick. He looked across the bay to the hills that were beginning to sharpen against the sky. Beyond the hills he knew the moon was coming up.

"I know it," Marjorie said happily.

"You know everything," Nick said.

"Oh, Nick, please cut it out! Please, please don't be that way!"

"I can't help it," Nick said. "You do. You know everything. That's the trouble. You know you do."

Marjorie did not say anything.

"I've taught you everything. You know you do. What don't you know, anyway?"

"Oh, shut up," Marjorie said. "There comes the moon."

They sat on the blanket without touching each other and watched the moon rise.

"You don't have to talk silly," Marjorie said. "What's really the matter?"

"I don't know."

"Of course you know."

"No I don't."

"Go on and say it."

Nick looked on at the moon, coming up over the hills.

"It isn't fun any more."

He was afraid to look at Marjorie. Then he looked at her. She sat there with her back toward him. He looked at her back. "It isn't fun any more. Not any of it."

28

She didn't say anything. He went on. "I feel as though everything was gone to hell inside of me. I don't know, Marge, I don't know what to say."

He looked on at her back.

"Isn't love any fun?" Marjorie said.

"No," Nick said. Marjorie stood up. Nick sat there his head in his hands.

"I'm going to take the boat," Marjorie called to him. "You can walk back around the point."

"All right," Nick said. "I'll push the boat off for you."

"You don't need to," she said. She was afloat in the boat on the water with the moonlight on it. Nick went back and lay down with his face in the blanket by the fire. He could hear Marjorie rowing on the water.

He lay there for a long time. He lay there while he heard Bill come into the clearing walking around through the woods. He felt Bill coming up to the fire. Bill didn't touch him, either.

"Did she go all right?" Bill said.

"Yes," Nick said, lying, his face on the blanket.

"Have a scene?"

"No, there wasn't any scene."

"How do you feel?"

"Oh, go away, Bill! Go away for a while."

Bill selected a sandwich from the lunch basket and walked over to have a look at the rods.

The Last Good Country (an excerpt)

Nick and his sister were lying on a browse bed under a lean-to that they had built together on the edge of the hemlock forest looking out over the slope of the hill to the cedar swamp and the blue hills beyond.

"If it isn't comfortable, Littless, we can feather in some more balsam on that hemlock. We'll be tired tonight and this will do. But we can fix it up really good tomorrow."

"It feels lovely," his sister said. "Lie loose and really feel it, Nickie."

"It's a pretty good camp," Nick said. "And it doesn't show. We'll only use little fires."

"Would a fire show across to the hills?"

"It might," Nick said. "A fire shows a long way at night. But I'll stake out a blanket behind it. That way it won't show."

"Nickie, wouldn't it be nice if there wasn't anyone after us and we were just here for fun?"

"Don't start thinking that way so soon," Nick said. "We just started. Anyway if we were just here for fun we wouldn't be here."

"I'm sorry, Nickie."

"You don't need to be," Nick told her. "Look, Littless, I'm going down to get a few trout for supper."

"Can I come?"

"No. You stay here and rest. You had a tough day. You read a while or just be quiet."

"It was tough in the slashings, wasn't it? I thought it was really hard. Did I do all right?"

"You did wonderfully and you were wonderful making camp. But you take it easy now."

"Have we got a name for this camp?"

"Let's call it Camp Number One," Nick said.

He went down the hill toward the creek and when he had come almost to the bank he stopped and cut himself a willow stick about four feet long and trimmed it, leaving the bark on. He could see the clear fast water of the stream. It was narrow and deep and the banks were mossy here before the stream entered the swamp. The dark clear water flowed fast and its rushing made bulges on the surface. Nick did not go close to it as he knew it flowed under the banks and he did not want to frighten a fish by walking on the bank.

There must be quite a few up here in the open now, he thought. It's pretty late in the summer.

He took a coil of silk line out of a tobacco pouch he carried in the left breast pocket of his shirt and cut a length that was not quite as long as the willow stick and fastened it to the tip where he had notched it lightly. Then he fastened on a hook that he took from the pouch; then holding the shank of the hook he tested the pull of the line and the bend of the willow. He laid his rod down now and went back to where the trunk of a small birch tree, dead for several years, lay on its side in the grove of birches that bordered the cedars by the stream. He rolled the log over and found several earthworms under it. They were not big. But they were red and lively and he put them in a flat round tin with holes punched in the top that had once held Copenhagen snuff. He put some dirt over them and rolled the log back. This was the third year he had found bait at this same place and he had always replaced the log so that it was as he had found it.

Nobody knows how big this creek is, he thought. It picks up an awful volume of water in that bad swamp up above. Now he looked up the creek and down it and up the hill to the hemlock forest where the camp was. Then he walked to where he had left the pole with the line and the hook and baited the hook carefully and spat on it for good luck. Holding the pole and the line with the baited hook in his right hand he walked very carefully and gently toward the bank of the narrow, heavy-flowing stream.

It was so narrow here that his willow pole would have spanned it and as he came close to the bank he heard the turbulent rush of the water. He stopped by the bank, out of sight of anything in the stream, and took two lead shot, split down one side, out of the tobacco pouch and bent them on the line about a foot above the hook, clinching them with his teeth.

He swung the hook on which the two worms curled out over the water and dropped it gently in so that it sank, swirling in the fast water, and he lowered the tip of the willow pole to let the current take the line and the baited hook under the bank. He felt the line straighten and a sudden heavy firmness. He swung up on the pole and it bent almost double in his hand. He felt the throbbing, jerking pull that did not yield as he pulled. Then it yielded, rising in the water with the line. There was a heavy wildness of movement in the narrow, deep current, and the trout was torn out of the water and, flopping in the air, sailed over Nick's shoulder and onto the bank behind him. Nick saw him shine in the sun and then he found him where he was tumbling in the ferns. He was strong and heavy in Nick's hands and he had a pleasant smell and Nick saw how dark his back was and how brilliant his spots were colored and how bright the edges of his fins were. They were white on the edge with a black line behind and then there was the lovely golden sunset color of his belly. Nick held him in his right hand and he could just reach around him.

He's pretty big for the skillet, he thought. But I've hurt him and I have to kill him.

He knocked the trout's head sharply against the handle of his hunting knife and laid him against the trunk of a birch tree.

"Damn," he said. "He's a perfect size for Mrs. Packard and her trout dinners. But he's pretty big for Littless and me."

I better go upstream and find a shallow and try to get a couple of small ones, he thought. Damn, didn't he feel like something when I horsed him out though? They can talk all they want about playing them but people that have never horsed them out don't know what they can make you feel. What if it only lasts that long? It's the time when there's no give at all and then they start to come and what they do to you on the way up and into the air.

This is a strange creek, he thought. It's funny when you have to hunt for small ones.

He found his pole where he had thrown it. The hook was bent and he straightened it. Then he picked up the heavy fish and started up the stream.

There's one shallow, pebbly part just after she comes out of the upper swamp, he thought. I can get a couple of small ones there. Littless might not like this big one. If she gets homesick I'll have to take her back. I wonder what those old boys are doing now? I don't think that goddam Evans kid knows about this place. That son of a bitch. I don't think anybody fished in here but Indians. You should have been an Indian, he thought. It would have saved you a lot of trouble.

He made his way up the creek, keeping back from the stream but once stepping onto a piece of bank where the stream flowed underground. A big trout broke out in a violence that made a slashing wake in the water. He was a trout so big that it hardly seemed he could turn in the stream.

"When did you come up?" Nick said when the fish had gone under the bank again further upstream. "Boy, what a trout."

At the pebbly shallow stretch he caught two small trout. They were beautiful fish, too, firm and hard and he gutted the three fish and tossed the guts into the stream, then washed the trout carefully in the cold water and then wrapped them in a small faded sugar sack from his pocket.

It's a good thing that girl likes fish, he thought. I wish we could have picked some berries. I know where I can always get some, though. He started back up the hill slope toward their camp. The sun was down behind the hill and the weather was good. He looked out across the swamp and up in the sky, above where the arm of the lake would be, he saw a fish hawk flying.

Now I Lay Me

That night we lay on the floor in the room and I listened to the silk-worms eating. The silk-worms fed in racks of mulberry leaves and all night you could hear them eating and a dropping sound in the leaves. I myself did not want to sleep because I had been living for a long time with the knowledge that if I ever shut my eyes in the dark and let myself go, my soul would go out of my body. I had been that way for a long time, ever since I had been blown up at night and felt it go out of me and go off and then come back. I tried never to think about it, but it had started to go since, in the nights, just at the moment of going off to sleep, and I could only stop it by a very great effort. So while now I am fairly sure that it would not really have gone out, yet then, that summer, I was unwilling to make the experiment.

I had different ways of occupying myself while I lay awake. I would think of a trout stream I had fished along when I was a boy and fish its whole length very carefully in my mind; fishing very carefully under all the logs, all the turns of the bank, the deep holes and the clear shallow stretches, sometimes catching trout and sometimes losing them. I would stop fishing at noon to eat my lunch; sometimes on a log over the stream; sometimes on a high bank under a tree, and I always ate my lunch very slowly and watched the stream below me while I ate. Often I ran out of bait because I would take only ten worms with me in a tobacco tin when I started. When I had used them all I had to find more worms, and sometimes it was very difficult digging in the bank of the stream where the cedar trees kept out the sun and there was no grass but only the bare moist earth and often I could find no worms. Always though I found some kind of bait, but one time in the swamp I could find no bait at all and had to cut up one of the trout I had caught and use him for bait.

Sometimes I found insects in the swamp meadows, in the grass or under ferns, and used them. There were beetles and insects with legs like grass stems, and grubs in old rotten logs; white grubs with brown pinching heads that would not stay on the hook and emptied into nothing in the cold water, and wood ticks under logs where sometimes I found angle-worms that slipped into the ground as soon as the log was raised. Once I used a salamander from under an old log. The salamander was very small and neat and agile and a lovely color. He had tiny feet that tried to hold on to the hook, and after that one time I never used a salamander, although I found them very often. Nor did I use crickets, because of the way they acted about the hook.

Sometimes the stream ran through an open meadow, and in the dry grass I would catch grasshoppers and use them for bait and sometimes I would catch grasshoppers and toss them into the stream and watch them float along swimming on the stream and circling on the surface as the current took them and then disappear as a trout rose. Sometimes I would fish four or five different streams in the night; starting as near as I could get to their source and fishing them down stream. When I had finished too quickly and the time did not go, I would fish the stream over again, starting where it emptied into the lake and fishing back up stream, trying for all the trout I had missed coming down. Some nights too I made up streams, and some of them were very exciting, and it was like being awake and dreaming. Some of those streams I still remember and think that I have fished in them, and they are confused with streams I really know. I gave them all names and went to them on the train and sometimes walked for miles to get to them.

But some nights I could not fish, and on those nights I was cold-awake and said my prayers over and over and tried to pray for all the people I had ever known. That took up a great amount of time, for if you try to remember all the people you have ever known, going back to the earliest thing you remember—which was, with me, the attic of the house where I was born and my mother and father's wedding-cake in a tin box hanging from one of the rafters, and, in the attic, jars of snakes and other specimens that my father had collected as a boy and preserved in alcohol, the alcohol sunken in the jars so the backs of some of the snakes and specimens were exposed and had turned white—if you thought back that far, you remembered a great many people. If you prayed for all of them, saying a Hail Mary and an Our Father for each one, it took a long time and finally it would be light, and then you could go to sleep, if you were in a place where you could sleep in the daylight.

On those nights I tried to remember everything that had ever happened to me, starting with just before I went to the war and remembering back from one thing to another. I found I could only remember back to that attic in my grandfather's house. Then I would start there and remember this way again, until I reached the war.

I remember, after my grandfather died we moved away from that house and to a new house designed and built by my mother. Many things that were not to be moved were burned in the backyard and I remember those jars from the attic being thrown in the fire, and how they popped in the heat and the fire flamed up from the alcohol. I remember the snakes burning in the fire in the backyard. But there were no people in that, only things. I could not remember who burned the things even, and I would go on until I came to people and then stop and pray for them.

About the new house I remember how my mother was always cleaning things out and making a good clearance. One time when my father was away on a hunting trip she made a good thorough cleaning out in the basement and burned everything that should not have been there. When my father came home and got down from his buggy and hitched the horse, the fire was still burning in the road beside the house. I went out to meet him. He handed me his shotgun and looked at the fire. "What's this?" he asked.

"I've been cleaning out the basement, dear," my mother said from the porch. She was standing there smiling, to meet him. My father looked at the fire and kicked at something. Then he leaned over and picked something out of the ashes. "Get a rake, Nick," he said to me. I went to the basement and brought a rake and my father raked very carefully in the ashes. He raked out some axes and stone skinning knives and tools for making arrow-heads and pieces of pottery and many arrow-heads. They had all been blackened and chipped by the fire. My father raked them all out very carefully and spread them on the grass by the road. His shotgun in its leather case and his game-bags were on the grass where he had left them when he stepped down from the buggy.

"Take the gun and the bags in the house, Nick, and bring me a paper," he said. My mother had gone inside the house. I took the shotgun, which was heavy to carry and banged against my legs, and the two game-bags and started toward the house. "Take them one at a time," my father said. "Don't try and carry too much at once." I put down the game-bags and took in the shotgun and brought out a newspaper from the pile in my father's office. My father spread all the blackened, chipped stone implements on the paper and then wrapped them up. "The best arrow-heads went all to pieces," he said. He walked into the house with the paper package and I stayed outside on the grass with the two game-bags. After a while I took them in. In remembering that, there were only two people, so I would pray for them both.

Some nights, though, I could not remember my prayers even. I could only get as far as "On earth as it is in heaven" and then have to start all over and be absolutely unable to get past that. Then I would have to recognize that I could not remember and give up saying my prayers that night and try something else. So on some nights I would try to remember all the animals in the world by name and then the birds and then fishes and then countries and cities and then kinds of food and the names of all the streets I could remember in Chicago, and when I could not remember anything at all any more I would just listen. And I do not remember a night on which you could not hear things. If I could have a light I was not afraid to sleep, because I knew my soul would only go out of me if it were dark. So, of course, many nights I was where I could have a light and then I slept because I was nearly always tired and often very sleepy. And I am sure many times too that I slept without knowing it—but I never slept knowing it, and on this night I listened to the silk-worms eating very clearly in the night and I lay with my eyes open and listened to them.

There was only one other person in the room and he was awake too. I listened to him being awake, for a long time. He could not lie as quietly as I could because, perhaps, he had not had as much practice being awake. We were lying on blankets spread over straw and when he moved the straw was noisy, but the silk-worms were not frightened by any noise we made and ate on steadily. There were the noises of night seven kilometres behind the lines outside but they were different from the small noises inside the room in the dark. The other man in the room tried lying quietly. Then he moved again. I moved too, so he would know I was awake. He had lived ten years in Chicago. They had taken him for a soldier in nineteen fourteen when he had come back to visit his family, and they had given him me for an orderly because he spoke English. I heard him listening, so I moved again in the blankets.

"Can't you sleep, Signor Tenente?" he asked.

"No."

"I can't sleep, either."

"What's the matter?"

"I don't know. I can't sleep."

"You feel all right?"

"Sure. I feel good. I just can't sleep."

"You want to talk a while?" I asked.

"Sure. What can you talk about in this damn place."

"This place is pretty good," I said.

"Sure," he said. "It's all right."

"Tell me about out in Chicago," I said.

"Oh," he said, "I told you all that once."

"Tell me about how you got married."

"I told you that."

"Was the letter you got Monday—from her?"

"Sure. She writes me all the time. She's making good money with the place."

"You'll have a nice place when you go back."

"Sure. She runs it fine. She's making a lot of money."

"Don't you think we'll wake them up, talking?" I asked.

"No. They can't hear. Anyway, they sleep like pigs. I'm different," he said. "I'm nervous."

"Talk quiet," I said. "Want a smoke?"

We smoked skilfully in the dark.

"You don't smoke much, Signor Tenente."

"No. I've just about cut it out."

"Well," he said, "it don't do you any good and I suppose you get so you don't miss it. Did you ever hear a blind man won't smoke because he can't see the smoke come out?"

"I don't believe it."

"I think it's all bull, myself," he said. "I just heard it somewhere. You know how you hear things."

We were both quiet and I listened to the silk-worms.

"You hear those damn silk-worms?" he asked. "You can hear them chew."

"It's funny," I said.

"Say, Signor Tenente, is there something really the matter that you can't sleep? I never see you sleep. You haven't slept nights ever since I been with you."

"I don't know, John," I said. "I got in pretty bad shape along early last spring and at night it bothers me."

"Just like I am," he said. "I shouldn't have ever got in this war. I'm too nervous."

"Maybe it will get better."

"Say, Signor Tenente, what did you get in this war for, anyway?"

"I don't know, John. I wanted to, then."

"Wanted to," he said. "That's a hell of a reason."

"We oughtn't to talk out loud," I said.

"They sleep just like pigs," he said. "They can't understand the English language, anyway. They don't know a damn thing. What are you going to do when it's over and we go back to the States?"

"I'll get a job on a paper."

"In Chicago?"

"Maybe."

"Do you ever read what this fellow Brisbane writes? My wife cuts it out for me and sends it to me."

"Sure."

"Did you ever meet him?"

"No, but I've seen him."

"I'd like to meet that fellow. He's a fine writer. My wife don't read English but she takes the paper just like when I was home and she cuts out the editorials and the sport page and sends them to me."

"How are your kids?""

"They're fine. One of the girls is in the fourth grade now. You know, Signor Tenente, if I didn't have the kids I wouldn't be your orderly now. They'd have made me stay in the line all the time."

"I'm glad you've got them."

"So am I. They're fine kids but I want a boy. Three girls and no boy. That's a hell of a note."

"Why don't you try and go to sleep?"

"No, I can't sleep now. I'm wide awake now, Signor Tenente. Say, I'm worried about you not sleeping though."

"It'll be all right, John."

"Imagine a young fellow like you not to sleep."

"I'll get all right. It just takes a while."

"You got to get all right. A man can't get along that don't sleep. Do you worry about anything? You got anything on your mind?"

"No, John, I don't think so."

"You ought to get married, Signor Tenente. Then you wouldn't worry."

"I don't know."

"You ought to get married. Why don't you pick out some nice Italian girl with plenty of money? You could get any one you want. You're young and you got good decorations and you look nice. You been wounded a couple of times."

"I can't talk the language well enough."

"You talk it fine. To hell with talking the language. You don't have to talk to them. Marry them."

"I'll think about it."

"You know some girls, don't you?"

"Sure."

"Well, you marry the one with the most money. Over here, the way they're brought up, they'll all make you a good wife."

"I'll think about it."

"Don't think about it, Signor Tenente. Do it."

"All right."

"A man ought to be married. You'll never regret it. Every man ought to be married."

"All right," I said. "Let's try and sleep a while."

"All right, Signor Tenente. I'll try it again. But you remember what I said."

"I'll remember it," I said. "Now let's sleep a while, John."

"All right," he said. "I hope you sleep, Signor Tenente."

I heard him roll in his blankets on the straw and then he was very quiet and I listened to him breathing regularly. Then he started to snore. I listened to him snore for a long time and then I stopped listening to him snore and listened to the silk-worms eating. They ate steadily, making a dropping in the leaves. I had a new thing to think about and I lay in the dark with my eyes open and thought of all the girls I had ever known and what kind of wives they would make. It was a very interesting thing to think about and for a while it killed off trout-fishing and interfered with my prayers. Finally, though, I went back to trout-fishing, because I found that I could remember all the streams and there was always something new about them, while the girls, after I had thought about them a few times, blurred and I could not call them into my mind and finally they all blurred and all became rather the same and I gave up thinking about them almost altogether. But I kept on with my prayers and I prayed very often for John in the nights and his class was removed from active service before the October offensive. I was glad he was not there, because he would have been a great worry to me. He came to the hospital in Milan to see me several months after and was very disappointed that I had not yet married, and I know he would feel very badly if he knew that, so far, I have never married. He was going back to America and he was very certain about marriage and knew it would fix up everything.

"Fishermen of the Seine"

(from *A Moveable Feast*)

I would walk along the quais when I finished work or when I was
trying to think something out. It was easier to think if I was walking and doing something or seeing people doing something that
they understood. At the head of the Ile de la Cité below the Pont
Neuf where there was the statue of Henri Quatre, the island
ended in a point like the sharp bow of a ship and there was a small
park at the water's edge with fine chestnut trees, huge and spreading,
and in the currents and back waters that the Seine made flowing
past, there were excellent places to fish. You went down a stairway
to the park and watched the fishermen there and under the great
bridge. The good spots to fish changed with the height of the river
and the fishermen used long, jointed, cane poles but fished with
very fine leaders and light gear and quill floats and expertly baited
the piece of water that they fished. They always caught some fish
and often they made excellent catches of the dace-like fish that
were called *goujon*. They were delicious fried whole and I could eat
a plateful. They were plump and sweet-fleshed with a finer flavor

than fresh sardines even, and were not at all oily, and we ate them bones and all.

One of the best places to eat them was at an open-air restaurant built out over the river at Bas Meudon where we would go when we had money for a trip away from our quarter. It was called La Pêche Miraculeuse and had a splendid white wine that was a sort of Muscadet. It was a place out of a Maupassant story with the view over the river as Sisley had painted it. You did not have to go that far to eat *goujon*. You could get a very good *friture* on the Île St.-Louis.

I knew several of the men who fished the fruitful parts of the Seine between the Ile St.-Louis and the Place du Verte Galente and sometimes, if the day was bright, I would buy a liter of wine and a piece of bread and some sausage and sit in the sun and read one of the books I had bought and watch the fishing.

Travel writers wrote about the men fishing in the Seine as though they were crazy and never caught anything; but it was serious and productive fishing. Most of the fishermen were men who had small pensions, which they did not know then would become worthless with inflation, or keen fishermen who fished on their days or half-days off from work. There was better fishing at Charenton, where the Marne came into the Seine, and on either side of Paris, but there was very good fishing in Paris itself. I did not fish because I did not have the tackle and I preferred to save my money to fish in Spain. Then too I never knew when I would be through working, nor when I would have to be away, and I did not want to become involved in the fishing which had its good times and its slack times. But I followed it closely and it was interesting and good to know about, and it always made me happy that there were men fishing in the city itself, having sound, serious fishing and taking a few *fritures* home to their families.

With the fishermen and the life of the river, the beautiful barges with their own life on board, the tugs with their smokestacks that folded back to pass under the bridges, pulling a tow of barges, the great elms on the stone banks of the river, the plane trees and in some places the poplars, I could never be lonely along the river. With so many trees in the city, you could see the spring coming each day until a night of warm wind would bring it suddenly in one morning. Sometimes the heavy cold rains would beat it back so that it would seem that it would never come and that you were losing a season out of your life. This was the only truly sad time in Paris because it was unnatural. You expected to be sad in the fall. Part of you died each year when the leaves fell from the trees and their branches were bare against the wind and the cold, wintry light. But you knew there would always be the spring, as you knew the river would flow again after it was frozen. When the cold rains kept on and killed the spring it was as though a young person had died for no reason.

In those days, though, the spring always came finally but it was frightening that it had nearly failed.

"On the Irati"

(from *The Sun Also Rises*)

It was baking hot in the square when we came out after lunch with our bags and the rod-case to go to Burguete. People were on top of the bus, and others were climbing up a ladder. Bill went up and Robert sat beside Bill to save a place for me, and I went back in the hotel to get a couple of bottles of wine to take with us. When I came out the bus was crowded. Men and women were sitting on all the baggage and boxes on top, and the women all had their fans going in the sun. It certainly was hot. Robert climbed down and I fitted into the place he had saved on the one wooden seat that ran across the top.

Robert Cohn stood in the shade of the arcade waiting for us to start. A Basque with a big leather wine-bag in his lap lay across the top of the bus in front of our seat, leaning back against our legs. He offered the wine-skin to Bill and to me, and when I tipped it up to drink he imitated the sound of a klaxon motor-horn so well and so suddenly that I spilled some of the wine, and everybody laughed. He apologized and made me take another drink. He made the klaxon again a little later, and it fooled me the second time. He was very good at it. The Basques liked it. The man next to Bill was talking to him in Spanish and Bill was not getting it, so he offered the man one of the bottles of wine. The man waved it away. He said it was too hot and he had drunk too much at lunch. When Bill offered the bottle the second time he took a long drink, and then the bottle went all over that part of the bus. Every one took a drink very politely, and then they made us cork it up and put it away. They all wanted us to drink from their leather wine-bottles. They were peasants going up into the hills.

Finally, after a couple more false klaxons, the bus started, and Robert Cohn waved good-by to us, and all the Basques waved good-by to him. As soon as we started out on the road outside of town it was cool. It felt nice riding high up and close under the trees. The bus went quite fast and made a good breeze, and as we went out along the road with the dust powdering the trees and down the hill, we had a fine view, back through the trees, of the town rising up from the bluff above the river. The Basque lying against my knees pointed out the view with the neck of the wine-bottle, and winked at us. He nodded his head.

"Pretty nice, eh?"

"These Basques are swell people," Bill said.

The Basque lying against my legs was tanned the color of saddle-leather. He wore a black smock like all the rest. There were wrinkles in his tanned neck. He turned around and offered his wine-bag to Bill. Bill handed him one of our bottles. The Basque wagged a fore-finger at him and handed the bottle back, slapping in the cork with the palm of his hand. He shoved the wine-bag up.

"Arriba! Arriba!" he said. "Lift it up."

Bill raised the wine-skin and let the stream of wine spurt out and into his mouth, his head tipped back. When he stopped drinking and tipped the leather bottle down a few drops ran down his chin.

"No! No!" several Basques said. "Not like that." One snatched the bottle away from the owner, who was himself about to give a demonstration. He was a young fellow and he held the wine-bottle at full arms' length and raised it high up, squeezing the leather bag with his hand so the stream of wine hissed into his mouth. He held the bag out there, the wine making a flat, hard trajectory into his mouth, and he kept on swallowing smoothly and regularly.

"Hey!" the owner of the bottle shouted. "Whose wine is that?"

The drinker waggled his little finger at him and smiled at us with his eyes. Then he bit the stream off sharp, made a quick lift with the wine-bag and lowered it down to the owner. He winked at us. The owner shook the wine-skin sadly.

We passed through a town and stopped in front of the posada, and the driver took on several packages. Then we started on again, and outside the town the road commenced to mount. We were going through farming country with rocky hills that sloped down into the fields. The grain-fields went up the hillsides. Now as we went higher there was a wind blowing the grain. The road was white and dusty, and the dust rose under the wheels and hung in the air behind us. The road climbed up into the hills and left the rich grain-fields below. Now there were only patches of grain on the bare hill-sides and on each side of the water-courses. We turned sharply out to the side of the road to give room to pass to a long string of six mules, following one after the other, hauling a high-hooded wagon loaded with freight. The wagon and the mules were covered with dust. Close behind was another string of mules and another wagon. This was loaded with lumber, and the arriero driving the mules leaned back and put on the thick wooden brakes as we passed. Up here the country was quite barren and the hills were rocky and hard-baked clay furrowed by the rain.

We came around a curve into a town, and on both sides opened out a sudden green valley. A stream went through the centre of the town and fields of grapes touched the houses.

The bus stopped in front of a posada and many of the passengers got down, and a lot of the baggage was unstrapped from the roof from under the big tarpaulins and lifted down. Bill and I got down and went into the posada. There was a low, dark room with saddles and harness, and hay-forks made of white wood, and clusters of canvas rope-soled shoes and hams and slabs of bacon and white garlics and long sausages hanging from the roof. It was cool and dusky, and we stood in front of a long wooden counter with two women behind it serving drinks. Behind them were shelves stacked with supplies and goods.

We each had an aguardiente and paid forty centimes for the two drinks. I gave the woman fifty centimes to make a tip, and she gave me back the copper piece, thinking I had misunderstood the price.

Two of our Basques came in and insisted on buying a drink. So they bought a drink and then we bought a drink, and then they slapped us on the back and bought another drink. Then we bought, and then we all went out into the sunlight and the heat, and climbed back on top of the bus. There was plenty of room now for every one to sit on the seat, and the Basque who had been lying on the tin roof now sat between us. The woman who had been serving drinks came out wiping her hands on her apron and talked to somebody inside the bus. Then the driver came out swinging two flat leather mail-pouches and climbed up, and everybody waving we started off.

The road left the green valley at once, and we were up in the hills again. Bill and the wine-bottle Basque were having a conversation. A man leaned over from the other side of the seat and asked in English: "You're American?"

"Sure."

"I been there," he said. "Forty years ago."

He was an old man, as brown as the others, with the stubble of a white beard.

"How was it?"

"What you say?"

"How was America?"

"Oh, I was in California. It was fine."

"Why did you leave?"

"What you say?"

"Why did you come back here?"

"Oh! I come back to get married. I was going to go back but my wife she don't like to travel. Where you from?"

"Kansas City."

"I been there," he said. "I been to Chicago, St. Louis, Kansas City, Denver, Los Angeles, Salt Lake City."

He named them carefully.

"How long were you over?"

"Fifteen years. Then I come back and got married."

"Have a drink?"

"All right," he said. "You can't get this in America, eh?"

"There's plenty if you can pay for it."

"What you come over here for?"

"We're going to the fiesta at Pamplona."

"You like the bull-fights?"

"Sure. Don't you?"

"Yes," he said. "I guess I like them."

Then after a little:

"Where you go now?"

"Up to Burguete to fish."

"Well," he said, "I hope you catch something."

He shook hands and turned around to the back seat again. The other Basques had been impressed. He sat back comfortably and smiled at me when I turned around to look at the country. But the effort of talking American seemed to have tired him. He did not say anything after that.

The bus climbed steadily up the road. The country was barren and rocks stuck up through the clay. There was no grass beside the road. Looking back we could see the country spread out below. Far back the fields were squares of green and brown on the hillsides. Making the horizon were the brown mountains. They were strangely shaped. As we climbed higher the horizon kept changing.

As the bus ground slowly up the road we could see other mountains coming up in the south. Then the road came over the crest, flattened out, and went into a forest. It was a forest of cork oaks, and the sun came through the trees in patches, and there were cattle grazing back in the trees. We went through the forest and the road came out and turned along a rise of land, and out ahead of us was a rolling green plain, with dark mountains beyond it. These were not like the brown, heat-baked mountains we had left behind. These were wooded and there were clouds coming down from them. The green plain stretched off. It was cut by fences and the white of the road showed through the trunks of a double line of trees that crossed the plain toward the north. As we came to the edge of the rise we saw the red roofs and white houses of Burguete ahead strung out on the plain, and away off on the shoulder of the first dark mountain was the gray metal-sheathed roof of the monastery of Roncesvalles.

"There's Roncevaux," I said.

"Where?"

"Way off there where the mountain starts."

"It's cold up here," Bill said.

"It's high," I said. "It must be twelve hundred metres."

"It's awful cold," Bill said.

The bus levelled down onto the straight line of road that ran to Burguete. We passed a crossroads and crossed a bridge over a stream. The houses of Burguete were along both sides of the road. There were no side-streets. We passed the church and the school-yard, and the bus stopped. We got down and the driver handed down our bags and the rod-case. A carabineer in his cocked hat and yellow leather cross-straps came up.

"What's in there?" he pointed to the rod-case.

I opened it and showed him. He asked to see our fishing permits and I got them out. He looked at the date and then waved us on.

"Is that all right?" I asked.

"Yes. Of course."

We went up the street, past the whitewashed stone houses, families sitting in their doorways watching us, to the inn.

The fat woman who ran the inn came out from the kitchen and shook hands with us. She took off her spectacles, wiped them, and put them on again. It was cold in the inn and the wind was starting to blow outside. The woman sent a girl up-stairs with us to show the room. There were two beds, a washstand, a clothes-chest, and a big, framed steel-engraving of Nuestra Señora de Roncesvalles. The wind was blowing against the shutters. The room was on the north side of the inn. We washed, put on sweaters, and came down-stairs into the dining-room. It had a stone floor, low ceiling, and was oak-panelled. The shutters were all up and it was so cold you could see your breath.

"My God!" said Bill. "It can't be this cold to-morrow. I'm not going to wade a stream in this weather."

There was an upright piano in the far corner of the room beyond the wooden tables and Bill went over and started to play.

"I got to keep warm," he said.

I went out to find the woman and ask her how much the room and board was. She put her hands under her apron and looked away from me.

"Twelve pesetas."

"Why, we only paid that in Pamplona."

She did not say anything, just took off her glasses and wiped them on her apron.

"That's too much," I said. "We didn't pay more than that at a big hotel."

"We've put in a bathroom."

"Haven't you got anything cheaper?"

"Not in the summer. Now is the big season."

We were the only people in the inn. Well, I thought, it's only a few days.

"Is the wine included?"

"Oh, yes."

"Well," I said. "It's all right."

I went back to Bill. He blew his breath at me to show how cold it was, and went on playing. I sat at one of the tables and looked at the pictures on the wall. There was one panel of rabbits, dead, one of pheasants, also dead, and one panel of dead ducks. The panels were all dark and smoky-looking. There was a cupboard full of liqueur bottles. I looked at them all. Bill was still playing. "How about a hot rum punch?" he said. "This isn't going to keep me warm permanently."

I went out and told the woman what a rum punch was and how to make it. In a few minutes a girl brought a stone pitcher, steaming, into the room. Bill came over from the piano and we drank the hot punch and listened to the wind.

"There isn't too much rum in that."

I went over to the cupboard and brought the rum bottle and poured a half-tumblerful into the pitcher.

"Direct action," said Bill. "It beats legislation."

The girl came in and laid the table for supper.

"It blows like hell up here," Bill said.

The girl brought in a big bowl of hot vegetable soup and the wine. We had fried trout afterward and some sort of stew and a big bowl of wild strawberries. We did not lose money on the wine, and the girl was shy but nice about bringing it. The old woman looked in once and counted the empty bottles.

After supper we went up-stairs and smoked and read in bed to keep warm. Once in the night I woke and heard the wind blowing. It felt good to be warm and in bed.

When I woke in the morning I went to the window and looked out. It had cleared and there were no clouds on the mountains. Outside under the window were some carts and an old diligence, the wood of the roof cracked and split by the weather. It must have been left from the days before the motor-buses. A goat hopped up on one of the carts and then to the roof of the diligence. He jerked his head at the other goats below and when I waved at him he bounded down.

Bill was still sleeping, so I dressed, put on my shoes outside in the hall, and went down-stairs. No one was stirring down-stairs, so I unbolted the door and went out. It was cool outside in the early morning and the sun had not yet dried the dew that had come when the wind died down. I hunted around in the shed behind the inn and found a sort of mattock, and went down toward the stream to try and dig some worms for bait. The stream was clear and shallow but it did not look trouty. On the grassy bank where it was damp I drove the mattock into the earth and loosened a chunk of sod. There were worms underneath. They slid out of sight as I lifted the sod and I dug carefully and got a good many. Digging at the edge of the damp ground I filled two empty tobacco-tins with worms and sifted dirt onto them. The goats watched me dig.

When I went back into the inn the woman was down in the kitchen, and I asked her to get coffee for us, and that we wanted a lunch. Bill was awake and sitting on the edge of the bed.

"I saw you out of the window," he said. "Didn't want to interrupt you. What were you doing? Burying your money?"

"You lazy bum!"

"Been working for the common good? Splendid. I want you to do that every morning."

"Come on," I said. "Get up."

"What? Get up? I never get up."

He climbed into bed and pulled the sheet up to his chin.

"Try and argue me into getting up."

I went on looking for the tackle and putting it all together in the tackle-bag.

"Aren't you interested?" Bill asked.

"I'm going down and eat."

"Eat? Why didn't you say eat? I thought you just wanted me to get up for fun. Eat? Fine. Now you're reasonable. You go out and dig some more worms and I'll be right down."

"Oh, go to hell!"

"Work for the good of all." Bill stepped into his underclothes. "Show irony and pity."

I started out of the room with the tackle-bag, the nets, and the rod-case.

"Hey! come back!"

I put my head in the door.

"Aren't you going to show a little irony and pity?"

I thumbed my nose.

"That's not irony."

As I went down-stairs I heard Bill singing, "Irony and Pity. When you're feeling . . . Oh, Give them Irony and Give them Pity. Oh, give them Irony. When they're feeling . . . Just a little irony. Just a little pity . . ." He kept on singing until he came down-stairs. The tune was: "The Bells are Ringing for Me and my Gal." I was reading a week-old Spanish paper.

"What's all this irony and pity?"

"What? Don't you know abut Irony and Pity?"

"No. Who got it up?"

"Everybody. They're mad about it in New York. It's just like the Fratellinis used to be."

The girl came in with the coffee and buttered toast. Or, rather, it was bread toasted and buttered.

"Ask her if she's got any jam," Bill said. "Be ironical with her."

"Have you got any jam?"

"That's not ironical. I wish I could talk Spanish."

The coffee was good and we drank it out of big bowls. The girl brought in a glass dish of raspberry jam.

"Thank you."

"Hey! that's not the way," Bill said. "Say something ironical. Make some crack about Primo de Rivera."

"I could ask her what kind of a jam they think they've gotten into in the Riff."

"Poor," said Bill. "Very poor. You can't do it. That's all. You don't understand irony. You have no pity. Say something pitiful."

"Robert Cohn."

"Not so bad. That's better. Now why is Cohn pitiful? Be ironic."

He took a big gulp of coffee.

"Aw, hell!" I said. "It's too early in the morning."

"There you go. And you claim you want to be a writer, too. You're only a newspaper man. An expatriated newspaper man. You ought to be ironical the minute you get out of bed. You ought to wake up with your mouth full of pity."

"Go on," I said. "Who did you get this stuff from?"

"Everybody. Don't you read? Don't you ever see anybody? You know what you are? You're an expatriate. Why don't you live in New York? Then you'd know these things. What do you want me to do? Come over here and tell you every year?"

"Take some more coffee," I said.

"Good. Coffee is good for you. It's the caffeine in it. Caffeine, we are here. Caffeine puts a man on her horse and a woman in his grave. You know what's the trouble with you? You're an expatriate. One of the worst type. Haven't you heard that? Nobody that ever left their own country ever wrote anything worth printing. Not even in the newspapers."

He drank the coffee.

"You're an expatriate. You've lost touch with the soil. You get precious. Fake European standards have ruined you. You drink yourself to death. You become obsessed by sex. You spend all your time talking, not working. You are an expatriate, see? You hang around cafés."

"It sounds like a swell life," I said. "When do I work?"

"You don't work. One group claims women support you. Another group claims you're impotent."

"No," I said. "I just had an accident."

"Never mention that," Bill said. "That's the sort of thing that can't be spoken of. That's what you ought to work up into a mystery. Like Henry's bicycle."

He had been going splendidly, but he stopped. I was afraid he thought he had hurt me with that crack about being impotent. I wanted to start him again.

"It wasn't a bicycle," I said. "He was riding horseback."

"I heard it was a tricycle."

"Well," I said. "A plane is sort of like a tricycle. The joystick works the same way."

"But you don't pedal it."

"No," I said, "I guess you don't pedal it."

"Let's lay off that," Bill said.

"All right. I was just standing up for the tricycle."

"I think he's a good writer, too," Bill said. "And you're a hell of a good guy. Anybody ever tell you you were a good guy?"

"I'm not a good guy."

"Listen. You're a hell of a good guy, and I'm fonder of you than anybody on earth. I couldn't tell you that in New York. It'd mean I was a faggot. That was what the Civil War was about. Abraham Lincoln was a faggot. He was in love with General Grant. So was Jefferson Davis. Lincoln just freed the slaves on a bet. The Dred Scott case was framed by the Anti-Saloon League. Sex explains it all. The Colonel's Lady and Judy O'Grady are Lesbians under their skin."

He stopped.

"Want to hear some more?"

"Shoot," I said.

"I don't know any more. Tell you some more at lunch."

"Old Bill," I said.

"You bum!"

We packed the lunch and two bottles of wine in the rucksack, and Bill put it on. I carried the rod-case and the landing-nets slung over my back. We started up the road and then went across a meadow and found a path that crossed the fields and went toward the woods on the slope of the first hill. We walked across the fields on the sandy path. The fields were rolling and grassy and the grass was short from the sheep grazing. The cattle were up in the hills. We heard their bells in the woods.

The path crossed a stream on a foot-log. The log was surfaced off, and there was a sapling bent across for a rail. In the flat pool beside the stream tadpoles spotted the sand. We went up a steep bank and across the rolling fields. Looking back we saw Burguete, white houses and red roofs, and the white road with a truck going along it and the dust rising.

Beyond the fields we crossed another faster-flowing steam. A sandy road led down to the ford and beyond into the woods. The path crossed the stream on another foot-log below the ford, and joined the road, and we went into the woods.

It was a beech wood and the trees were very old. Their roots bulked above the ground and the branches were twisted. We walked on the road between the thick trunks of the old beeches and the sunlight came through the leaves in light patches on the grass. The trees were big, and the foliage was thick but it was not gloomy. There was no undergrowth, only the smooth grass, very green and fresh, and the big gray trees well spaced as though it were a park.

"This is country," Bill said.

The road went up a hill and we got into thick woods, and the road kept on climbing. Sometimes it dipped down but rose again steeply. All the time we heard the cattle in the woods. Finally, the road came out on the top of the hills. We were on the top of the height of land that was the highest part of the range of wooded hills we had seen from Burguete. There were wild strawberries growing on the sunny side of the ridge in a little clearing in the trees.

Ahead the road came out of the forest and went along the shoulder of the ridge of hills. The hills ahead were not wooded, and there were great fields of yellow gorse. Way off we saw the steep bluffs, dark with trees and jutting with gray stone, that marked the course of the Irati River.

"We have to follow this road along the ridge, cross these hills, go through the woods on the far hills, and come down to the Irati valley," I pointed out to Bill.

"That's a hell of a hike."

"It's too far to go and fish and come back the same day, comfortably."

"Comfortably. That's a nice word. We'll have to go like hell to get there and back and have any fishing at all."

It was a long walk and the country was very fine, but we were tired when we came down the steep road that led out of the wooded hills into the valley of the Rio de la Fabrica.

The road came out from the shadow of the woods into the hot sun. Ahead was a river-valley. Beyond the river was a steep hill. There was a field of buckwheat on the hill. We saw a white house under some trees on the hillside. It was very hot and we stopped under some trees beside a dam that crossed the river.

Bill put the pack against one of the trees and we jointed up the rods, put on the reels, tied on leaders, and got ready to fish.

"You're sure this thing has trout in it?" Bill asked.

"It's full of them."

"I'm going to fish a fly. You got any McGintys?"

"There's some in there."

"You going to fish bait?"

"Yeah. I'm going to fish the dam here."

"Well, I'll take the fly-book, then." He tied on a fly. "Where'd I better go? Up or down?"

"Down is the best. They're plenty up above, too."

Bill went down the bank.

"Take a worm can."

"No, I don't want one. If they won't take a fly I'll just flick it around."

Bill was down below watching the stream.

"Say," he called up against the noise of the dam. "How about putting the wine in that spring up the road?"

"All right," I shouted. Bill waved his hand and started down the stream. I found the two wine-bottles in the pack, and carried them up the road to where the water of a spring flowed out of an iron pipe. There was a board over the spring and I lifted it and, knocking the corks firmly into the bottles, lowered them down into the water. It was so cold my hand and wrist felt numbed. I put back the slab of wood, and hoped nobody would find the wine.

I got my rod that was leaning against the tree, took the bait-can and landing-net, and walked out onto the dam. It was built to provide a head of water for driving logs. The gate was up, and I sat on one of the squared timbers and watched the smooth apron of water before the river tumbled into the falls. In the white water at the foot of the dam it was deep. As I baited up, a trout shot up out of the white water into the falls and was carried down. Before I could finish baiting, another trout jumped at the falls, making the same lovely arc and disappearing into the water that was thundering down. I put on a good-sized sinker and dropped into the white water close to the edge of the timbers of the dam.

I did not feel the first trout strike. When I started to pull up I felt that I had one and brought him, fighting and bending the rod almost double, out of the boiling water at the foot of the falls, and swung him up and onto the dam. He was a good trout, and I banged his head against the timber so that he quivered out straight, and then slipped him into my bag.

While I had him on, several trout had jumped at the falls. As soon as I baited up and dropped in again I hooked another and brought him in the same way. In a little while I had six. They were all about the same size. I laid them out, side by side, all their heads pointing the same way, and looked at them. They were beautifully colored and firm and hard from the cold water. It was a hot day, so I slit them all and shucked out the insides, gills and all, and tossed them over across the river. I took the trout ashore, washed them in the cold, smoothly heavy water above the dam, and then picked some ferns and packed them all in the bag, three trout on a layer of ferns, then another layer of ferns, then three more trout, and then covered them with ferns. They looked nice in the ferns, and now the bag was bulky, and I put it in the shade of the tree.

It was very hot on the dam, so I put my worm-can in the shade with the bag, and got a book out of the pack and settled down under the tree to read until Bill should come up for lunch.

It was a little past noon and there was not much shade, but I sat against the trunk of two of the trees that grew together, and read. The book was something by A. E. W. Mason, and I was reading a wonderful story about a man who had been frozen in the Alps and then fallen into a glacier and disappeared, and his bride was going to wait twenty-four years exactly for his body to come out on the moraine, while her true love waited too, and they were still waiting when Bill came up.

"Get any?" he asked. He had his rod and his bag and his net all in one hand, and he was sweating. I hadn't heard him come up, because of the noise from the dam.

"Six. What did you get?"

Bill sat down, opened up his bag, laid a big trout on the grass. He took out three more, each one a little bigger than the last, and laid them side by side in the shade from the tree. His face was sweaty and happy.

"How are yours?"

"Smaller."

"Let's see them."

"They're packed."

"How big are they really?"

"They're all about the size of your smallest."

"You're not holding out on me?"

"I wish I were."

"Get them all on worms?"

"Yes."

"You lazy bum!"

Bill put the trout in the bag and started for the river, swinging the open bag. He was wet from the waist down and I knew he must have been wading the stream.

I walked up the road and got out the two bottles of wine. They were cold. Moisture beaded on the bottles as I walked back to the trees. I spread the lunch on a newspaper, and uncorked one of the bottles and leaned the other against a tree. Bill came up drying his hands, his bag plump with ferns.

"Let's see that bottle," he said. He pulled the cork, and tipped up the bottle and drank. "Whew! That makes my eyes ache."

"Let's try it."

The wine was icy cold and tasted faintly rusty.

"That's not such filthy wine," Bill said.

"The cold helps it," I said.

We unwrapped the little parcels of lunch.

"Chicken."

"There's hard-boiled eggs."

"Find any salt?"

"First the egg," said Bill. "Then the chicken. Even Bryan could see that."

"He's dead. I read it in the paper yesterday."

"No. Not really?"

"Yes. Bryan's dead."

Bill laid down the egg he was peeling.

"Gentlemen," he said, and unwrapped a drumstick from a piece of newspaper. "I reverse the order. For Bryan's sake. As a tribute to the Great Commoner. First the chicken; then the egg."

"Wonder what day God created the chicken?"

"Oh," said Bill, sucking the drumstick, "how should we know? We should not question. Our stay on earth is not for long. Let us rejoice and believe and give thanks."

"Eat an egg."

Bill gestured with the drumstick in one hand and the bottle of wine in the other.

"Let us rejoice in our blessings. Let us utilize the fowls of the air. Let us utilize the product of the vine. Will you utilize a little, brother?"

"After you, brother."

Bill took a long drink.

"Utilize a little, brother," he handed me the bottle. "Let us not doubt, brother. Let us not pry into the holy mysteries of the hencoop with simian fingers. Let us accept on faith and simply say—I want you to join with me in saying—What shall we say, brother?" He pointed the drumstick at me and went on. "Let me tell you. We will say, and I for one am proud to say—and I want you to say with me, on your knees, brother. Let no man be ashamed to kneel here in the great out-of-doors. Remember the woods were God's first temples. Let us kneel and say: 'Don't eat that, Lady—that's Mencken.'"

"Here," I said. "Utilize a little of this."

We uncorked the other bottle.

"What's the matter?" I said. "Didn't you like Bryan?"

"I loved Bryan," said Bill. "We were like brothers."

"Where did you know him?"

"He and Mencken and I all went to Holy Cross together."

"And Frankie Fritsch."

"It's a lie. Frankie Fritsch went to Fordham."

"Well," I said, "I went to Loyola with Bishop Manning."

"It's a lie," Bill said. "I went to Loyola with Bishop Manning myself."

"You're cock-eyed," I said.

"On wine?"

"Why not?

"It's the humidity," Bill said. "They ought to take this damn humidity away."

"Have another shot."

"Is this all we've got?"

"Only the two bottles."

"Do you know what you are?" Bill looked at the bottle affectionately.

"No," I said.

"You're in the pay of the Anti-Saloon League."

"I went to Notre Dame with Wayne B. Wheeler."

"It's a lie," said Bill. "I went to Austin Business College with Wayne B. Wheeler. He was class president."

"Well," I said, "the saloon must go."

"You're right there, old classmate," Bill said. "The saloon must go, and I will take it with me."

"You're cock-eyed."

"On wine?"

"On wine."

"Well, maybe I am."

"Want to take a nap?"

"All right."

We lay with our heads in the shade and looked up into the trees.

"You asleep?"

"No," Bill said. "I was thinking."

I shut my eyes. It felt good lying on the ground.

"Say," Bill said, "what about this Brett business?"

"What about it?"

"Were you ever in love with her?"

"Sure."

"For how long?"

"Off and on for a hell of a long time."

"Oh, hell!" Bill said. "I'm sorry, fella."

"It's all right," I said. "I don't give a damn any more."

"Really?"

"Really. Only I'd a hell of a lot rather not talk about it."

"You aren't sore I asked you?"

"Why the hell should I be?"

"I'm going to sleep," Bill said. He put a newspaper over his face.

"Listen, Jake," he said, "are you really a Catholic?"

"Technically."

"What does that mean?"

"I don't know."

"All right, I'll go to sleep now," he said. "Don't keep me awake by talking so much."

I went to sleep, too. When I woke up Bill was packing the rucksack. It was late in the afternoon and the shadow from the trees was long and went out over the dam. I was stiff from sleeping on the ground.

"What did you do? Wake up?" Bill asked. "Why didn't you spend the night?" I stretched and rubbed my eyes.

"I had a lovely dream," Bill said. "I don't remember what it was about, but it was a lovely dream."

"I don't think I dreamt."

"You ought to dream," Bill said. "All our biggest business men have been dreamers. Look at Ford. Look at President Coolidge. Look at Rockefeller. Look at Jo Davidson."

I disjointed my rod and Bill's and packed them in the rod-case. I put the reels in the tackle-bag. Bill had packed the rucksack and we put one of the trout-bags in. I carried the other.

"Well," said Bill, "have we got everything?"

"The worms."

"Your worms. Put them in there."

He had the pack on his back and I put the worm-cans in one of the outside flap pockets.

"You got everything now?"

I looked around on the grass at the foot of the elm-trees.

"Yes."

We started up the road into the woods. It was a long walk home to Burguete, and it was dark when we came down across the fields to the road, and along the road between the houses of the town, their windows lighted, to the inn.

We stayed five days at Burguete and had good fishing. The nights were cold and the days were hot, and there was always a breeze even in the heat of the day. It was hot enough so that it felt good to wade in a cold stream, and the sun dried you when you came out and sat on the bank. We found a stream with a pool deep enough to swim in. In the evenings we played three-handed bridge with an Englishman named Harris, who had walked over from Saint Jean Pied de Port and was stopping at the inn for the fishing. He was very pleasant and went with us twice to the Irati River. There was no word from Robert Cohn nor from Brett and Mike.

One morning I went down to breakfast and the Englishman, Harris, was already at the table. He was reading the paper through spectacles. He looked up and smiled.

"Good morning," he said. "Letter for you. I stopped at the post and they gave it me with mine."

The letter was at my place at the table, leaning against a coffee-cup. Harris was reading the paper again. I opened the letter. It had been forwarded from Pamplona. It was dated San Sebastian, Sunday:

Dear Jake,

We got here Friday, Brett passed out on the train, so brought her here for 3 days rest with old friends of ours. We go to Montoya Hotel Pamplona Tuesday, arriving at I don't know what hour. Will you send a note by the bus to tell us what to do to rejoin you all on Wednesday. All our love and sorry to be late, but Brett was really done in and will be quite all right by Tues. and is practically so now. I know her so well and try to look after her but it's not so easy. Love to all the chaps,

MICHAEL.

"What day of the week is it?" I asked Harris.

"Wednesday, I think. Yes, quite. Wednesday. Wonderful how one loses track of the days up here in the mountains."

"Yes. We've been here nearly a week."

"I hope you're not thinking of leaving?"

"Yes. We'll go in on the afternoon bus, I'm afraid."

"What a rotten business. I had hoped we'd all have another go at the Irati together."

"We have to go into Pamplona. We're meeting people there."

"What rotten luck for me. We've had a jolly time here at Burguete."

"Come on in to Pamplona. We can play some bridge there, and there's going to be a damned fine fiesta."

"I'd like to. Awfully nice of you to ask me. I'd best stop on here, though. I've not much more time to fish."

"You want those big ones in the Irati."

"I say, I do, you know. They're enormous trout there."

"I'd like to try them once more."

"Do. Stop over another day. Be a good chap."

"We really have to get into town," I said.

"What a pity."

After breakfast Bill and I were sitting warming in the sun on a bench out in front of the inn and talking it over. I saw a girl coming up the road from the centre of the town. She stopped in front of us and took a telegram out of the leather wallet that hung against her skirt.

"Por ustedes?"

I looked at it. The address was: "Barnes, Burguete."

"Yes. It's for us."

She brought out a book for me to sign, and I gave her a couple of coppers. The telegram was in Spanish: "Vengo Jueves Cohn."

I handed it to Bill.

"What does the word Cohn mean?" he asked.

"What a lousy telegram!" I said. "He could send ten words for the same price. 'I come Thursday'. That gives you a lot of dope, doesn't it?"

"It gives you all the dope that's of interest to Cohn."

"We're going in, anyway," I said. "There's no use trying to move Brett and Mike out here and back before the fiesta. Should we answer it?"

"We might as well," sid Bill. "There's no need for us to be snooty."

We walked up to the post-office and asked for a telegraph blank.

"What will we say?" Bill asked.

"'Arriving to-night.' That's enough."

We paid for the message and walked back to the inn. Harris was there and the three of us walked up to Roncesvalles. We went through the monastery.

"It's a remarkable place," Harris said, when we came out. "But you know I'm not much on those sort of places."

"Me either," Bill said.

"It's a remarkable place, though," Harris said. "I wouldn't not have seen it. I'd been intending coming up each day."

"It isn't the same as fishing, though, is it?" Bill asked. He liked Harris.

"I say not."

We were standing in front of the old chapel of the monastery.

"Isn't that a pub across the way?" Harris asked. "Or do my eyes deceive me?"

"It has the look of a pub," Bill said.

"It looks to me like a pub," I said.

"I say," said Harris, "let's utilize it." He had taken up utilizing from Bill.

We had a bottle of wine apiece. Harris would not let us pay. He talked Spanish quite well, and the innkeeper would not take our money.

"I say. You don't know what it's meant to me to have you chaps up here."

73

"We've had a grand time, Harris."

Harris was a little tight.

"I say. Really you don't know how much it means. I've not had much fun since the war."

"We'll fish together again, some time. Don't you forget it, Harris."

"We must. We *have* had such a jolly good time."

"How about another bottle around?"

"Jolly good idea," said Harris.

"This is mine," said Bill. "Or we don't drink it."

"I wish you'd let me pay for it. It *does* give me pleasure, you know."

"This is going to give me pleasure," Bill said.

The innkeeper brought in the fourth bottle. We had kept the same glasses. Harris lifted his glass.

"I say. You know this does utilize well."

Bill slapped him on the back.

"Good old Harris."

"I say. You know my name isn't really Harris. It's Wilson-Harris. All one name. With a hyphen, you know."

"Good old Wilson-Harris," Bill said. "We call you Harris because we're so fond of you."

"I say, Barnes. You don't know what this all means to me."

"Come on and utilize another glass," I said.

"Barnes. Really, Barnes, you can't know. That's all."

"Drink up, Harris."

We walked back down the road from Roncesvalles with Harris between us. We had lunch at the inn and Harris went with us to the bus. He gave us his card, with his address in London and his club and his business address, and as we got on the bus he handed us each an envelope. I opened mine and there were a dozen flies in it. Harris had tied them himself. He tied all his own flies.

"I say, Harris—" I began.

"No, no!" he said. He was climbing down from the bus.

"They're not first-rate flies at all. I only thought if you fished them some time it might remind you of what a good time we had."

The bus started. Harris stood in front of the post-office. He waved. As we started along the road he turned and walked back toward the inn.

"Say, wasn't that Harris nice?" Bill said.

"I think he really did have a good time."

"Harris? You bet he did."

"I wish he'd come into Pamplona."

"He wanted to fish."

"Yes. You couldn't tell how English would mix with each other, anyway."

"I suppose not."

"The River"

(from *A Moveable Feast*)

What did I know best that I had not written about and lost? What did
I know about truly and care for the most? There was no choice at all.
There was only the choice of streets to take you back fastest to
where you worked. I went up Bonaparte to Guynemer, then to the
rue d'Assas, up the rue Notre-Dame-des-Champs to the Closerie
des Lilas.

I sat in a corner with the afternoon light coming in over my
shoulder and wrote in the notebook. The waiter brought me a *café
crème* and I drank half of it when it cooled and left it on the table
while I wrote. When I stopped writing I did not want to leave the
river where I could see the trout in the pool, its surface pushing and
swelling smooth against the resistance of the log-driven piles of the
bridge. The story was about coming back from the war but there
was no mention of the war in it.

But in the morning the river would be there and I must make it
and the country and all that would happen. There were days ahead
to be doing that each day. No other thing mattered. In my pocket

was the money from Germany so there was no problem. When that was gone some other money would come in.

All I must do now was stay sound and good in my head until morning when I would start to work again.

"Three Big Trout"

(from *Green Hills of Africa*)

"What about time?"

"We've got to get out. Make it back tomorrow night if you can. Use your own judgment. I think this is the turning point. You'll get a kudu."

"Do you know what it's like?" I said. "It's just like when we were kids and we heard about a river no one had ever fished out on the huckleberry plains beyond the Sturgeon and the Pigeon."

"How did the river turn out?"

"Listen. We had a hell of a time to get in and the night we got there, just before dark, and saw it, there was a deep pool and a long straight stretch and the water so cold you couldn't keep your hand in it and they kept snapping it up and spitting it out as it floated until it went to pieces."

"Big trout?"

"The biggest kind."

"God save us," said Pop. "What did you do then?"

"Rigged up my rod and made a cast and it was dark and there

was a nighthawk swooping around and it was cold as a bastard and then I was fast to three fish the second the flies hit the water."

"Did you land them?"

"The three of them."

"You damned liar."

"I swear to God."

"I believe you. Tell me the rest when you come back. Were they big trout?"

"The biggest bloody kind."

"God save us," said Pop. "You're going to get a kudu. Get started."

"The Stream"

(from *Green Hills of Africa*)

If you serve time for society, democracy, and the other things quite
young, and declining any further enlistment make yourself respon-
sible only to yourself, you exchange the pleasant, comforting stench
of comrades for something you can never feel in any other way than
by yourself. That something I cannot yet define completely but the
feeling comes when you write well and truly of something and
know impersonally you have written in that way and those who are
paid to read it and report on it do not like the subject so they say it
is all a fake, yet you know its value absolutely; or when you do
something which people do not consider a serious occupation and
yet you know, truly, that it is as important and has always been as
important as all the things that are in fashion, and when, on the sea,
you are alone with it and know that this Gulf Stream you are living
with, knowing, learning about, and loving, has moved, as it moves,
since before man, and that it has gone by the shoreline of that long,
beautiful, unhappy island since before Columbus sighted it and
that the things you find out about it, and those that have always

lived in it are permanent and of value because that stream will flow, as it has flowed, after the Indians, after the Spaniards, after the British, after the Americans and after all the Cubans and all the systems of governments, the richness, the poverty, the martyrdom, the sacrifice and the venality and the cruelty are all gone as the high-piled scow of garbage, bright-colored, white-flecked, ill-smelling, now tilted on its side, spills off its load into the blue water, turning it a pale green to a depth of four or five fathoms as the load spreads across the surface, the sinkable part going down and the flotsam of palm fronds, corks, bottles, and used electric light globes, seasoned with an occasional condom or a deep floating corset, the torn leaves of a student's exercise book, a well-inflated dog, the occasional rat, the no-longer-distinguished cat; all this well shepherded by the boats of the garbage pickers who pluck their prizes with long poles, as interested, as intelligent, and as accurate as historians; they have the viewpoint; the stream, with no visible flow, takes five loads of this a day when things are going well in La Habana and in ten miles along the coast it is as clear and blue and unimpressed as it was ever before the tug hauled out the scow; and the palm fronds of our victories, the worn light bulbs of our discoveries and the empty condoms of our great loves float with no significance against one single, lasting thing—the stream.

II

Dispatches from Various Waters—
The Soo to the
Great Blue River

The Best Rainbow Trout Fishing

Toronto Star Weekly, August 28, 1920

Rainbow trout fishing is as different from brook fishing as prize fighting is from boxing. The rainbow is called *Salmo iridescens* by those mysterious people who name the fish we catch and has recently been introduced into Canadian waters. At present the best rainbow trout fishing in the world is in the rapids of the Canadian Soo.

There the rainbow have been taken as large as fourteen pounds from canoes that are guided through the rapids and halted at the pools by Ojibway and Chippewa boatmen. It is a wild and nerve-frazzling sport and the odds are in favor of the big trout who tear off thirty or forty yards of line at a rush and then will sulk at the base of a big rock and refuse to be stirred into action by the pumping of a stout fly rod aided by a fluent monologue of Ojibwayian profanity. Sometimes it takes two hours to land a really big rainbow under those circumstances.

The Soo affords great fishing. But it is a wild nightmare kind of fishing that is second only in strenuousness to angling for tuna off Catalina Island. Most of the trout too take a spinner and refuse a fly and to the 99 per cent pure fly fisherman, there are no one hundred per centers, that is a big drawback.

Of course the rainbow trout of the Soo will take a fly but it is rough handling them in that tremendous volume of water on the light tackle a fly fisherman loves. It is dangerous wading in the spots that can be waded, too, for a mis-step will take the angler over his head in the rapids. A canoe is a necessity to fish the very best water.

Altogether it is a rough, tough, mauling game, lacking in the meditative qualities of the Izaak Walton school of angling. What would make a fitting Valhalla for the good fisherman when he dies would be a regular trout river with plenty of rainbow trout in it jumping crazy for the fly.

There is such a one not forty miles from the Soo called the— well, called the river. It is about as wide as a river should be and a little deeper than a river ought to be and to get the proper picture you want to imagine in rapid succession the following fade-ins:

A high pine covered bluff that rises steep up out of the shadows. A short sand slope down to the river and a quick elbow turn with a little flood wood jammed in the bend and then a pool.

A pool where the moselle colored water sweeps into a dark swirl and expanse that is blue-brown with depth and fifty feet across.

There is the setting.

The action is supplied by two figures that slog into the picture up the trail along the river bank with loads on their backs that would tire a pack horse. These loads are pitched over the heads onto the patch of ferns by the edge of the deep pool. That is incorrect. Really the figures lurch a little forward and the tump line loosens and the pack slumps onto the ground. Men don't pitch loads at the end of an eight mile hike.

One of the figures looks up and notes the bluff is flattened on top and that there is a good place to put a tent. The other is lying on his back and looking straight up in the air. The first reaches over and picks up a grasshopper that is stiff with the fall of the evening dew and tosses him into the pool.

The hopper floats spraddle legged on the water of the pool an instant, an eddy catches him and then there is a yard long flash of flame, and a trout as long as your forearm has shot into the air and the hopper has disappeared.

"Did you see that?" gasped the man who had tossed in the grasshopper.

It was a useless question, for the other, who a moment before would have served as a model for a study entitled "Utter Fatigue," was jerking his fly rod out of the case and holding a leader in his mouth.

We decided on a McGinty and a Royal Coachman for the flies and at the second cast there was a swirl like the explosion of a depth bomb, the line went taut and the rainbow shot two feet out of water. He tore down the pool and the line went out until the core of the reel showed. He jumped and each time he shot into the air we lowered the tip and prayed. Finally he jumped and the line went slack and Jacques reeled in. We thought he was gone and then he jumped right under our faces. He had shot upstream towards us so fast that it looked as though he were off.

When I finally netted him and rushed him up the bank and could feel his huge strength in the tremendous muscular jerks he made when I held him flat against the bank, it was almost dark. He measured twenty-six inches and weighed nine pounds and seven ounces.

That is rainbow trout fishing.

The rainbow takes the fly more willingly than he does bait. The McGinty, a fly that looks like a yellow jacket, is the best. It should be tied on a number eight or ten hook.

The smaller flies get more strikes but are too small to hold the really big fish. The rainbow trout will live in the same streams with brook trout but they are found in different kinds of places. Brook trout will be forced into the shady holes under the bank and where alders hang over the banks, and the rainbow will dominate the clear pools and the fast shallows.

Magazine writers and magazine covers to the contrary the brook or speckled trout does not leap out of water after he has been hooked. Given plenty of line he will fight a deep rushing fight. Of course if you hold the fish too tight he will be forced by the rush of the current to flop on top of the water.

But the rainbow always leaps on a slack or tight line. His leaps are not mere flops, either, but actual jumps out of and parallel with the water of from a foot to five feet. A five-foot jump by any fish sounds improbable, but it is true.

If you don't believe it tie onto one in fast water and try and force him. Maybe if he is a five-pounder he will throw me down and only jump four feet eleven inches.

Tuna Fishing in Spain

Toronto Star Weekly, February 18, 1922

Vigo, Spain.—Vigo is a pasteboard looking village, cobble streeted, white and orange plastered, set up on one side of a big, almost land-locked harbor that is large enough to hold the entire British navy. Sun-baked brown mountains slump down to the sea like tired old dinosaurs, and the color of the water is as blue as a chromo of the bay at Naples.

A grey pasteboard church with twin towers and a flat, sullen fort that tops the hill where the town is set up look out on the blue bay, where the good fishermen will go when snow drifts along the north-ern streams and trout lie nose to nose in deep pools under a scum of ice. For the bright, blue chromo of a bay is alive with fish.

It holds schools of strange, flat, rainbow-colored fish, hunting-packs of long, narrow Spanish mackerel, and big, heavy-shouldered sea-bass with odd, soft-sounding names. But principally it holds the king of all fish, the ruler of the Valhalla of fishermen.

The fisherman goes out on the bay in a brown lateen sailed boat that lists drunkenly and determinedly and sails with a skimming pull. He baits with a silvery sort of amulet and lets his line out to troll. As the boat moves along, close hauled to keep the bait under water, there is a silver splatter in the sea as though a bushel full of buckshot had been tossed in. It is a school of sardines jumping out of water, forced out by the swell of a big tuna who breaks water with a boiling crash and shoots his entire length six feet into the air. It is then that the fisherman's heart lodges against his palate, to sink to his heels when the tuna falls back into the water with the noise of a horse driving off a dock.

A big tuna is silver and slate blue, and when he shoots up into the air from close beside the boat it is like a blinding flash of quicksilver. He may weigh 300 pounds and he jumps with the eagerness and ferocity of a mammoth rainbow trout. Sometimes five and six tuna will be in the air at once in Vigo Bay, shouldering out of the water like porpoises as they herd the sardines, then leaping in a towering jump that is as clean and beautiful as the first leap of a well-hooked rainbow.

The Spanish boatmen will take you out to fish for them for a dollar a day. There are plenty of tuna and they take the bait. It is a back-sickening, sinew-straining, man-sized job even with a rod that looks like a hoe handle. But if you land a big tuna after a six-hour fight, fight him man against fish when your muscles are nauseated with the unceasing strain, and finally bring him up alongside the boat, green-blue and silver in the lazy ocean, you will be purified and be able to enter unabashed into the presence of the very elder gods and they will make you welcome.

For the cheerful, brown-face gods that judge over the happy hunting grounds live up in the old, crumbly mountains that wall the bright, blue bay of Vigo. They live there wondering why the good, dead fishermen don't come down to Vigo where the happy hunting grounds are waiting.

Fishing the Rhone Canal

Toronto Daily Star, June 10, 1922

Geneva, Switzerland.—In the afternoon a breeze blows up the Rhone valley from Lake Geneva. Then you fish up-stream with the breeze at your back, the sun on the back of your neck, the tall white mountains on both sides of the green valley and the fly dropping very fine and far off on the surface and under the edge of the banks of the little stream, called the Rhone canal, that is barely a yard wide, and flows swift and still.

Once I caught a trout that way. He must have been surprised at the strange fly and he probably struck from bravado, but the hook set and he jumped into the air twice and zigged nobly back and forth toward every patch of weed at the current bottom until I slid him up the side of the bank.

He was such a fine trout that I had to keep unwrapping him to take a look and finally the day got so hot that I sat under a pine tree on the back of the stream and unwrapped the trout entirely and ate a paper-bag full of cherries I had and read the trout-dampened Daily Mail. It was a hot day, but I could look out across the green, slow valley past the line of trees that marked the course of the

Rhone and watch a waterfall coming down the brown face of the mountain. The fall came out of a glacier that reached down toward a little town with four grey houses and three grey churches that was planted on the side of the mountain and looked solid, the waterfall, that is, until you saw it was moving. Then it looked cool and flickering, and I wondered who lived in the four houses and who went to the three churches with the sharp stone spires.

Now if you wait until the sun gets down behind the big shoulder of the Savoie Alps where France joins on to Switzerland, the wind changes in the Rhone valley and a cool breeze comes down from the mountains and blows down stream toward the Lake of Geneva. When this breeze comes and the sun is going down, great shadows come out from the mountains, the cows with their manypitched bells begin to be driven along the road, and you fish down the stream.

There are a few flies over the water and every little while some big trout rises and goes "plop" where a tree hangs over the water. You can hear the "plop" and look back of you up the stream and see the circles on the water where the fish jumped. Then is the time to rewrap the trout in Lord Northcliff's latest speech reported verbatim, the reported imminent demise of the coalition, the thrilling story of the joking earl and the serious widow, and, saving the [Horatio] Bottomley [fraud] case to read on the train going home, put the trout filled paper in your jacket pocket. There are great trout in the Canada du Rhone, and it is when the sun has dropped back of the mountains and you can fish down the stream with the evening breeze that they can be taken.

Fishing slowly down the edge of the stream, avoiding the willow trees near the water and the pines that run along the upper edge of what was once the old canal bank with your back cast, you drop the fly on to the water at every likely looking spot. If you are lucky, sooner or later there will be a swirl or a double swirl where the trout strikes and misses and strikes again, and then the old, deathless thrill of the plunge of the rod and the irregular plunging, circling, cutting up stream and shooting into the air fight the big trout puts up, no matter what country he may be in. It is a clear stream and there is no excuse for losing him when he is once hooked, so you tire him by working him against the current and then, when he shows a flash of white belly, slide him up against the bank and snake him up with a hand on the leader.

It is a good walk in to Aigle. There are horse chestnut trees along the road with their flowers that look like wax candles and the air is warm from the heat the earth absorbed from the sun. The road is white and dusty, and I thought of Napoleon's grand army, marching along it through the white dust on the way to the St. Bernard pass and Italy. Napoleon's batman may have gotten up at sun up before the camp and sneaked a trout or two out of the Rhone canal for the Little Corporal's breakfast. And before Napoleon, the Romans came along the valley and built this road and some Helvetian in the road gang probably used to sneak away from the camp in the evening to try for a big one in one of the pools under the willows. In the Roman days the trout perhaps weren't as shy.

So I went along the straight white road to Aigle through the evening and wondered about the grand army and the Romans and the Huns that traveled light and fast, and yet must have had time to try the stream along towards daylight, and very soon I was in Aigle, which is a very good place to be. I have never seen the town of Aigle, it straggles up the hillside, but there is a cafe across the station that has a galloping gold horse on top, a great wisteria vine as thick through as a young tree that branches out and shades the porch with hanging bunches of purple flowers that bees go in and out of all day long and that glisten after a rain; green tables with green chairs, and seventeen per cent dark beer. The beer comes foaming out in great glass mugs that hold a quart and cost forty centimes, and the barmaid smiles and asks about your luck.

Trains are always at least two hours apart in Aigle, and those waiting in the station buffet, this cafe with the golden horse and the wisteria hung porch is a station buffet, mind you, wish they would never come.

93

Trout Fishing in Europe

Toronto Star Weekly, November 17, 1923

Bill Jones went to visit a French financier who lives near Deauville and has a private trout stream. The financier was very fat. His stream was very thin.

"Ah, Monsieur Zshones, I will show you the fishing." The financier purred over the coffee. "You have the trout in Canada, is it not? But here! Here we have the really charming trout fishing of Normandy. I will show you. Rest yourself content. You will see it."

The financier was a very literal man. His idea of showing Bill the fishing was for Bill to watch and the financier to fish. They started out. It was a trying sight.

If undressed and put back on the shelf piece by piece the financier would have stocked a sporting goods store. Placed end to end his collection of flies would have reached from Keokuk, Ill., to Paris, Ont. The price of his rod would have made a substantial dent in the interallied debt or served to foment a central American revolution.

The financier flung a pretty poisonous fly, too. At the end of two hours one trout had been caught. The financier was elated. The trout was a beauty, fully five and a half inches long and perfectly proportioned. The only trouble with him was some funny black spots along his sides and belly.

"I don't believe he's healthy," Bill said doubtfully.

"Healthy? You don't think he's healthy? That lovely trout? Why, he's a wonder. Did you not see the terrible fight he made before I netted him?" The financier was enraged. The beautiful trout lay in his large, fat hand.

"But what are those black spots?" Bill asked.

"Those spots? Oh, absolutely nothing. Perhaps worms. Who can say? All of our trout here have them at this season. But do not be afraid of that, Monsieur Zshones. Wait until you taste this beautiful trout for your breakfast!"

It was probably the proximity to Deauville that spoiled the financier's trout stream. Deauville is supposed to be a sort of combination of Fifth Avenue, Atlantic City, and Sodom and Gomorrah. In reality it is a watering place that has become so famous that the really smart people no longer go to it and the others hold a competitive spending contest and take each other for duchesses, dukes, prominent pugilists, Greek millionaires and the Dolly sisters.

The real trout fishing of Europe is in Spain, Germany and Switzerland. Spain has probably the best fishing of all in Galicia. But the Germans and the Swiss are right behind.

In Germany the great difficulty is to get permission to fish. All the fishing water is rented by the year to individuals. If you want to fish you have first to get permission of the man who has rented the fishing. Then you go back to the township and get a permission, and then you finally get the permission of the owner of the land.

If you have only two weeks to fish, it will probably take about all of it to get these different permissions. A much easier way is simply to carry a rod with you and fish when you see a good stream. If anyone complains, begin handing out marks. If the complaints keep up, keep handing out marks. If this policy is pursued far enough the complaints will eventually cease and you will be allowed to continue fishing.

If, on the other hand, your supply of marks runs out before the complaints cease you will probably go either to jail or the hospital. It is a good plan, on this account, to have a dollar bill secreted somewhere in your clothes. Produce the dollar bill. It is ten to one your assailant will fall to his knees in an attitude of extreme thanksgiving and on arising break all existing records to the nearest, deepest and wooliest German hand knitted sock, the south German's savings bank.

Following this method of obtaining fishing permits, we fished all through the Black Forest. With rucksacks and fly-rods, we hiked across country, sticking to the high ridges and the rolling crests of the hills, sometimes through deep pine timber, sometimes coming out into a clearing and farmyards and again going, for miles, without seeing a soul except occasional wild looking berry pickers. We never knew where we were. But we were never lost because at any time we could cut down from the high country into a valley and know we would hit a stream. Sooner or later every stream flowed into a river and a river meant a town.

At night we stopped in little inns or gasthofs. Some of these were so far from civilization that the innkeepers did not know the mark was rapidly becoming worthless and continued to charge the old German prices. At one place, room and board, in Canadian money, were less than ten cents a day.

One day we started from Triberg and toiled up a long, steadily ascending hill road until we were on top of the high country and could look out at the Black Forest rolling away from us in every direction. Away off across country we could see a range of hills, and we figured that at their base must flow a river. We cut across the high, bare country, dipping down into valleys and walking through woods, cool and dim as a cathedral on the hot August day. Finally we hit the upper end of the valley at the foot of the hills we had seen.

In it flowed a lovely trout stream and there was not a farmhouse in sight. I jointed up the rod, and while Mrs. Hemingway sat under a tree on the hillside and kept watch both ways up the valley, caught four real trout. They averaged about three-quarters of a pound apiece. Then we moved down the valley. The stream broadened out and Herself took the rod while I found a look-out post.

She caught six in about an hour, and two of them I had to come down and net for her. She had hooked a big one, and after he was triumphantly netted we looked up to see an old German in peasant clothes watching us from the road.

"Gut tag," I said.

"Tag," he said. "Have you good fishing?"

"Yes. Very good."

"Good," he said. "It is good to have somebody fishing." And went hiking along the road.

In contrast to him were the farmers in Ober-Prechtal, where we had obtained full fishing permits, who came down and chased us away from the stream with pitchforks because we were Auslanders.

In Switzerland I discovered two valuable things about trout fishing. The first was while I was fishing a stream that parallels the Rhone river and that was swollen and grey with snow water. Flies were useless, and I was fishing with a big gob of worms. A fine, juicy-looking bait. But I wasn't getting any trout or even any strikes.

An old Italian who had a farm up the valley was walking behind me while I fished. As there was nothing doing in a stream I knew from experience was full of trout, it got more and more irritating. Somebody just back of you while you are fishing is as bad as someone looking over your shoulder while you write a letter to your girl. Finally I sat down and waited for the Italian to go away. He sat down, too.

He was an old man, with a face like a leather water bottle.

"Well, Papa, no fish to-day," I said.

"Not for you," he said solemnly.

"Why not for me? For you, maybe?" I said.

"Oh yes," he said, not smiling. "For me trout always. Not for you. You don't know how to fish with worms." And spat into the stream.

This touched a tender spot, a boyhood spent within forty miles of the Soo, hoisting out trout with a cane pole and all the worms the hook would hold.

"You're so old you know everything. You are probably a rich man from your knowledge of fishworms," I said.

This bagged him.

"Give me the rod," he said.

He took it from me, cleaned off the fine wriggling gob of trout food, and selected one medium-sized angleworm from my box. This he threaded a little way on the number 10 hook, and let about three-fourths of the worm wave free.

"Now that's a worm," he said with satisfaction.

He reeled the line up till there was only the six feet of leader out and dropped the free swinging worm into a pool where the stream swirled under the bank. There was nothing doing. He pulled it slowly out and dropped it in a little lower down. The tip of the rod twisted. He lowered it just a trifle. Then it shot down in a jerk, and he struck and horsed out a 15-inch trout and sent him back over his head in a telephone pole swing.

I fell on him while he was still flopping.

The old Italian handed me the rod. "There, young one. That is the way to use a worm. Let him be free to move like a worm. The trout will take the free end and then suck him all in, hook and all. I have fished this stream for twenty years and I know. More than one worm scares the fish. It must be natural."

"Come, use the rod and fish now," I urged him.

"No. No. I only fish at night," he smiled. "It is much too expensive to get a permit."

But by my watching of the river guard while he fished and our using the rod alternately until each caught a fish, we fished all day and caught 18 trout. The old Italian knew all the holes, and only fished where there were big ones. We used a free wriggling worm, and the 18 trout averaged a pound and a half apiece.

He also showed me how to use grubs. Grubs are only good in clear water, but are a deadly bait. You can find them in any rotten tree or sawlog, and the Swiss and Swiss-Italians keep them in grub boxes. Flat pieces of wood bored full of auger holes with a sliding metal top. The grub will live as well in his hole in the wood as in the log and is one of the greatest hot weather baits known. Trout will take a grub when they will take nothing else in the low water days of August.

The Swiss, too, have a wonderful way of cooking trout. They boil them in a liquor made of wine vinegar, bay leaves, and a dash of red pepper. Not too much of any of the ingredients in the boiling water, and cook until the trout turns blue. It preserves the true trout flavor better than almost any way of cooking. The meat stays firm and pink and delicate. Then they serve them with drawn butter. They drink the clear Sion wine when they eat them.

It is not a well-known dish at the hotels. You have to go back in the country to get trout cooked that way. You come up from the stream to a chalet and ask them if they know how to cook blue trout. If they don't you walk on away. If they do, you sit down on the porch with the goats and the children and wait. Your nose will tell you when the trout are boiling. Then after a little while you will hear a pop. That is the Sion being uncorked. Then the woman of the chalet will come to the door and say, "It is prepared, Monsieur."

Then you can go away and I will do the rest myself.

Marlin Off the Morro: A Cuban Letter

Esquire, Autumn 1933

The rooms on the northeast corner of the Ambos Mundos Hotel in Havana look out, to the north, over the old cathedral, the entrance to the harbor, and the sea, and to the east to Casablanca peninsula, the roofs of all houses in between and the width of the harbor. If you sleep with your feet toward the east, this may be against the tenets of certain religions, the sun, coming up over the Casablanca side and into your open window, will shine on your face and wake you no matter where you were the night before. If you do not choose to get up you can turn around the other way in the bed or roll over. That will not help for long because the sun will be getting stronger and the only thing to do is close the shutter.

Getting up to close the shutter you look across the harbor to the flag on the fortress and see it is straightened out toward you. You look out the north window past the Morro and see that the smooth morning sheen is rippling over and you know the trade wind is coming up early. You take a shower, pull on an old pair of khaki pants and a shirt, take the pair of moccasins that are dry, put the other pair in the window so they will be dry next night, walk to the elevator, ride down, get a paper at the desk, walk across the corner to the cafe and have breakfast.

There are two opposing schools about breakfast. If you knew you were not going to be into fish for two or three hours, a good big breakfast would be the thing. Maybe it is a good thing any way but I do not want to trust it, so drink a glass of vichy, a glass of cold milk and eat a piece of Cuban bread, read the papers and walk down to the boat. I have hooked them on a full stomach in that sun and I do not want to hook any more of them that way.

We have an ice-box that runs across the stern of the boat with bait iced down on one side and beer and fruit iced on the other. The best bait for big marlin is fresh cero mackerel or kingfish of a pound to three pounds weight. The best beer is Hatuey, the best fruits, in season, are Filipino mangoes, iced pineapple, and alligator pears. Ordinarily we eat the alligator pears for lunch with a sandwich, fixing them with pepper and salt and a freshly squeezed lime. When we run into the beach to anchor, swim and cook a hot lunch on days when fish are not running you can make a French dressing for the pears, adding a little mustard. You can get enough fine, big avocados to feed five people for fifteen cents.

The boat is the Anita, thirty-four feet long, very able in a sea, with plenty of speed for these fish, owned and skippered by Capt. Joe Russell of Key West who brought the first load of liquor that ever came into that place from Cuba and who knows more about swordfish than most Keywesters do about grunts. The other man on board is the best marlin and swordfisherman around Cuba, Carlos Gutierrez, of Zapata, 31, Havana, 54 years old, who goes Captain on a fishing smack in the winter and fishes marlin commercially in the summer. I met him six years ago in Dry Tortugas and first heard about the big marlin that run off Cuba from him. He can, literally, gaff a dolphin through the head back-handed and he has studied the habits of the marlin since he first went fishing for them as a boy of twelve with his father.

As the boat leaves the San Francisco wharf, tarpon are rolling in the slip. Going out of the harbor you see more of them rolling near the live fish cars that are buoyed alongside the line of anchored fishing smacks. Off the Morro in the entrance to the harbor there is a good coral bottom with about twenty fathoms of water and you pass many small boats bottom fishing for mutton fish and red snappers and jigging for mackerel and occasional kingfish. Outside the breeze freshens and as far as you can see the small boats of the marlin fishermen are scattered. They are fishing with four to six heavy handlines in from forty to seventy fathoms drifting for the fish that are travelling deep. We troll for the ones that are on the surface feeding, or travelling, or cruising fifteen or twenty fathoms down. They see the two big teasers or the baits and come up with a smash, usually going head and shoulders out of water on the strike.

Marlin travel from east to west against the current of the gulf stream. No one has ever seen them working in the other direction, although the current of the gulf stream is not so stable; sometimes, just before the new moon, being quite slack and at others running strongly to the westward. But the prevailing wind is the northeast trade and when this blows the marlin come to the top and cruise with the wind, the scythe tail, a light, steely lavender, cutting the swells as it projects and goes under; the big fish, yellow looking in the water, swimming two or three feet under the surface, the huge pectoral fins tucked close to the flanks, the dorsal fin down, the fish looking a round, fast-moving log in the water except for the erect curve of that slicing tail.

The heavier the current runs to the eastward the more marlin there are; travelling along the edge of the dark, swirling current from a quarter of a mile to four miles off shore; all going in the same direction like cars along a highway. We have been fighting a fish, on days when they were running well, and seen six others pass close to the boat during a space of half an hour.

As an indication of how plentiful they are, the official report from the Havana markets from the middle of March to the 18th of

July this year showed eleven thousand small marlin and one hundred and fifty large marlin were brought into the market by the commercial fishermen of Santa Cruz del Norte, Jaruco, Guanabo, Cojimar, Havana, Chorrera, Marianso, Jaimanitas, Baracoa, Banes, Mariel and Cabañas. Marlin are caught at Matanzas and Cardenas to the east and at Bahai Honda to the west of the towns mentioned but those fish are not shipped to Havana. The big fish had only been running two weeks when this report was compiled.

Fishing with rod and reel from the middle of April through the 18th of July of this season we caught fifty-two marlin and two sailfish. The largest black marlin was 468 pounds, and 12 feet 8 inches long. The largest striped marlin was 343 pounds and 10 feet five inches. The biggest white marlin weighed 87 pounds and was 7 feet 8 inches in length.

The white marlin run first in April and May, then come the immature striped marlin with brilliant stripes which fade after the fish dies. These are most plentiful in May and run into June. Then come the black and striped marlin together. The biggest run of striped marlin is in July and as they get scarce the very big black marlin come through until into September and later. Just before the striped marlin are due to run the smaller marlin drop off altogether and it seems, except for an occasional school of small tuna and bonito, as though the gulf stream were empty. There are so many color variations, some of them caused by feed, others by age, others by the depth of water, in these marlin that anyone seeking notoriety for himself by naming new species could have a field day along the north Cuba coast. For me they are all color and sexual variations of the same fish. This is too complicated a theory to go into a letter.

The marlin hit a trolled bait in four different ways. First, with hunger, again with anger, then simply playfully, last with indifference. Anyone can hook a hungry fish who gives him enough line, doesn't backlash and sets the hook hard enough. What happens then is something else. The main thing is to loosen your drag quickly enough when he starts to jump and make his run, and get the boat after him as he heads out to sea. The hungry marlin smashes at the bait with bill, shoulders, top fin and tail out. If he gets one bait he will turn and charge the other. If you pull the bait out of his mouth he will come for it again as long as there is any bait on the hook.

The angry fish puzzled us for a long time. He would come from below and hit the bait with a smash like a bomb exploding in the water. But as you slacked line to him he has dropped it. Screw down on the drag and race the bait in and he would slam it again without taking it. There is no way to hook a fish acting that way except to strike hard as he smashes. Put the drag on, speed up the boat and sock him as he crashes it. He slams the bait to kill it as long as it seems to believe.

The playful marlin, probably one who has fed well, will come behind a bait with his fin high, shove his bill clear out of water and take the bait lightly between his bill and pointed lower jaw. When you turn it loose to him he drops it. I am speaking of absolutely fresh bait caught that same day; if the bait were stale you might expect them all to refuse it once they had tasted it. This sort of fish can often be made to hit by speeding the boat up and skipping the bait over the top of the water with the rod. If he does take it, do not give him too much line before you hit him.

The indifferent fish will follow the boat for as many as three or four miles. Looking the baits over, sheering away, coming back to swim deep down below them and follow, indifferent to the bait, yet curious. If such a fish swims with his pectoral fins tucked close to his sides he will not bite. He is cruising and you are on his course. That is all. The minute a marlin sees the bait, if he is going to strike, he raises his dorsal fin and spreads those wide, bright blue pectorals so that he looks like some great, under-sea bird in the water as he follows.

The black marlin is a stupid fish. He is immensely powerful, can jump wonderfully and will break your back sounding but he has not the stamina of the striped marlin, nor his intelligence. I believe they are mostly old, female fish, past their prime and that it is age that gives them that black color. When they are younger they are much bluer and the meat, too, is whiter. If you fight them fast, never letting up, never resting, you can kill them quicker than you could ever kill a striped marlin of the same size. Their great strength makes them very dangerous for the first forty minutes. I mean dangerous to the tackle; no fish is dangerous to a man in a launch. But if you can take what they have to give during that time and keep working on them they will tire much quicker than any striped marlin. The 468 pounder was hooked in the roof of the mouth, was in no way tangled in the leader, jumped eight times completely clear, towed the boat stern first when held tight, sounded four times, but was brought to gaff at the top of the water, fin and tail out, in sixty-five minutes. But if I had not lost a much larger striped marlin the day before after two hours and twenty minutes, and fought a black one the day before for forty-five I would not have been in shape to work him so hard.

Fishing in a five-mile-an-hour current, where a hooked fish will always swim against the current, where the water is from four hundred to seven hundred fathoms deep, there is much to learn about tactics in fighting big fish. But one myth that can be dissipated is the old one that the water pressure at one thousand feet will kill the fish. A marlin dies at the bottom only if he has been hooked in the belly. These fish are used to going to the bottom. They often feed there. They are not built like bottom fish which live always at the same depth but are built to be able to go up and down in any depth. I have had a marlin sound four hundred yards straight down, all the rod under water over the side, bent double with that weight going down, down, down, watching the line go, putting on all pressure possible on the reel to check him, him going down and down until you are sure every inch of line will go. Suddenly he stops sounding and you straighten up, get onto your feet, get the butt in the socket and work him up slowly, finally you have the double line on the reel and think he is coming to gaff and then the line begins to rip out as he hooks up and heads off to sea just under the surface to come out in ten long, clean jumps. This after an hour and a half of fight. Then to sound again. They are a fish all right. The 343 pounder jumped 44 times.

You can fish for them in Cuba from April all through the summer. Big ones will be accidental until the middle of June and we only saw four broadbill all season. But in July and August it is even money any day you go out that you will hook into a fish from three hundred pounds up. Up means a very long way up. The biggest marlin ever brought into the market by the commercial fishermen weighed eleven hundred and seventy-five pounds with head cut off, gutted, tail cut off and flanks cut away; eleven hundred and seventy-five pounds when on the slab, nothing but the saleable meat ready to be cut into steaks. All right. You tell me. What did he weigh in the water and what did he look like when he jumped?

Out in the Stream: A Cuban Letter

Esquire, August 1934

The sun on the water is the toughest part of fishing the north coast of Cuba for marlin in July and August. Havana is cooler than most northern cities in those months because the northeast trades get up about ten o'clock in the forenoon and blow until four or five o'clock the next morning, and the northeast trade is a cool and pleasant wind, but out on the water even with a breeze, the sun gives you something to remember him by. You can avoid it by going to the eastward with the current in the morning, fishing with the boat headed into the sun, and then coming back against the current in the afternoon with the sun at your back again as you troll, but sometimes all the fish will be in the short stretch between Havana and Cojimar and there is nothing to do but work back and forth in and out of the sun and take it. I do not believe it is very bad for the eyes if you wear glasses with Crookes lenses. My eyes were much better after a hundred days in the gulf than they were when we started. But it gives you a schnozzle like some rare and unattractive tropical vegetable and in the evening the sun slants up off the water like molten lead and comes up under the long visor of one of those down east swordfishing caps and broils as it works toward that sun's ideal of a nose, the monumental proboscis of J. P. Morgan the elder.

You have a lot of time to think out in the gulf and you can touch the schnozzle with a little coconut oil with the left hand while the right holds the big reel and watch the bait bounce and the two teasers dip and dive and zig in and out in the wake and still have time to speculate on higher and lower things. Yes, you say, but why do they have to work into the sun? Why can't they work in and out, north and south instead of east and west?

It would be fine if you could but when the breeze gets up out of the northeast and blows against the current it makes a big sea and you cannot work in the trough of it but have to go either with it or against it.

Of course you may not ask that question at all. You may be bored blind with the whole thing and be waiting for the action to begin or the conversation to start. Gentlemen, I'd like to oblige you but this is one of those instructive ones. This is one of those contemplative pieces of the sort that Izaak Walton used to write (I'll bet you never read him either. You know what a classic is, don't you? A book that everyone mentions and no one reads) except that the charm, and quaintness and the literary value of Walton are omitted. Are they omitted intentionally? Ah, reader, thank you. Thank you and that's mighty white of you.

Well, here we have Piscator, as Walton puts it, sitting on a chair which, with the heat, has given him that unattractive condition called fisherman's seat, holding now in his hand a cold bottle of Hatuey beer, and trying to peer past his monumental schnozzle and out over the sea which is doing considerable rising and falling. The boat has been headed in the sun and if a fish comes now Piscator can see him. He can see the slicing wake of a fin, if he cuts toward the bait, or the rising and lowering sickle of a tail if he is travelling, or if he comes from behind he can see the bulk of him under water, great blue pectorals widespread like the wings of some huge, underwater bird, and the stripes around him like purple bands around a brown barrel, and then the sudden upthrust waggle of a bill. He can see the marlin's mouth open as the bill comes out of the water and see him slice off to the side and go down with the bait, sometimes to swim deep down with the boat so that the line seems slack and Piscator cannot come up against him solidly to hook him. Then when he is hooked he makes a sweeping turn, the drag screwed down, the line zings out and he breaks water, the drag loosed now, to go off jumping, throwing water like a speedboat, in those long, loping, rhythmic, pounding leaps of twenty feet and more in length.

To see that happen, to feel that fish in his rod, to feel that power and that great rush, to be a connected part of it and then to dominate it and master it and bring that fish to gaff, alone and with no one else touching rod, reel or leader, is something worth waiting many days for, sun and all, and as said, while you wait there is plenty of time to think. A good part of the things you think about are not put into a magazine printed on shiny paper and designed to go through the mails. Some they can put you in jail for if you write and others are simply no one's business but a great part of the time you think about fish.

Why does the south wind stop all fish biting off the north coast of Cuba while it makes them bite off the Florida keys?

Why will a mako shark not eat a hooked or dead marlin or swordfish when all other sharks will?

Is there a connection between the mako and the swordfish just as the wahoo, or peto, seems to be a connecting link between the kingfish and the sailfish and marlin?

What makes intelligence and courage in a fish like the mako who will refuse to pull, when hooked, unless you pull on him; who will deliberately charge a fisherman in a boat (I have a moving picture of this); who seems to be thinking while you are fighting him and will try different tactics to escape and come to the top of the water and rest during the fight; and who will swim around and round a hooked marlin and never hit him? The mako is a strange fish. His skin is not like a shark, his eye is not like a shark, his fins are more like a broadbill swordfish than a shark and his smell is sweet and not sharky. Only his mouth, full of those curved-in teeth that give him his Cuban name of *dentuso*, is a shark's mouth. And he has shark's gills.

What use is the sailfish's sail to that fish? Why should this fish which seems to be an unsuccessful model, an earlier and more fantastic model for the marlin, thin where the marlin is rounded, weak where the marlin is strong, provided with insufficient pectoral fins and too small a tail for its size, have survived? There must be a good reason for the sail. What is it?

Why do marlin always travel from east to west against the current and where do they go after they reach Cape San Antonio at the western end of Cuba? Is there a counter current hundreds of fathoms below the surface current and do they return working against that? Or do they make a circle through the Caribbean?

Why in the years of great abundance of marlin off the California coast are the fish equally plentiful off Cuba? Is it possible that marlin, the same fish, follow the warm currents of all the oceans, or that they have certain circuits that they make? They are caught in New Zealand, Tahiti, Honolulu, the Indian ocean, off Japan, off the west coast of South America, off the west coast of Mexico and as far north on the west coast of the United States as California. This year there were many small marlin taken off Miami, and the big ones appear off Bimini just across the gulf stream several months before they run in Cuba. Last summer they caught striped marlin as far north as Montauk Point off Long Island.

Are not the white marlin, the striped marlin and the black marlin all sexual and age variations of the same fish?

For me, with what data I have been able to get so far, they are all one fish. This may be wrong and I would be glad to have any one disprove the theory as what we want is knowledge, not the pride of proving something to be true. So far I believe that the white marlin, the common marlin caught off Miami and Palm Beach, whose top limit in weight is from 125 to 150 lbs., are the young fish of both sexes. These fish when caught have either a very faint stripe which shows in the water but disappears when the fish is taken from the sea or no stripe at all. The smallest I have ever seen weighed twenty-three pounds. At a certain weight, around seventy pounds and over, the male fish begin to have very pronounced and fairly wide stripes which show brightly in the water but fade when the fish dies and disappear an hour or so after death. These fish are invariably well rounded, obviously maturing marlin, are always males, and are splendid leapers and fighters in the style of the striped marlin. I believe they are the adolescent males of the marlin.

The striped marlin is characterized by his small head, heavily rounded body, rapier-like spear, and by the broad lavender stripes that, starting immediately behind the gills, encircle his body at irregular intervals all the way back to his tail. These stripes do not fade much after the fish is dead and will come up brightly hours after the fish has been caught if water is thrown over him.

All varieties of marlin breed off the Cuban coast and as the roe brings from forty cents to a dollar and a quarter a pound in the Havana market all fish are carefully opened for roe. Market fishermen say that all the striped marlin are males. On the other hand they claim all the black marlin are females.

But what is the immediate stage in the development of the female of the white marlin from the handsome, gleaming, well proportioned though rather large headed fish that it is as we know it at a hundred pounds, before it becomes the huge, ugly headed, thick billed, bulky, dark purple, coarse fleshed, comparatively ugly fish that has been called the black marlin?

I believe that its mature life is passed as what we call the silver marlin. This is a handsome, silvery marlin, unstriped, reaching a thousand pounds or more in weight and a terrific leaper and fighter. The market fishermen claim these fish are always females.

That leaves one type of marlin unaccounted for; the so-called blue marlin. I do not know whether these are a color variation stemming from the white, whether they are both male and female, or whether they are a separate species. This summer may show.

We have caught and examined some ninety-one marlin in the last two years and will need to catch and examine several hundred more before any conclusions can be drawn with even a pretense of accuracy. And all the fish should be examined by a scientist who should note the details of each fish.

The trouble is that to study them you have to catch them and catching them is a fairly full time job although it allows plenty of time for thinking.

It really should be subsidized too, because, by the time you buy gas in Havana at thirty cents a gallon to run twelve hours a day for a hundred days a year, get up at daylight every morning, sleep on your belly half the time because of what the fish do to your back— pay a man to gaff—another to be at the wheel, buy bait, reels at two hundred and fifty dollars apiece, six hundred yards of thirty-six thread line at a time, good rods, hooks and leaders, and try to do this out of the money you fenagle out of publishers and editors, you are too exhausted physically and financially to sit up nights counting the number of rays in the fins and putting a calipers on the ventral spikes with four hundred water front Cubans wanting to know why the fish isn't being cut up and distributed. Instead you are sitting in the stern of the boat, feeling pretty good and having a drink while the fish is being butchered out. You can't do everything.

All the people I know with enough wealth to subsidize anything are either busy studying how to get more wealth, or horses, or what is wrong with themselves with psychoanalysts, or horses, or how not to lose what wealth they have, or horses, or the moving picture business, or horses or all of these things together, and, possibly, horses. Also I freely admit that I would fish for marlin with great enjoyment even if it were of no scientific value at all and you cannot expect anyone to subsidize anything that anybody has a swell time out of. As a matter of fact I suppose we are lucky to be able to fish for them without being put in jail. This time next year they may have gotten out a law against it.

Curiosity, I suppose, is what makes you fish as much as anything and here is a very curious thing. This time last year we caught a striped marlin with a roe in it. It wasn't much of a roe it is true. It was the sort of a roe you would expect to find in certain moving picture actresses if they had roe, or in many actors. Examining it carefully it looked about like the sort of roe an interior decorator would have if he decided to declare himself and roe out. But it was a roe and the first one any of the commercial fishermen had ever seen in a striped marlin.

Until we saw this roe, and I wish I could describe it to you without getting too medical, all striped marlin were supposed to be males. All right then. Was this striped marlin how shall we put it or, as I had believed for a long time, do all marlin, white, striped, silver, etc. end their lives as black marlin, becoming females in the process? The jewfish becomes a female in the last of its life no matter how it starts and I believe the marlin does the same thing. The real black marlin are all old fish. You can see it in the quality of the flesh, the coarseness of the bill, and, above all in fighting them, in the way they live. Certainly they grow to nearly a ton in weight. But to me they are all old fish, all represent the last stages of the marlin, and they are all females.

Now you prove me wrong.

On Being Shot Again:
A Gulf Stream Letter

Esquire, June 1935

If you ever have to shoot a horse stand so close to him that you cannot miss and shoot him in the forehead at the exact point where a line drawn from his left ear to his right eye and another line drawn from his right ear to his left eye would intersect. A bullet there from a .22 caliber pistol will kill him instantly and without pain and all of him will race all the rest of him to the ground and he will never move except to stiffen his legs out so he falls like a tree.

If you ever have to shoot a shark shoot him anywhere along a straight line down the center of his head, flat, running from the tip of his nose to a foot behind his eyes. If you can, with your eye, intersect this line with a line running between his eyes and can hit that place it will kill him dead. A .22 will kill him as dead as a .45. But never think he may not move plenty afterwards simply because you know he is dead. He will have no more ideas after you hit him there, but he is capable of much undirected movement. What paralyzes him is clubbing him over the head.

If you want to kill any large animal instantly you shoot it in the brain if you know where that shot is and can call it. If you want to kill it, but it does not make any difference whether it moves after the shot, you can shoot for the heart. But if you want to stop any large animal you should always shoot for the bone. The best bone to break is the neck or any part of the spinal column; then the shoulders. A heavy four-legged animal can move with a broken leg but a broken shoulder will break him down and anchor him.

Your correspondent's mind has been turned to shooting and he is inspired to offer this information on account of just having shot himself in the calves of both legs. This difficult maneuver to perform with a single bullet was not undertaken as an experiment in ballistics but was quite casual. Your correspondent was once criticized in a letter by a reader of this magazine for not being a casual enough traveller. Trying to become more casual, your correspondent finally ends up by shooting himself through both legs with one hand while gaffing a shark with the other. This is as far as he will go in pleasing a reader. If the reader wants to break your correspondent down by smashing a large bone, or drop him cold with a well directed brain shot, or watch him race for the ice box with a bullet through the heart the reader will have to do the shooting himself.

We had left Key West early in the morning and were about twenty miles out in the Gulf Stream trolling to the eastward along a heavy, dark current of stream en route to Bimini in the Bahama Islands. The wind was in the south, blowing across the current; it was moderately rough fishing, but it was a pretty day. We had sighted a green turtle scudding under the surface and were rigging a harpoon to strike him, planning to salt him down in a keg, a layer of meat, a layer of salt, for meat for the trip, when Dos hooked a very large dolphin. While he played the dolphin we lost sight of the turtle.

Another dolphin hit Henry Strater, President of The Maine Tuna Club, hereinafter referred to as the President, and while the President was working on him a while a school of dolphin

showed green in the water and from below them a large black
shark of the type we call *galanos* on the Cuban coast came up to
cut the surface of the water behind the President's dolphin which
went into the air wildly. He kept in the air, wildly, the shark going
half out of water after him. The President worked on him with
Presidential skill and intelligence, giving him a free spool to run
away from the shark, and on the slack he threw the hook.

The dolphin were still around the stern and while Dos took
motion pictures we put another bait on the President's hook and he
slacked out to a dolphin and was still slacking to this or another dolphin when the shark had taken the bait in to what Old Bread, the
wheelsman, referred to in other terms as the outlet of his colon.

With the President hooked into this shark and sweating heavily
your correspondent slacked out from a gigantic new 14/0 reel with a
lot of discarded line on it (we had been testing the reel for capacity
and to see how the new VomHofe drag worked and had not put a
good line on it yet) and a very large *galano* swung up to the bait,
turned and started off with it, popping the old line. "Fornicate the
illegitimate," said your correspondent and slacked out another bait
on the same line. The *galano* with a length of double line streaming
out of his mouth like one whisker on a catfish turned and took this
bait too and, when your correspondent came back on him, popped
the old line again. At this your correspondent again addressed the
galano in the third person and slacked out a third bait on the President's heavy tackle. This bait the *galano* swam around several times
before taking; evidently he was tickled by the two lengths of double line which now streamed in catfishlike uncatfishivity (your correspondent has been reading, and admiring, *Pylon* by Mr. William
Faulkner), but finally swallowed the bait and started off, bending
the President's heavy hickory with the pull of the new thirty-nine
thread line while your correspondent addressed the *galano*, saying,
"All right you illegitimate, let's see you pull, you illegitimate."

For a few minutes your correspondent and the President
sweated, each busy with his own shark (the President's was on a light

outfit so he had to go easy with him), then your correspondent's came alongside, and while Saca, the cook, took hold of the leader your correspondent gaffed the *galano* and holding him with the big gaff shot him in the top of the head with the .22 caliber Colt automatic pistol shooting a greased, hollow-point, long rifle bullet. Dos was up on top of the boat, forward, taking some pictures of the shark going into a flurry and your correspondent was watching for a chance to shoot him again to quiet him enough so we could bring him up on the stern to club him into a state where we could cut the hooks out when the gaff broke with a loud crack, the shaft striking your correspondent across the right hand, and, looking down, your correspondent saw that he was shot through the calf of the left leg.

"I'll be of unsavoury parentage," remarked your correspondent. "I'm shot."

There was no pain and no discomfort; only a small hole about three inches below the knee-cap, another ragged hole bigger than your thumb, and a number of small lacerations on the calves of both legs. Your correspondent went over and sat down. The crack of the gaff shaft breaking and the report of the pistol had been at the same instant and no one else had heard the pistol go off. I could not see how there could have been more than one shot then. But where did the other wounds come from? Could I have pulled the trigger twice or three times without knowing it the way former mistresses did in the testimony regarding Love Nest Killings. Hell no, thought your correspondent. But where did all the holes come from then?

"Get the iodine, Bread."

"What did it, Cap?"

"I got shot when the gaff broke."

All this time the President was working hard on his *galano*.

"I can't figure it," I said. "There's a regular wound from a bullet that has mushroomed, but what in hell is all the little stuff? Look and see if you can find a hole in the cockpit where I was standing, or a bullet."

"Do you want a drink, Cap?" Bread asked.

"Later on."

"There ain't no bullet, Cap," Saca said. "Nowhere there at all."

"It's in there then. We've got to hook the hell up and go in."

"We got to pick up the dinghy, Cap," Bread said. "That we turned loose when you hung the sharks."

"Jeez Hem that's a hell of a note," Dos said. "We better go in."

"We better cut Mike loose," I said.

Saca went back to tell the President who was still working on the *galano*. The Pres. cut his line and came up to where I was sitting. "Hell, kid, I didn't know you were shot," he said. "I thought you were kidding. I felt some splatters hit my shoes. I thought you were joking. I wouldn't have kept on with the damned shark."

Your correspondent stood up and went back to the stern. There, on the top of the brass strip on top of the combing, slanted a little inside, was the starry splash the bullet had made when it ricocheted. That explained the fragments. The body of the bullet was in my left calf evidently. There was absolutely no pain at all. That is why your correspondent wrote at the head of this letter that if you want to stop large animals you should shoot for bone.

We boiled some water, scrubbed with an antiseptic soap, poured the holes all full of iodine while running into Key West. Your correspondent has to report that he made an equally skillful shot on his lunch into a bucket while running in, that Doctor Warren in Key West removed the fragments, probed, had an X-ray made, decided not to remove the large piece of bullet which was about three or four inches into the calf, and that his judgment was vindicated by the wound keeping clean and not infecting and that the trip was delayed only six days. The next of these letters will be from Bimini. Your correspondent hopes to keep them informative and casual.

One thing I am willing to state definitely now, in spite of all the literature on the subject that you have ever read, is that sailfish do not tap a bait to kill it. They take hold of a bait, more or less gingerly, between their lower jaw and the bill. Their lower jaw is movable and their upper jaw is fixed and is elongated into the bill or rostrum. What is mistaken for a tap is when the fish takes hold of the bait lightly and pulls on it tentatively. When the fish comes at the bait from directly behind it in order to take it in his mouth he must push his bill out of water to bring the bait within seizing range of the lower jaw. This is an awkward position to swim in and the fish's bill wobbles from side to side with the effort. While it is wobbling it might tap the leader or the bait even. But it would be accidental rather than a tap given to kill the bait.

If sailfish tap the bait rather than take it how would they be caught on baits fished from outriggers as they are fished on the charter boats at Miami and Palm Beach? The baited line is held by a wooden clothespin and the fish *must take hold of it to pull it loose.*

I came to consider the possibility of sailfish not tapping through watching more than four hundred marlin swordfish hit a bait without tapping it in spite of all I had read about them tapping. This winter I began to think about the question of whether sailfish tapped or not and we all watched their swimming action in the water very closely and also watched the way they hit. All this winter I did not see a single sailfish tap a bait; and on one day we hooked nine. Now I believe they never tap a bait to kill it any more than a marlin does.

One other thing we have found out this winter and spring. Large fish, marlin, big dolphin and sailfish, hang about the turtles, both green and loggerhead, that you see scudding, floating, or feeding in the Gulf Stream.

Always pass a bait close to a turtle when you see one out there. I believe the large fish hang around to feed on the small fish that congregate in the shade and the shelter of the turtle; exactly as they will congregate around your own boat if you are broke down or drifting in the stream.

Blue marlin also turned up this winter off Key West. One was caught and three others were hooked and broke away. We raised five during the winter; had strikes from two, and failed to hook either one. They surged at the strip bait, then followed for awhile and went down. Two were raised just outside the reef in about twelve fathoms of water. The other three were out better than ten miles in the stream.

On the way to Bimini we want to troll well out toward the axis of the Gulf Stream and see what we can raise. There is a lot of very fine looking current out there with a world of flying fish in it, that we have had to cross going back and forth to Cuba and you cannot tell what we may hit. Your correspondent plans not to hit himself in the leg.

On the Blue Water:
A Gulf Stream Letter

Esquire, April 1936

Certainly there is no hunting like the hunting of man and those who have hunted armed men long enough and liked it, never really care for anything else thereafter. You will meet them doing various things with resolve, but their interest rarely holds because after the other thing ordinary life is as flat as the taste of wine when the taste buds have been burned off your tongue. Wine, when your tongue has been burned clean with lye and water, feels like puddle water in your mouth, while mustard feels like axle-grease, and you can smell crisp, fried bacon, but when you taste it, there is only a feeling of crinkly lard.

You can learn about this matter of the tongue by coming into the kitchen of a villa on the Riviera late at night and taking a drink from what should be a bottle of Evian water and which turns out to be *Eau de Javel*, a concentrated lye product used for cleaning sinks. The taste buds on your tongue, if burned off by *Eau de Javel*, will begin to function again after about a week. At what rate other things regenerate one does not know, since you lose track of friends and the things one could learn in a week were mostly learned a long time ago.

The other night I was talking with a good friend to whom all hunting is dull except elephant hunting. To him there is no sport in anything unless there is great danger and, if the danger is not enough, he will increase it for his own satisfaction. A hunting companion of his had told me how this friend was not satisfied with the risks of ordinary elephant hunting but would, if possible, have the elephants driven, or turned, so he could take them head-on, so it was a choice of killing them with the difficult frontal shot as they came, trumpeting, with their ears spread, or having them run over him. This is to elephant hunting what the German cult of suicide climbing is to ordinary mountaineering, and I suppose it is, in a way, an attempt to approximate the old hunting of the armed man who is hunting you.

This friend was speaking of elephant hunting and urging me to hunt elephant, as he said that once you took it up no other hunting would mean anything to you. I was arguing that I enjoyed all hunting and shooting, any sort I could get, and had no desire to wipe this capacity for enjoyment out with the *Eau de Javel* of the old elephant coming straight at you with his trunk up and his ears spread.

"Of course you like that big fishing too," he said rather sadly. "Frankly, I can't see where the excitement is in that."

"You'd think it was marvelous if the fish shot at you with Tommy guns or jumped back and forth through the cockpit with swords on the ends of their noses."

"Don't be silly," he said. "But frankly I don't see where the thrill is."

"Look at so and so," I said. "He's an elephant hunter and this last year he's gone fishing for big fish and he's goofy about it. He must get a kick out of it or he wouldn't do it."

"Yes," my friend said. "There must be something about it but I can't see it. Tell me where you get a thrill out of it."

"I'll try to write it in a piece sometime," I told him.

"I wish you would," he said. "Because you people are sensible on other subjects. Moderately sensible I mean."

"I'll write it."

In the first place the Gulf Stream and the other great ocean currents are the last wild country there is left. Once you are out of sight of land and of the other boats you are more alone than you can ever be hunting and the sea is the same as it has been since before men ever went on it in boats. In a season fishing you will see it oily flat as the becalmed galleons saw it while they drifted to the westward; white-capped with a fresh breeze as they saw it running with the trades; and in high, rolling blue hills, the tops blowing off them like snow as they were punished by it, so that sometimes you will see three great hills of water with your fish jumping from the top of the farthest one and if you tried to make a turn to go with him without picking your chance, one of those breaking crests would roar down in on you with a thousand tons of water and you would hunt no more elephants, Richard, my lad.

There is no danger from the fish, but anyone who goes on the sea the year around in a small power boat does not seek danger. You may be absolutely sure that in a year you will have it without seeking, so you try always to avoid it all you can.

Because the Gulf Stream is an unexploited country, only the very fringe of it ever being fished, and then only at a dozen places in thousands of miles of current, no one knows what fish live in it, or how great size they reach or what age, or even what kinds of fish and animals live in it at different depths. When you are drifting, out of sight of land, fishing four lines, sixty, eighty, one hundred and one hundred fifty fathoms down, in water that is seven hundred fathoms deep you never know what may take the small tuna that you use for bait, and every time the line starts to run off the reel, slowly first, then with a scream of the click as the rod bends and you feel it double and the huge weight of the friction of the line rushing through that depth of water while you pump and reel, pump and reel, pump and reel, trying to get the belly out of the line before the fish jumps, there is always a thrill that needs no danger to make it real. It may be a marlin that will jump high and clear off to your right and then go off in a series of leaps, throwing a splash like a speedboat in a sea as you shout for the boat to turn with him watching the line melting off the reel before the boat can get around. Or it may be a broadbill that will show wagging his great broadsword. Or it may be some fish that you will never see at all that will head straight out to the northwest like a submerged submarine and never show and at the end of five hours the angler has a straightened-out hook. There is always a feeling of excitement when a fish takes hold when you are drifting deep.

In hunting you know what you are after and the top you can get is an elephant. But who can say what you will hook sometime when drifting in a hundred and fifty fathoms in the Gulf Stream? There are probably marlin and swordfish to which the fish we have seen caught are pygmies; and every time a fish takes the bait drifting you have a feeling perhaps you are hooked to one of these.

Carlos, our Cuban mate, who is fifty-three years old and has been fishing for marlin since he went in the bow of a skiff with his father when he was seven, was fishing drifting deep one time when he hooked a white marlin. The fish jumped twice and then sounded and when he sounded suddenly Carlos felt a great weight and he could not hold the line which went out and down and down irresistibly until the fish had taken out over a hundred and fifty fathoms. Carlos says it felt as heavy and solid as though he were hooked to the bottom of the sea. Then suddenly the strain was loosened but he could feel the weight of his original fish and pulled it up stone dead. Some toothless fish like a swordfish or marlin had closed his jaws across the middle of the eighty pound white marlin and squeezed it and held it so that every bit of the insides of the fish had been crushed out while the huge fish moved off with the eighty-pound fish in its mouth. Finally it let go. What size of a fish would that be? I thought it might be a giant squid but Carlos said there were no sucker marks on the fish and that it showed plainly the shape of the marlin's mouth where he had crushed it.

Another time an old man fishing alone in a skiff out of Cabañas hooked a great marlin that, on the heavy sashcord handline, pulled the skiff far out to sea. Two days later the old man was picked up by fishermen sixty miles to the eastward, the head and forward part of the marlin lashed alongside. What was left of the fish, less than half, weighed eight hundred pounds. The old man had stayed with him a day, a night, a day and another night while the fish swam deep and pulled the boat. When he had come up the old man had pulled the boat up on him and harpooned him. Lashed alongside the sharks had hit him and the old man had fought them out alone in the Gulf Stream in a skiff, clubbing them, stabbing at them, lunging at them with an oar until he was exhausted and the sharks had eaten all that they could hold. He was crying in the boat when the fishermen picked him up, half crazy from his loss, and the sharks were still circling the boat.

But what is the excitement in catching them from a launch? It comes from the fact that they are strange and wild things of unbelievable speed and power and a beauty, in the water and leaping, that is indescribable, which you would never see if you did not fish for them, and to which you are suddenly harnessed so that you feel their speed, their force and their savage power as intimately as if you were riding a bucking horse. For half an hour, an hour, or five hours, you are fastened to the fish as much as he is fastened to you and you tame him and break him the way a wild horse is broken and finally lead him to the boat. For pride and because the fish is worth plenty of money in the Havana market, you gaff him at the boat and bring him on board, but the having him in the boat isn't the excitement; it is while you are fighting him that is the fun.

If the fish is hooked in the bony part of the mouth I am sure the hook hurts him no more than the harness hurts the angler. A large fish when he is hooked often does not feel the hook at all and will swim toward the boat, unconcerned, to take another bait. At other times he will swim away deep, completely unconscious of the hook, and it is when he feels himself held and pressure exerted to turn him, that he knows something is wrong and starts to make his fight. Unless he is hooked where it hurts he makes his fight not against the pain of the hook, but against being captured and if, when he is out of sight, you figure what he is doing, in what direction he is pulling when deep down, and why, you can convince him and bring him to the boat by the same system you break a wild horse. It is not necessary to kill him, or even completely exhaust him to bring him to the boat.

To kill a fish that fights deep you pull against the direction he wants to go until he is worn out and dies. It takes hours and when the fish dies the sharks are liable to get him before the angler can raise him to the top. To catch such a fish quickly you figure, by trying to hold him absolutely, which direction he is working (a sounding fish is going in the direction the line slants in the water when you have put enough pressure on the drag so the line would break if you held it any tighter); then get ahead of him on that direction and he can be brought to the boat without killing him. You do not tow him or pull him with the motor boat; you use the engine to shift your position just as you would walk up or downstream with a salmon. A fish is caught most surely from a small boat such as a dory since the angler can shut down on his drag and simply let the fish pull the boat. Towing the boat will kill him in time. But the most satisfaction is to dominate and convince the fish and bring him intact in everything but spirit to the boat as rapidly as possible.

"Very instructive," says the friend. "But where does the thrill come in?"

The thrill comes when you are standing at the wheel drinking a cold bottle of beer and watching the outriggers jump the baits so they look like small live tuna leaping along and then behind one you see a long dark shadow wing up and then a big spear thrust out followed by an eye and head and dorsal fin and the tuna jumps with the wave and he's missed it.

"Marlin," Carlos yells from the top of the house and stamps his feet up and down, the signal that a fish is raised. He swarms down to the wheel and you go back to where the rod rests in its socket and there comes the shadow again, fast as the shadow of a plane moving over the water, and the spear, head, fin and shoulders smash out of water and you hear the click the closepin makes as the line pulls out and the long bight of line whishes through the water as the fish turns and as you hold the rod, you feel it double and the butt kicks you in the belly as you come back hard and feel his weight, as you strike him again and again, and again.

Then the heavy rod arc-ing out toward the fish, and the reel in a hand-saw zinging scream, the marlin leaps clear and long, silver in the sun long, round as a hogshead and banded with lavender stripes and, when he goes up into the water, it throws a column of spray like a shell lighting.

Then he comes out again, and the spray roars, and again, then the line feels slack and out he bursts headed across and in, then jumps wildly twice more seeming to hang high and stiff in the air before falling to throw the column of water and you can see the hook in the corner of his jaw.

Then in a series of jumps like a greyhound he heads to the northwest and standing up, you follow him in the boat, the line taut as a banjo string and little drops coming from it until you finally get the belly of it clear of that friction against the water and have a straight pull out toward the fish.

And all the time Carlos is shouting, "Oh, God the bread of my children! Oh look at the bread of my children! Joseph and Mary look at the bread of my children jump! There it goes the bread of my children! He'll never stop the bread the bread the bread of my children!"

This striped marlin jumped, in a straight line to the northwest, fifty-three times, and every time he went out it was a sight to make your heart stand still. Then he sounded and I said to Carlos, "Get me the harness. Now I've got to pull him up the bread of your children."

"I couldn't stand to see it," he says. "Like a filled pocketbook jumping. He can't go down deep now. He's caught too much air jumping."

"Like a race horse over obstacles," Julio says. "Is the harness all right? Do you want water?"

"No." Then kidding Carlos, "What's this about the bread of your children?"

"He always says that," says Julio. "You should hear him curse me when we would lose one in the skiff."

"What will the bread of your children weigh?" I ask with mouth dry, the harness taut across shoulders, the rod a flexible prolongation of the sinew pulling ache of arms, the sweat salty in my eyes.

"Four hundred and fifty," says Carlos.

"Never," says Julio.

"Thou and thy never," says Carlos. "The fish of another always weighs nothing to thee."

"Three seventy-five," Julio raises his estimate. "Not a pound more."

Carlos says something unprintable and Julio comes up to four hundred.

The fish is nearly whipped now and the dead ache is out of raising him, and then, while lifting, I feel something slip. It holds for an instant and then the line is slack.

"He's gone," I say and unbuckle the harness.

"The bread of your children," Julio says to Carlos.

"Yes," Carlos says. "Yes. Joke and no joke yes. *El pan de mis hijos.* Three hundred and fifty pounds at ten cents a pound. How many days does a man work for that in the winter? How cold is it at three o'clock in the morning on all those days? And the fog and the rain in a norther. Every time he jumps the hook cutting the hole a little bigger in his jaw. Ay how he could jump. How he could jump!"

"The bread of your children," says Julio.

"Don't talk about that any more," said Carlos.

No it is not elephant hunting. But we get a kick out of it. When you have a family and children, your family, or my family, or the family of Carlos, you do not have to look for danger. There is always plenty of danger when you have a family.

And after a while the danger of others is the only danger and there is no end to it nor any pleasure in it nor does it help to think about it.

But there is great pleasure in being on the sea, in the unknown wild suddenness of a great fish; in his life and death which he lives for you in an hour while your strength is harnessed to his; and there is satisfaction in conquering this thing which rules the sea it lives in.

Then in the morning of the day after you have caught a good fish, when the man who carried him to the market in a handcart brings the long roll of heavy silver dollars wrapped in a newspaper onboard it is very satisfactory money. It really feels like money.

"There's the bread of your children," you say to Carlos.

"In the time of the dance of the millions," he says, "a fish like that was worth two hundred dollars. Now it is thirty. On the other hand a fisherman never starves. The sea is very rich."

"And the fisherman always poor."

"No. Look at you. You are rich."

"Like hell," you say. "And the longer I fish the poorer I'll be. I'll end up fishing with you for the market in a dinghy."

"That I never believe," says Carlos devoutly. "But look. That fishing in a dinghy is very interesting. You would like it."

"I'll look forward to it," you say.

"What we need for prosperity is a war," Carlos says. "In the time of the war with Spain and in the last war the fishermen were actually rich."

"All right," you say. "If we have a war you get the dinghy ready.

The Clark's Fork Valley, Wyoming

Vogue, February 1939

At the end of summer, the big trout would be out in the centre of the stream; they were leaving the pools along the upper part of the river and dropping down to spend the winter in the deep water of the canyon. It was wonderful fly-fishing then in the first weeks of September. The native trout were sleek, shining, and heavy, and nearly all of them leaped when they took the fly. If you fished two flies, you would often have two big trout on and the need to handle them very delicately in that heavy current.

The nights were cold, and, if you woke in the night, you would hear the coyotes. But you did not want to get out on the stream too early in the day because the nights were so cold they chilled the water, and the sun had to be on the river until almost noon before the trout would start to feed.

You could ride in the morning, or sit in front of the cabin, lazy in the sun, and look across the valley where the hay was cut so the meadows were cropped brown and smooth to the line of quaking aspens along the river, now turning yellow in the fall. And on the hills rising beyond, the sage was silvery grey.

Up the river were the two peaks of Pilot and Index, where we would hunt mountain-sheep later in the month, and you sat in the sun and marvelled at the formal, clean-lined shape mountains can have at a distance, so that you remember them in the shapes they show from far away, and not as the broken rockslides you crossed, the jagged edges you pulled up by, and the narrow shelves you sweated along, afraid to look down, to round that peak that looked so smooth and geometrical. You climbed around it to come out on a clear space to look down to where an old ram and three young rams were feeding in the juniper bushes in a high, grassy pocket cupped against the broken rock of the peak.

The old ram was purple-grey, his rump was white, and when he raised his head you saw the great heavy curl of his horns. It was the white of his rump that had betrayed him to you in the green of the junipers when you had lain in the lee of a rock, out of the wind, three miles away, looking carefully at every yard of the high country through a pair of good Zeiss glasses.

Now as you sat in front of the cabin, you remembered that down-hill shot and the young rams standing, their heads turned, staring at him, waiting for him to get up. They could not see you on that high ledge, nor wind you, and the shot made no more impression on them than a boulder falling.

You remembered the year we had built a cabin at the head of Timber Creek, and the big grizzly that tore it open every time we were away. The snow came late that year, and this bear would not hibernate, but spent his autumn tearing open cabins and ruining a trap-line. But he was so smart you never saw him in the day. Then you remembered coming on the three grizzlies in the high country at the head of Crandall Creek. You heard a crash of timber and thought it was a cow elk bolting, and then there they were, in the broken shadow, running with an easy, lurching smoothness, the afternoon sun making their coats a soft, bristling silver.

You remembered elk bugling in the fall, the bull so close you could see his chest muscles swell as he lifted his head, and still not

136

see his head in the thick timber; but hear that deep, high mounting whistle and the answer from across another valley. You thought of all the heads you had turned down and refused to shoot, and you were pleased about every one of them.

You remembered the children learning to ride; how they did with different horses; and how they loved the country. You remembered how this country had looked when you first came into it, and the year you had to stay four months after you had brought the first car ever to come in for the swamp roads to freeze solid enough to get the car out. You could remember all the hunting and all the fishing and the riding in the summer sun and the dust of the pack-train, the silent riding in the hills in the sharp cold of fall going up after the cattle on the high range, finding them wild as deer and as quiet, only bawling noisily when they were all herded together being forced along down into the lower country.

Then there was the winter; the trees bare now, the snow blowing so you could not see, the saddle wet, then frozen as you came down-hill, breaking a trail through the snow, trying to keep your legs moving, and the sharp, warming taste of whiskey when you hit the ranch and changed your clothes in front of the big open fireplace. It's a good country.

The Great Blue River

Holiday, July 1949

People ask you why you live in Cuba and you say it is because you like it. It is too complicated to explain about the early morning in the hills above Havana where every morning is cool and fresh on the hottest day in summer. There is no need to tell them that one reason you live there is because you can raise your own fighting cocks, train them on the place, and fight them anywhere that you can match them and that this is all legal.

Maybe they do not like cockfighting anyway.

You do not tell them about the strange and lovely birds that are on the farm the year around, nor about all the migratory birds that come through, nor that quail come in the early mornings to drink at the swimming pool, nor about the different types of lizards that live and hunt in the thatched arbor at the end of the pool, nor the eighteen different kinds of mangoes that grow on the long slope up to the house. You do not try to explain about our ball team—hardball, not softball—where, if you are over forty, you can have a boy run for you and still stay in the game, nor which are the boys in our town that are really the fastest on the base paths.

You do not tell them about the shooting club just down the road, where we used to shoot the big live-pigeon matches for the large money, with Winston Guest, Tommy Shevlin, Thorwald Sanchez and Pichon Aguilera, and where we used to shoot matches against the Brooklyn Dodgers when they had fine shots like Curt Davis, Billy Herman, Augie Galan and Hugh Casey. Maybe they think live-pigeon shooting is wrong. Queen Victoria did and barred it in England. Maybe they are right. Maybe it is wrong. It certainly is a miserable spectator sport. But with strong, really fast birds it is still the best participant sport for betting I know; and where we live it is legal.

You could tell them that you live in Cuba because you only have to put shoes on when you come into town, and that you can plug the bell in the party-line telephone with paper so that you won't have to answer, and that you work as well there in those cool early mornings as you ever have worked anywhere in the world. But those are professional secrets.

There are many other things you do not tell them. But when they talk to you about salmon fishing and what it costs them to fish the Restigouche, then, if they have not talked too much about how much it costs, and have talked well, or lovingly, about the salmon fishing, you tell them the biggest reason you live in Cuba is the great, deep blue river, three quarters of a mile to a mile deep and sixty to eighty miles across, that you can reach in thirty minutes from the door of your farmhouse, riding through beautiful country to get to it, that has, when the river is right, the finest fishing I have ever known.

When the Gulf Stream is running well, it is a dark blue and there are whirlpools along the edges. We fish in a forty-foot cabin cruiser with a flying bridge equipped with topside controls, oversize outriggers big enough to skip a ten-pound bait in summer, and we fish four rods.

Sometimes we keep Pilar, the fishing boat, in Havana harbor, sometimes in Cojimar, a fishing village seven miles east of Havana, with a harbor that is safe in summer and imminently unsafe in winter when there are northers or nor'westers. Pilar was built to be a fishing machine that would be a good sea boat in the heaviest kind of weather, have a minimum cruising range of five hundred miles, and sleep seven people. She carries three hundred gallons of water. On a long trip she can carry another hundred gallons of gas in small drums in her forward cockpit and the same extra amount of water in demijohns. She carries, when loaded full, 2400 pounds of ice.

Wheeler Shipyard, of New York, built her hull and modified it to our specifications, and we have made various changes in her since. She is a really sturdy boat, sweet in any kind of sea, and she has a very low-cut stern with a large wooden roller to bring big fish over. The flying bridge is so sturdy and so reinforced below you can fight fish from the top of the house.

Ordinarily, fishing out of Havana, we get a line out with a Japanese feather squid and a strip of pork rind on the hook, while we are still running out of the harbor. This is for tarpon, which feed around the fishing smacks anchored along the Morro Castle-Cabañas side of the channel, and for kingfish, which are often in the mouth of the main ship channel and over the bar, where the bottom fishermen catch snappers just outside the Morro.

This bait is fished on a twelve-foot No. 10 piano-wire leader from a 6/0 reel, full of fifteen-thread line and from a nine-ounce Tycoon tip. The biggest tarpon I ever caught with this rig weighed 135 pounds. We have hooked some that were much bigger but lost them to outgoing or incoming ships, to port launches, to bumboats and to the anchor chains of the fishing smacks. You can plead with or threaten launches and bumboats when you have a big fish on and they are headed so that they will cut him off. But there is nothing you can do when a big tanker, or a cargo ship, or a liner is coming down the channel. So we usually put out this line when we can see the channel is clear and nothing is coming out; or after seven o'clock in the evening when ships will usually not be entering the harbor due to the extra port charges made after that hour.

Coming out of the harbor I will be on the flying bridge steering and watching the traffic and the line that is fishing the feather astern. As you go out, seeing friends along the water front—lottery-ticket sellers you have known for years, policemen you have given fish to and who have done favors in their turn, bumboatmen who lose their earnings standing shoulder to shoulder with you in the betting pit at the jai-alai fronton, and friends passing in motorcars along the harbor and ocean boulevard who wave and you wave to but cannot recognize at that distance, although they can see the Pilar and you on her flying bridge quite clearly—your feather jig is fishing all the time.

Behind the boulevards are the parks and buildings of old Havana and on the other side you are passing the steep slopes and walls of the fortress of Cabañas, the stone weathered pink and yellow, where most of your friends have been political prisoners at one time or another; and then you pass the rocky headland of the Morro, with O'Donnell, 1844, on the tall white light tower and then, two hundred yards beyond the Morro, when the stream is running well, is the great river.

Sometimes as you leave the gray-green harbor water and Pilar's bows dip into the dark blue water a covey of flying fish will rise from under her bows and you will hear the slithering, silk-tearing noise they make when they leave the water.

If they are the usual size flying fish it does not mean so much as a sign, unless you see a man-of-war hawk working, dipping down after them if they go up again; but if they are the big three-pound, black-winged Bahian flyers that come out of the water as though they were shot out, and at the end of their soaring flight drop their tails to give the flight a new impulse and fly again and again, then it is a very good sign. Seeing the big Bahian flyers is as sure a sign as any, except seeing fish themselves.

By now, Gregorio, the mate, has gotten the meat line out. The meat line is a new trick that I'll tell about later because once it is out, and he wants to get it out fast to cover this patch of bottom before we get outside of the hundred-fathom curve, he must get outrigger baits out, since marlin will come in over this bottom any time the stream is running and the water is blue and clear.

Gregorio Fuentes has been mate on Pilar since 1938. He is fifty years old this summer and went to sea in sail from Lanzarote, one of the smaller Canary Islands, when he was four. I met him at Dry Tortugas when he was captain of a fishing smack and we were both stormbound there in a very heavy northeast gale in 1928. We went on board his smack to get some onions. We wanted to buy the onions, but he gave them to us, and some rum as well, and I remember thinking he had the cleanest ship that I had ever seen. Now after ten years I know that he would rather keep a ship clean, and paint and varnish, than he would fish. But I know, too, that he would rather fish than eat or sleep.

We had a great mate before Gregorio, named Carlos Gutierrez, but someone hired him away from me when I was away at the Spanish Civil War. It was wonderful luck to find Gregorio, and his seamanship has saved Pilar in three hurricanes. So far, knocking on wood, we have never had to put in a claim on the all-risk marine insurance policy carried on her; and Gregorio was the only man to stay on board a small craft in the October, 1944, hurricane when it blew 180 mph true, and small craft and Navy vessels were blown up onto the harbor boulevard and up onto the small hills around the harbor. He also rode out the 1948 hurricane on her.

By now, as you have cleared the harbor, Gregorio has the meat line out and is getting the outrigger baits out and, it being a good day, you are getting flying fish up and pushing to the eastward into the breeze. The first marlin you see can show within ten minutes of leaving our moorings, and so close to the Morro that you can still see the curtains on the light.

He may come behind the big, white wooden teaser that is zigzagging and diving between the two inside lines. He may show behind an outrigger bait that is bouncing and jumping over the water. Or he may come racing from the side, slicing a wake through the dark water, as he comes for the feather.

When you see him from the flying bridge he will look first brown and then dark purple as he rises in the water, and his pectoral fins, spread wide as he comes to feed, will be a light lavender color and look like widespread wings as he drives just under the surface. He will look, in the sea, more like a huge submarine bird than a fish.

Gregorio, if he sees him first will shout, "Feesh! Feesh, Papa, feesh!"

If you see him first you leave the wheel, or turn it over to Mary, your wife, and go to the stern end of the house and say "Feesh" as calmly as possible to Gregorio, who has always seen him by then, too, and you lean over and he hands you up the rod the marlin is coming for, or, if he is after the teaser, he hands you up the rod with the feather and pork rind on.

All right, he is after the teaser and you are racing-in the feather. Gregorio is keeping the teaser, a tapering, cylindrical piece of wood two feet long, with a curve cut in its head that makes it dive and dance when towed, away from the marlin. The marlin is rushing it and trying to grab it. His bull comes out of water as he drives toward it. But Gregorio keeps it just out of his reach. If he pulled it all the way in, the fish might go down. So he is playing him as a bullfighter might play a bull, keeping the lure just out of his range, and yet never denying it to him, while you race-in the feather.

Mary is saying, "Isn't he beautiful? Oh, Papa, look at his stripes and that color and the color of his wings. Look at him!"

"I'm looking at him," you say, and you have the feather now abreast of the teaser, and Gregorio sees it and flicks the teaser clear, and the marlin sees the feather. The big thing that he chased, and that looked and acted like a crippled fish, is gone. But here is a squid, his favorite food, instead.

The marlin's bill comes clear out of water as he hits the feather

144

and you see his open mouth and, as he hits it, you lower the rod that you have held as high as you could, so the feather goes out of sight into his mouth. You see it go in, and the mouth shuts and you see him turn, shining silver, his stripes showing as he turns.

As he turns his head you hit him, striking hard, hard and hard again, to set the hook. Then, if he starts to run instead of jumping, you hit him three or four times more to make sure, because he might just be holding feather, hook and all, tight in his jaws and running away with it, still unhooked. Then he feels the hook and jumps clear. He will jump straight up all clear of the water, shaking himself. He will jump high and long, shedding drops of water as he comes out, and making a splash like a shell hitting when he enters the water again. And he will jump, and jump, and jump, sometimes on one side of the boat, then crossing to the other so fast you see the belly of the line whipping through the water, fast as a racing ski turn.

Sometimes he will get the leader over his shoulder (the hump on his back behind his head) and go off greyhounding over the water, jumping continuously and with such an advantage in pull, with the line in that position, that you cannot stop him, and so Mary has to back Pilar fast and then turn, gunning both motors, to chase him.

You lose plenty of line making the turn to chase him. But he is jumping against the friction of the belly of the line in the water which keeps it taut, and when, reeling, you recover that belly and have the fish now broadside, then astern again, you have control of him once more. He will sound now and circle, and then you will gradually work him closer and closer and then in to where Gregorio can gaff him, club him and take him on board.

That is the way it should go ideally; he should sound, circle, and you should work him gradually alongside or on either quarter of the stern, and then gaff him, club him and bring him on board. But it doesn't always go that way. Sometimes when he gets up to the boat he will start the whole thing all over again and head out for the northwest, jumping again as fresh, seemingly, as when he was first hooked, and you have to chase him again.

Sometimes, if he is a big striped marlin, you will get him within thirty feet of the boat and he will come no farther, swimming with his wings spread, at whatever speed and direction you elect to move. If you don't move, he will be up and under the boat. If you move away from him, he will stay there, refusing to come in one inch, as strong a fish for his weight as any in the world and as stubborn.

(Bonefish angler, on your way! You never saw a bonefish in mile-deep water, nor up against the tackle striped marlin have to face sometimes. Nor did you know how your bonefish would act after he had jumped forty-three times clean out of water. Your bonefish is a smart fish, very conservative, very strong too. Too smart by far to jump, even if he could. I do not think he can, myself. And the only nonjumping fish that has a patent of nobility in our books is the wahoo. He *can* jump, too, if he wants to. He will do it sometimes when he takes the bait. Also, bonefish angler, your fish might be as fat and as short of wind, at four hundred pounds, as some of the overstuffed Nova Scotia tuna are. But do not shoot, bonefish angler; at four hundred pounds, your fish might be the strongest thing in the sea, the strongest fish that ever lived; so strong no one wold ever want to hook into one. But tell me confidentially: would he jump . . . ? Thank you very much. I thought not.)

This dissertation has not helped you any if you have a strong, male, striped marlin on and he decides he won't be lifted any closer. Of course you could loosen up the drag and work away from him and wear him out that way. But that is the way sharks get fish. We like to fight them close to the boat and take them while they are still strong. We will gaff an absolutely green fish, one that has not been tired at all, if by any fluke we can get him close enough.

Since 1931, when I learned that was how to keep fish from being hit by sharks, I have never lost a marlin nor a tuna to a shark, no matter how shark-infested the waters fished. We try to fight them fast, but never rough. The secret is for the angler never to rest. Any time he rests the fish is resting. That gives the fish a chance to get strong again, or to get down to a greater depth; and the odds lengthen that something may close in on him.

So now, say, you have this marlin down thirty feet, pulling as strong as a horse. All you have to do is stay with him. Play him just this side of breaking strain, but do it softly. Never jerk on him. Jerking will only hurt him or anger him. Either or both will make him pull harder. He is as strong as a horse. Treat him like a horse. Keep your maximum possible strain on him and you will convince him and bring him in. Then you gaff him, club him for kindness and for safety, and bring him on board.

You do not have to kill a horse to break him. You have to convince him, and that is what you have to do with a truly strong, big fish after the first jumps, which correspond to a wild horse's bucking, are over. To do this, you have to be in good condition.

There is tackle made now, and there are fishing guides expert in ways of cheating with it, by which anybody who can walk up three flights of stairs, carrying a quart bottle of milk in each hand, can catch game fish over five hundred pounds without even having to sweat much.

There is old-fashioned tackle with which you can catch really big fish in short time, thus ensuring they will not be attacked by sharks. But you have to be a fisherman or, at least, in very good shape to use it. But this is the tackle that will give you the greatest amount of sport with the smaller and medium-sized marlin. You don't need to be an athlete to use it. You ought to be in good condition. If you are not, two or three fish will put you in condition. Or they may make you decide marlin fishing in the Gulf Stream is not your sport.

In almost any other sport requiring strength and skill to play or practice, those practicing the sport expect to know how to play it, to have at least moderate ability and to be in some sort of condition. In big-game fishing they will come on board in ghastly shape, incapable of reeling in 500 yards of line, simply line, with no question of there being a fish on it, and yet full of confidence that they can catch a fish weighing twice or three times their weight.

They are confident because it has been done. But it was never done honestly, to my knowledge, by completely inexperienced and untrained anglers, without physical assistance from the guides, mates and boatmen, until the present winch reels, unbreakable rods and other techniques were invented which made it possible for any angler, no matter how incompetent, to catch big fish if he could hold and turn the handle of a winch.

The International Game Fish Association, under the auspices of the American Museum of Natural History, has tried to set a standard of sporting fishing and to recognize records of fish taken honestly and sportingly according to these standards. It has had considerable success in these and other fields. But as long as charter boats are extremely expensive, and both guides and their anglers want results above everything else, big-game fishing will be closer to total war against big fish than to sport. Of course, it could never be considered an equal contest unless the angler had a hook in his mouth, as well as the fish. But insistence on that might discourage the sporting fishermen entirely.

Education as to what makes a big fish legitimately caught has been slow, but it has progressed steadily. Very few guides or anglers shoot or harpoon hooked fish any more. Nor is the flying gaff much used.

The use of wire line, our meat line, is a deadly way of fishing, and no fish caught that way could possibly be entered as a sporting record. But we use it as a way of finding out at what depths fish are when they are not on the surface. It is a scientific experiment, the results are carefully noted, and what it catches are classed in our books as fish caught commercially. Its carefully recorded results will surely provide valuable information for the commercial fisherman, and its use is justified for that end. It is also a very rough, tough, punishing way to catch big fish and it puts the angler who practices it, fishing standing up, not sitting in a chair, into the condition he needs to be able to fight fish honestly with the sporting tackle that allows the fish to run, leap and sound to his fullest ability and still be caught within an hour by the angler, if the angler knows how to handle big fish.

Fighting a really big fish, fast and unaided, never resting, nor letting the fish rest, is comparable to a ten-round fight in the ring in its requirements for good physical condition. Two hours of the same, not resting, not letting the fish rest, is comparable to a twenty-round fight. Most honest and skillful anglers who lose big fish do so because the fish whips them, and they cannot hold him when he decides, toward the end of the fight, to sound and, sounding, dies.

Once the fish is dead, sharks will eat him if any are about. If he is not hit by sharks, bringing him up, dead, from a great depth is one of the most difficult phases of fishing for big fish in deep water.

We have tried to work out tackle which would give the maximum sport with the different fish, small, medium, large and oversize, at the different months of the year when they run. Since their runs overlap it has been necessary to try to have always a margin of safety in the quantity of line. In a section at the end of the article this tackle is described. It would not suit purists, or members of some light-tackle clubs; but remember we fish five months out of the year in water up to a mile deep, in a current that can make a very big sea with the trade wind blowing against it, and in waters that are occasionally infested with sharks. We could catch fish with the very lightest tackle, I believe. It would prove nothing, since others have done it, and we would break many fish off to die. Our ideal is to catch the fish with tackle that you can really pull on and which still permits the fish to jump and run as freely as possible.

Then, altogether apart from that ideal, there is the meat line. This is 800 yards of monel wire of eight-five-pound test which, fished from an old Hardy six-inch reel and old Hardy No. 5 rod, will sink a feather jib down so that it can be trolled in thirty-five fathoms if you put enough wire out. When there are no fish on the surface at all, this goes down where they are. It catches everything: wahoo out of their season when no one has caught one on the surface for months; big grouper; huge dog snappers, red snappers, big kingfish; and it catches marlin when they are deep and not coming up at all. With it we eat, and fill the freezing unit, on days when you would not have caught a fish surface-trolling. The fight on the wire which actually tests no more than thirty-nine-thread line but is definitely wire, not line, is rugged, muscle-straining, punishing, short and anything but sweet. It is in a class with steer bulldogging, bronc riding and other ungentle sports. The largest marlin caught in 1948 on the meat line was a 210-pound striped fish. We caught him when we had fished three days on the surface and not seen a thing.

Now we are anxious to see what the meat line will dredge into during those days in August and September, when there are flat calms, and the huge fish are down deep and will not come up. When you hook a marlin on the wire he starts shaking his head, then he bangs it with his bill, then he sees if he can outpull you. Then if he can't, he finally comes up to see what is the matter. What we are anxious to find out is what happens if he ever gets the wire over his shoulder and starts to go. They can go, if they are big enough, wire and all. We plan to try to go with him. There is a chance we could make it, if Pilar makes the turn fast enough. That will be up to Mary.

The really huge fish always head out to the northwest when they make their first run. If you are ever flying across between Havana and Miami, and looking down on the blue sea, and you see something making splashes such as a horse dropped off a cliff might make, and behind these splashes a black boat with green topside and decks is chasing, leaving a white wake behind her—that will be us.

If the splashes look sizable from the height that you are flying, and they are going out to the northwest, then wish us plenty of luck. Because we will need it.

In the meantime, what we always hope for is fish feeding on the surface, up after the big flying fish, and that whoever is a guest on the boat, unless he or she has fished before, will hook something under one hundred and fifty pounds to start with. Any marlin from thirty pounds up, on proper tackle, will give a new fisherman all the excitement and all the exercise he can assimilate, and off the marlin grounds along the north Cuban coast he might raise twenty to thirty in a day, when they are running well. The most I ever caught in one day was seven. But Pepe Gomez-Mena and Martin Menocal caught twelve together in one day, and I would hate to bet that record would not be beaten by them, or by some of the fine resident and visiting sportsmen who love and know the marlin fishing of the great river that moves along Cuba's northern coast.

Ernest Hemingway's Tackle Specifications

White marlin run: April–May–Early June.

Gear for the feather jig, fished astern, with pork-rind strip on the hook:

Rod, 9 oz. or 12 oz. tip; Reel, 6/0; 500 yards #15 thread line; 12-foot piano-wire leader #9 or #10; 8/0 or 9/0 O'Shaughnessy hook, or 8/0 Mustad, smallest type of Japanese feather jig (white) and three-inch strip of pork rind attached. (This gives a beautiful motion in the water. Of white marlin hooked we average six out of ten on the feather compared to the baits.)

First rod (light for smaller bait) of the two outrigger rods:

Rod, 14 oz. tip; Reel, 9/0; 600 yards of #18 thread line; 14-foot piano-wire leader #10 or #11; 10/0 Mustad hook.

Baits: small mullet, strip bait, boned needle fish, small cero mackerel, small or medium size flying fish, fresh squid and cut baits.

Second rod of two outriggers:

14 oz. tip; Reel, 9/0; 400 yards of #18 thread line, spliced to 150 yards of #21 thread, on the outside for when the fish is close to the boat. 14-foot piano-wire leader #11; 11/0 or 12/0 Mustad hook.

Baits: big cero mackerel, medium and large mullet, large strip baits, flying fish and good-sized squid.

Above rod is designed to attract any big fish that might be mixed in with the smaller run.

Big marlin run: July–August–September–October.

(Fish from 250 to over 1000 pounds.)

Feather is fished same as ever, since after white marlin are gone it will catch school tuna, albacore, bonito and dolphin. An extra rod is in readiness, equipped with feather jig in case schools of above fish are encountered.

Outrigger rods: Either 22 or 24 oz tips. (The best I have found, outside of the old Hardy Hickory-Palakona bamboo #5, are those made by Frank O'Brien of Tycoon Tackle, Inc. His rods are incomparably the best I know made today.)

Reels: 12/0 or 14/0 Hardy, and two 14/0 Finor for guests. If inexperienced anglers want to catch big fish they need the advantage the Finor changeable gear ratio reel gives them.

Line: all the reels will hold without jamming of either 36 or 39 thread good Ashaway linen line. We use this line for years, testing it, discarding any rotted by the sun, and splicing on more as needed.

Leaders are 14 1/2 foot stainless-steel cable.

Hooks: 14/0 Mustad, bent in the crook of the shank to give the point an offset hooking drive.

Baits: Albacore and bonito, whole, up to seven pounds and barracuda, whole, up to five and six pounds. These are the best. Alternative baits are large cero mackerel, squid, big mullet and yellow jacks, runners and big needlefish. Of all baits, the whole bonito and albacore have proved, with us, the best for attracting really big marlin.

The wire line has been described in the article.

"A Situation Report" (an excerpt)

Look, September 4, 1956

No one can work every day in the hot months without going stale. To break up the pattern of work, we fish the Gulf Stream in the spring and summer months and in the fall. The changes of each season show in the sea as they do on the land. There is no monotony as long as the current is alive and moving, and each day you never know what you will meet with.

You go out early or later, depending on the tide which pushes the heavy blue water out or brings it close to shore. When the current is running well and the flying fish are coming into the air from under the bow of the *Pilar*, you have an even chance or better to catch dolphin and small tuna and to catch or lose white marlin.

When you have finished far enough down with the current, you go into some beach to swim and have a drink while Gregorio, the mate, cooks lunch. In the late afternoon, you fish back toward home against the current until sunset. The small marlin are there in the spring and early summer and the big fish in the summer and the fall.

This fishing is what brought you to Cuba in the old days. Then you took a break on a book, or between books, of a hundred days or more and fished every day from sunup to sundown. Now, living on the hill in the country, you fish the days you pick.

It was different in Peru where we went to try to photograph big fish for the picture. There the wind blew day and night. Sand blew in your room from the desert that makes the coast and the doors banged shut with the wind.

We fished 32 days from early morning until it was too rough to photograph and the seas ran like onrushing hills with snow blowing off the tops. If you looked from the crest of a sea toward shore you could see the haze of the sand blowing as the wind furrowed the hills and scoured and sculptured them each day.

The sea birds huddled in the lee of the cliffs, coming out in clouds to dive wildly when a scouting bird would sight schoolfish moving along the shore, and the condors ate dead pelicans on the beaches. The pelicans usually died from bursting their food pouches diving and a condor would walk backwards along the beach lifting a large dead pelican as though it weighed nothing.

The marlin were large and did not fight as the fish off Cuba do. But their weight and bulk in the heavy seas made it hard work, and a fish that you would bring to gaff in eight or twelve minutes you would let run again, holding him always in close camera range, feeling his weight through the soles of your feet, your forearms and your back, and finally when he was dead tired, have Gregorio harpoon him to try for the camera shot you needed in the picture.

It was steady punishing work each day and it was fun too because the people were nice and it was a strange new sea to learn. It was good too to be back in Cuba and on *Pilar* again.

III
The Sea—
Respite and Ultimate Challenge

from *The Garden of Eden*

They were living at le Grau du Roi then and the hotel was on a canal that ran from the walled city of Aigues Mortes straight down to the sea. They could see the towers of Aigues Mortes across the low plain of the Camargue and they rode there on their bicycles at some time of nearly every day along the white road that bordered the canal. In the evenings and the mornings when there was a rising tide sea bass would come into it and they would see the mullet jumping wildly to escape from the bass and watch the swelling bulge of the water as the bass attacked.

A jetty ran out into the blue and pleasant sea and they fished from the jetty and swam on the beach and each day helped the fishermen haul in the long net that brought the fish up onto the long sloping beach. They drank aperitifs in the cafe on the corner facing the sea and watched the sails of the mackerel fishing boats out in the Gulf of Lions. It was late in the spring and the mackerel were running and fishing people of the port were very busy. It was a cheerful and friendly town and the young couple liked the hotel, which had four rooms upstairs and a restaurant and two billiard tables downstairs facing the canal and the lighthouse. The room they lived in looked like the painting of Van Gogh's room at Arles except there was a double bed and two big windows and you could look out across the water and the marsh and sea meadows to the white town and bright beach of Palavas.

They were always hungry but they ate very well. They were hungry for breakfast which they ate at the cafe, ordering brioche and café au lait and eggs, and the type of preserve that they chose and the manner in which the eggs were to be cooked was an excitement. They were always so hungry for breakfast that the girl often had a headache until the coffee came. But the coffee took the headache away. She took her coffee without sugar and the young man was learning to remember that.

On this morning there was brioche and red raspberry preserve and the eggs were boiled and there was a pat of butter that melted as they stirred them and salted them lightly and ground pepper over them in the cups. They were big eggs and fresh and the girl's were not cooked quite as long as the young man's. He remembered that easily and he was happy with his which he diced up with the spoon and ate with only the flow of the butter to moisten them and the fresh early morning texture and the bite of the coarsely ground pepper grains and the hot coffee and the chickory-fragrant bowl of café au lait.

The fishing boats were well out. They had gone out in the dark with the first rising of the breeze and the young man and the girl had wakened and heard them and then curled together under the sheet of the bed and slept again. They had made love when they were half awake with the light bright outside but the room still shadowed and then had lain together and been happy and tired and then made love again. Then they were so hungry that they did not think they would live until breakfast and now they were in the cafe eating and watching the sea and the sails and it was a new day again.

"What are you thinking?" the girl asked.

"Nothing."

"You have to think something."

"I was just feeling."

"How?"

"Happy."

"But I get so hungry," she said. "Is it normal do you think? Do you always get so hungry when you make love?"

"When you love somebody."

"Oh, you know too much about it," she said.

"No."

"I don't care. I love it and we don't have to worry about anything do we?"

"Nothing."

"What do you think we should do?"

"I don't know," he said. "What do you?"

"I don't care at all. If you'd like to fish I should write a letter or maybe two and then we could swim before lunch."

"To be hungry?"

"Don't say it. I'm getting hungry already and we haven't finished breakfast."

"We can think about lunch."

"And then after lunch?"

"We'll take a nap like good children."

"That's an absolutely new idea," she said. "Why have we never thought of that?"

"I have these flashes of intuition," he said. "I'm the inventive type."

"I'm the destructive type," she said. "And I'm going to destroy you. They'll put a plaque up on the wall of the building outside the room. I'm going to wake up in the night and do something to you that you've never even heard of or imagined. I was going to last night but I was too sleepy."

"You're too sleepy to be dangerous."

"Don't lull yourself into any false security. Oh darling, let's have it hurry up and be lunch time."

They sat there in their striped fishermen's shirts and the shorts they had bought in the store that sold marine supplies, and they were very tan and their hair was streaked and faded by the sun and the sea. Most people thought they were brother and sister until they said they were married. Some did not believe that they were married and that pleased the girl very much.

In those years only a very few people had ever come to the Mediterranean in the summer time and no one came to le Grau du Roi except a few people from Nîmes. There was no casino and no entertainment and except in the hottest months when people came to swim there was no one at the hotel. People did not wear fishermen's shirts then and this girl that he was married to was the first girl he had ever seen wearing one. She had bought the shirts for them and then had washed them in the basin in their room at the hotel to take the stiffness out of them. They were stiff and built for hard wear but the washings softened them and now they were worn and softened enough so that when he looked at the girl now her breasts showed beautifully against the worn cloth.

No one wore shorts either around the village and the girl could not wear them when they rode their bicycles. But in the village it did not matter because the people were very friendly and only the local priest disapproved. But the girl went to mass on Sunday wearing a skirt and a long-sleeved cashmere sweater with her hair covered with a scarf and the young man stood in the back of the church with the men. They gave twenty francs which was more than a dollar then and since the priest took up the collection himself their attitude toward the church was known and the wearing of shorts in the village was regarded as an eccentricity by foreigners rather than an attempt against the morality of the ports of the Camargue. The priest did not speak to them when they wore shorts but he did not denounce them and when they wore trousers in the evening the three of them bowed to each other.

"I'll go up and write the letters," the girl said and she got up and smiled at the waiter and went out of the cafe.

"Monsieur is going to fish?" the waiter asked when the young man, whose name was David Bourne, called him over and paid him.

"I think so. How is the tide?"

"This tide is very good," the waiter said. "I have some bait if you want it."

"I can get some along the road."

"No. Use this. They're sandworms and there are plenty."

"Can you come out?"

"I'm on duty now. But maybe I can come out and see how you do. You have your gear?"

"It's at the hotel."

"Stop by for the worms."

At the hotel the young man wanted to go up to the room and see the girl but instead he found the long, jointed bamboo pole and the basket with his fishing gear behind the desk where the room keys hung and went back out into the brightness of the road and on down to the cafe and out onto the glare of the jetty. The sun was hot but there was a fresh breeze and the tide was just starting to ebb. He wished that he had brought a casting rod and spoons so that he might cast out across the flow of the water from the canal over the rocks on the far side but instead he rigged his long pole with its cork and quill float and let a sandworm float gently along at a depth where he thought fish might be feeding.

He fished for some time with no luck and watched the mackerel boats tacking back and forth out on the blue sea and the shadows the high clouds made on the water. Then his float went under in a sharp descent with the line angling stiffly and he brought the pole up against the pull of a fish that was strong and driving wildly and making the line hiss through the water. He tried to hold it as lightly as he could and the long pole was bent to the breaking point of the line and trace by the fish which kept trying to go toward the open sea. The young man walked with him on the jetty to ease the strain but the fish kept pulling so that as he drove a quarter of the rod was forced under water.

The waiter had come from the cafe and was very excited. He was talking by the young man's side saying, "Hold him. Hold him. Hold him as softly as you can. He'll have to tire. Don't let him break. Soft with him. Softly. Softly."

There was no way the young man could be softer with him except to get into the water with the fish and that did not make sense as the canal was deep. If I could only walk along the bank with him, he thought. But they had come to the very end of the jetty. More than half the pole was under water now.

"Just hold him softly," the waiter pleaded. "It's a strong trace."

The fish bored deep, ran, zig-zagged and the long bamboo pole bent with his weight and his rapid, driving strength. Then he came up thrashing at the surface and then was down again and the young man found that although the fish felt as strong as ever the tragic violence was lessened and now he could be led around the end of the jetty and up the canal.

"Softly does it," the waiter said. "Oh softly now. Softly for us all."

Twice more the fish forced his way out to the open sea and twice the young man led him back and now he was leading him gently along the jetty toward the cafe.

"How is he?" asked the waiter.

"He's fine but we've beaten him."

"Don't say it," the waiter said. "Don't say it. We must tire him. Tire him. Tire him."

"He's got my arm tired," the young man said.

"Do you want me to take him?" the waiter asked hopefully.

"My God no."

"Just easy, easy, easy. Softly, softly, softly," the waiter said.

The young man worked the fish past the terrace of the cafe and into the canal. He was swimming just under the surface but was still strong and the young man wondered if they would take him all the way up the canal through the length of the town. There were many other people now and as they went by the hotel the girl saw them out of the window and shouted, "Oh what a wonderful fish! Wait for me! Wait for me!"

She had seen the fish clearly from above and his length and the shine of him in the water and her husband with the bamboo pole bent almost double and the procession of people following. When she got down to the canal bank and, running, caught up with the people, the procession had stopped. The waiter was in the water at the edge of the canal and her husband was guiding the fish slowly against the bank where there was a clump of weeds growing. The fish was on the surface now and the waiter bent down and brought his hands together from either side and then lifted the fish with his thumbs in both his gills and moved up the bank of the canal with him. He was a heavy fish and the waiter held him high against his chest with the head under his chin and the tail flopping against his thighs.

Several men were pounding the young man on the back and putting their arms around him and a woman from the fish market kissed him. Then the girl had her arms around him and kissed him and he said, "Did you see him?"

Then they all went over to see him laid out on the side of the road silver as a salmon and dark gunmetal shining on his back. He was a handsome beautifully built fish with great live eyes and he breathed slowly and brokenly.

"What is he?"

"A *loup*," he said. "That's a sea bass. They call them *bar* too. They're a wonderful fish. This is the biggest one I've ever seen."

The waiter, whose name was André, came over and put his arms around David and kissed him and then he kissed the girl.

"Madame, it is necessary," he said. "It is truly necessary. No one ever caught such a fish on such tackle."

"We better have him weighed," David said.

They were at the cafe now. The young man had put the tackle

away, after the weighing, and washed up and the fish was on a block of ice that had come in the *camion* from Nîmes to ice the mackerel catch. The fish had weighed a little over fifteen pounds. On the ice he was still silver and beautiful but the color on his back had changed to gray. Only his eyes still looked alive. The mackerel fishing boats were coming in now and the women were unloading the shining blue and green and silver mackerel from the boats into baskets and carrying the heavy baskets on their heads to the fish house. It was a very good catch and the town was busy and happy.

"What are we going to do with the big fish?" the girl asked.

"They're going to take him in and sell him," the young man said. "He's too big to cook here and they say it would be wicked to cut him up. Maybe he'll go right up to Paris. He'll end in some big restaurant. Or somebody very rich will buy him."

"He was so beautiful in the water," she said. "And when André held him up. I couldn't believe him when I saw him out of the window and you with your mob following you."

"We'll get a small one for us to eat. They're really wonderful. A small one ought to be grilled with butter and with herbs. They're like striped bass at home."

"I'm excited about the fish," she said. "Don't we have wonderful simple fun?"

They were hungry for lunch and the bottle of white wine was cold and they drank it as they ate the celery *rémoulade* and the small radishes and the home pickled mushrooms from the big glass jar. The bass was grilled and the grill marks showed on the silver skin and the butter melted on the hot plate. There was sliced lemon to press on the bass and fresh bread from the bakery and the wine cooled their tongues of the heat of the fried potatoes. It was good light, dry, cheerful unknown white wine and the restaurant was proud of it.

from *Islands in the Stream*

When the sun woke Thomas Hudson he went down to the beach and swam and then had breakfast before the rest of them were up. Eddy said he did not think they would have much of a breeze and it might even be a calm. He said the gear was all in good shape on the boat and he had a boy out after bait.

Thomas Hudson asked him if he had tested the lines since the boat had not been out for big fish in quite a while and Eddy said he had tested them and taken off all the line that was rotten. He said they were going to have to get some more thirty-six thread in and plenty more twenty-four thread and Thomas Hudson promised to send for it. In the meantime Eddy had spliced enough good line on to replace the discarded line and both the big reels had all they would hold. He had cleaned and sharpened all of the big hooks and checked all the leaders and swivels.

"When did you do all this?"

"I sat up last night splicing," he said. "Then I worked on that new cast net. Couldn't sleep with the goddam moon."

"Does a full moon bother you for sleeping too?"

"Gives me hell," Eddy said.

"Eddy, do you think it's really bad for you to sleep with it shining on you?"

"That's what the old heads say. I don't know. Always makes me feel bad, anyway."

"Do you think we'll do anything today?"

"Never know. There's some awfully big fish out there this time of year. Are you going clean up to the Isaacs?"

"The boys want to go up there."

"We ought to get going right after breakfast. I'm not figuring to cook lunch. I've got conch salad and potato salad and beer and I'll make up sandwiches. We've got a ham that came over on the last run-boat and I've got some lettuce and we can use mustard and that chutney. Mustard doesn't hurt kids, does it?"

"I don't think so."

"We never had it when I was a kid. Say, that chutney's good, too. You ever eat it in a sandwich?"

"No."

"I didn't know what it was for when you first got it and I tried some of it like a marmalade. It's damned good. I use it sometimes on grits."

"Why don't we have some curry pretty soon?"

"I got a leg of lamb coming on the next run-boat. Wait till we eat off it a couple of times—once, I guess, with that young Tom and Andrew eating, and we'll have a curry."

"Fine. What do you want me to do about getting off?"

"Nothing, Tom. Just get them going. Want me to make you a drink? You aren't working today. Might as well have one."

"I'll drink a cold bottle of beer with breakfast."

"Good thing. Cut that damn phlegm."

"Is Joe here yet?"

"No. He went after the boy that's gone for bait. I'll put your breakfast out there."

"No, let me take her."

166

"No, go on in there and drink a cold bottle of beer and read the paper. I've got her all ironed out for you. I'll bring the breakfast."

Breakfast was corned-beef hash, browned, with an egg on top of it, coffee and milk, and a big glass of chilled grapefruit juice. Thomas Hudson skipped the coffee and the grapefruit juice and drank a very cold bottle of Heineken beer with the hash.

"I'll keep the juice cold for the kids," Eddy said. "That's some beer, isn't it, for early in the morning?"

"It would be pretty easy to be a rummy, wouldn't it, Eddy?"

"You'd never make a rummy. You like to work too well."

"Drinking in the morning feels awfully good, though."

"You're damned right it does. Especially something like that beer."

"I couldn't do it and work, though."

"Well, you're not working today so what's the goddamn problem? Drink that one up and I'll get you another."

"No. One's all I want."

They got off by nine o'clock and went down the channel with the tide. Thomas Hudson was steering on the topside and he headed her out over the bar and ran straight out toward where he could see the dark line of the Gulf. The water was so calm and so very clear that they could see the bottom clearly in thirty fathoms, see that sea fans bent with the tide current, still see it, but cloudily, at forty fathoms, and then it deepened and was dark and they were out in the dark water of the stream.

"It looks like a wonderful day, papa," Tom said. "It looks like a good stream."

"It's a fine stream. Look at the little curl of the whirlpools along the edge."

"Isn't this the same water that we have in on the beach in front of the house?"

"Sometimes, Tommy. Now the tide is out and it has pushed the Stream out from in front of the mouth of the harbor. See in there along the beach, where there is no opening, it's made in again."

"It looks almost as blue in there as it is out here. What makes the Gulf water so blue?"

"It's a different density of water. It's an altogether different type of water."

"The depth makes it darker, though."

"Only when you look down into it. Sometimes the plankton in it make it almost purple."

"Why?"

"Because they add red to the blue I think. I know they call the Red Sea red because the plankton make it look really red. They have terrific concentrations of them there "

"Did you like the Red Sea, papa?"

"I loved it. It was awfully hot but you never saw such wonderful reefs and it's full of fish on the two monsoons. You'd like it, Tom."

"I read two books about it in French by Mr. de Montfried. They were very good. He was in the slave trade. Not the white slave trade. The olden days slave trade. He's a friend of Mr. Davis."

"I know," Thomas Hudson said. "I know him, too."

"Mr. Davis told me that Mr. de Montfried came back to Paris one time from the slave trade and when he would take a lady out anywhere he would have the taxi driver put down the top of the taxi and he would steer the taxi driver wherever he wanted to go by the stars. Say Mr. de Montfried was on the Pont de la Concorde and he wanted to go to the Madeleine. He wouldn't just tell the taxi driver to take him to the Madeleine, or to cross the Place de la Concorde and go up the Rue Royale the way you or I would do it, papa. Mr. de Montfried would steer himself to the Madeleine by the North Star."

"I never heard that one about Mr. de Montfried," Thomas Hudson said. "I heard quite a lot of others."

"It's quite a complicated way to get around in Paris, don't you think? Mr. Davis wanted to go in the slave trade at one time with Mr. de Montfried but there was some sort of a hitch. I don't remember what it was. Yes, now I do. Mr. de Montfried had left the slave trade and gone into the opium trade. That was it."

"Didn't Mr. Davis want to go in the opium trade?"

"No. I remember he said he thought he'd leave the opium trade to Mr. De Quincey and Mr. Coceau. He said they'd done so well in it that he didn't think it was right to disturb them. That was one of those remarks that I couldn't understand. Papa, you explain anything to me that I ask but it used to slow the conversation up so much to be asking all the time that I would just remember certain things I didn't understand to ask about sometime and that's one of those things."

"You must have quite a backlog of those things."

"I've got hundreds of them. Possibly thousands. But I get rid of a lot of them every year by getting to understand them myself. But some I know I'll have to ask you about. At school this year I may write a list of them for an English composition. I've got some awfully good ones for a composition of that sort."

"Do you like school, Tom?"

"It's just one of those things you have to take. I don't think anyone likes school, do they, that has ever done anything else?"

"I don't know. I hated it."

"Didn't you like art school either?"

"No. I liked to learn to draw but I didn't like the school part."

"I don't really mind it," Tom said. "But after you've spent your life with men like Mr. Joyce and Mr. Pascin and you and Mr. Davis, being with boys seems sort of juvenile."

"You have fun, though, don't you?"

"Oh yes. I have lots of friends and I like any of the sports that aren't built around throwing or catching balls and I study quite hard. But papa, it isn't much of a life."

"That was the way I always felt about it," Thomas Hudson said. "You liven it up as much as you can, though."

"I do. I liven it up all I can and still stay in it. Sometimes it's a pretty close thing, though."

Thomas Hudson looked astern where the wake ran crisply in the calm sea and the two baits from the outriggers were dragging; dipping and leaping in the curl of the waves the wake raised as it cut the calm. David and Andrew sat in the two fishing chairs holding rods. Thomas Hudson saw their backs. Their faces were astern watching the baits. He looked ahead at some bonito jumping, not working and threshing the water, but coming up out and dropping back into the water singly and in pairs, making hardly any disturbance of the surface as they rose, shining in the sun, and returning, heavy heads down, to enter the water almost without splash.

"Fish!" Thomas Hudson heard young Tom shout. "Fish! Fish! There he comes up. Behind you, Dave. Watch him!"

Thomas Hudson saw a huge boil in the water but could not see the fish. David had the rod butt in the gimble and was looking up at the clothespin on the outrigger line. Thomas Hudson saw the line fall from the outrigger in a long, slow loop that tightened as it hit the water and now was racing out at a slant, slicing the water as it went.

"Hit him, Dave. Hit him hard," Eddy called from the companionway.

"Hit him, Dave. For God's sake, hit him," Andrew begged.

"Shut up," David said. "I'm handling him."

He hadn't struck yet and the line was steadily going out at that angle, the rod bowed, the boy holding back on it as the line moved out. Thomas Hudson had throttled the motors down so they were barely turning over.

"Oh for God's sake, hit him," Andrew pleaded. "Or let me hit him."

David just held back on the rod and watched the line moving out at that same steady angle. He had loosened the drag.

"He's a broadbill, papa," he said without looking up. "I saw his sword when he took it."

"Honest to God?" Andrew asked. "Oh boy."

"I think you ought to hit him now," Roger was standing with

the boy now. He had the back out of the chair and he was buckling the harness on the reel. "Hit him now, Dave, and really hit him."

"Do you think he's had it long enough?" David asked. "You don't think he's just carrying it in his mouth and swimming with it?"

"I think you better hit him before he spits it out."

David braced his feet, tightened the drag well down with his right hand, and struck back hard against the great weight. He struck again and again bending the rod like a bow. The line moved out steadily. He had made no impression on the fish.

"Hit him again, Dave," Roger said. "Really put it into him."

David struck again with all his strength and the line started zizzing out, the rod bent so that he could hardly hold it.

"Oh God," he said devoutly. "I think I've got it into him."

"Ease up on your drag," Roger told him "Turn with him, Tom, and watch the line."

"Turn with him and watch the line," Thomas Hudson repeated. "You all right, Dave?"

"I'm wonderful, papa," Dave said. "Oh God, if I can catch this fish."

Thomas Hudson swung the boat around almost on her stern. Dave's line was fading off the reel and Thomas Hudson moved up on the fish.

"Tighten up and get that line in now," Roger said. "Work on him, Dave."

David was lifting and reeling as he lowered, lifting and reeling as he lowered, as regularly as a machine, and was getting back a good quantity of line onto his reel.

"Nobody in our family's ever caught a broadbill," Andrew said.

"Oh keep your mouth off him, please," David said. "Don't put your mouth on him."

"I won't," Andrew said. "I've been doing nothing but pray ever since you hooked him."

"Do you think his mouth will hold?" young Tom whispered to his father, who was holding the wheel and looking down into the stern and watching the slant of the white line in the dark water.

"I hope so. Dave isn't strong enough to be rough with him."

"I'll do anything if we can get him," young Tom said. "Anything. I'll give up anything. I'll promise anything. Get him some water, Andy."

"I've got some," Eddy said. "Stay with him, old Dave boy."

"I don't want him any closer," Roger called up. He was a great fisherman and he and Thomas Hudson understood each other perfectly in a boat.

"I'll put him astern," Thomas Hudson called and swung the boat around very softly and easily so the stern hardly disturbed the calm sea.

The fish was sounding now and Thomas Hudson backed the boat very slowly to ease the pressure on the line all that he could. But with only a touch of reverse with the stern moving slowly toward the fish the angle was all gone from the line and the rod tip was pointing straight down and the line kept going out in a series of steady jerks, the rod bucking each time in David's hands. Thomas Hudson slipped the boat ahead just a thought so that the boy would not have the line so straight up and down in the water. He knew how it was pulling on his back in that position, but he had to save all the line he could.

"I can't put any more drag on or it will break," David said. "What will he do, Mr. Davis?"

"He'll just keep on going down until you stop him" Roger said. "Or until he stops. Then you've got to try to get him up."

The line kept going out and down, out and down, out and down. The rod was bent so far it looked as though it must break and the line was taut as a tuned cello string and there was not much more of it on the reel.

"What can I do, papa?"

"Nothing. You're doing what there is to do."

"Won't he hit the bottom?" Andrew asked.

"There isn't any bottom," Roger told him.

"You hold him, Davy," Eddy said. "He'll get sick of it and come up."

"These damned straps are killing me," David said. "They cut my shoulders off."

"Do you want me to take him?" Andrew asked.

"No, you fool," David said. "I just said what they were doing to me. I don't care about it."

"See if you can rig him the kidney harness," Thomas Hudson called down to Eddy. "You can tie it on with line if the straps are too long."

Eddy wrapped the broad, quilted pad across the small of the boy's back and fastened the rings on the web straps that ran across it to the reel with heavy line.

"That's much better," David said. "Thank you very much, Eddy."

"Now you can hold him with your back as well as your shoulders," Eddy told him.

"But there isn't going to be any line," David said. "Oh goddam him, why does he have to keep on sounding?"

"Tom," Eddy called up. "Ease her a little northwest. I think he's moving."

Thomas Hudson turned the wheel and moved her softly, slowly, softly out to sea. There was a big patch of yellow gulf weed ahead with a bird on it and the water was calm and so blue and clear that, as you looked down into it, there were lights in it like the reflections from a prism.

"You see?" Eddy told David. "You're not losing any now."

The boy could not raise the rod; but the line was no longer jerking down into the water. It was as taut as ever and there weren't fifty yards left on the reel. But it was not going out. David was holding him and the boat was on his course. Thomas Hudson could see the just perceptible slant of the white line deep down in the blue water as the boat barely moved, its engines turning so quietly he could not hear them.

"You see, Davy, he went down to where he liked it and now he's moving out to where he wants to go. Pretty soon you'll get some line on him."

The boy's brown back was arched, the rod bent, the line moved slowly through the water, and the boat moved slowly on the surface, and a quarter of a mile below the great fish was swimming. The gull left the patch of weed and flew toward the boat. He flew around Thomas Hudson's head while he steered, then headed off toward another patch of yellow weed on the water.

"Try to get some on him now," Roger told the boy. "If you can hold him you can get some."

"Put her ahead just a touch more," Eddy called the bridge and Thomas Hudson eased her ahead as softly as he could.

David lifted and lifted, but the rod only bent and the line only tightened. It was as though he were hooked to a moving anchor.

"Never mind," Roger told him. "You'll get it later. How are you, Davy?"

"I'm fine," David said. "With that harness across my back I'm fine."

"Do you think you can stay with him?" Andrew asked.

"Oh shut up," David said. "Eddy, can I have a drink of water?"

"Where'd I put it?" Eddy asked. "I guess I spilled it."

"I'll get one," Andrew went below.

"Can I do anything, Dave?" young Tom asked. "I'm going up so I won't be in the way."

"No, Tom. Goddam it, *why* can't I lift on him?"

"He's an awfully big fish, Dave," Roger told him. "You can't bull him around. You've got to lead him and try to convince him where he has to come."

"You tell me what to do and I'll do it until I die," David said. "I trust you."

"Don't talk about dying," Roger said. "That's no way to talk."

"I mean it," David said. "I mean it really."

Young Tom came back up on the flying bridge with his father.

They were looking down at David, bent and harnessed to his fish, with Roger standing by him and Eddy holding the chair. Andrew was putting the glass of water to Dave's mouth. He took some in and spat it out.

"Pour some on my wrists, will you, Andy?" he asked.

"Papa, do you think he can really stay with this fish?" Tom said to his father very softly.

"It's an awful lot of fish for him."

"It scares me," Tom said. "I love David and I don't want any damned fish to kill him."

"Neither do I and neither does Roger and neither does Eddy."

"Well, we've got to look after him. If he gets in really bad shape, Mr. Davis ought to take the fish or you take him."

"He's a long way from bad shape yet."

"But you don't know him like we do. He *would* kill himself to get the fish."

"Don't worry, Tom."

"I can't help it," young Tom said. "I'm the one in the family that always worries. I hope I'll get over it."

"I wouldn't worry about this now," Thomas Hudson said.

"But papa, how is a boy like David going to catch a fish like that? He's never caught anything bigger than sailfish and amber-jack."

"The fish will get tired. It's the fish that has the hook in his mouth."

"But he's monstrous," Tom said. "And Dave's fastened to him just as much as he is to Dave. It's so wonderful! I can't believe it if Dave catches him, but I wish you or Mr. Davis had him."

"Dave's doing all right."

They were getting farther out to sea all the time but it was still a flat calm. There were many patches of Gulf weed now, sunburned so that they were yellow on the purple water, and sometimes the slow-moving taut white line ran through a patch of weed and Eddy reached down and cleared any weed that clung to the line. As he

175

leaned over the coaming and pulled the yellow weed off the line and tossed it away, Thomas Hudson saw his wrinkled red brown neck and old felt hat and heard him say to Dave, "He's practically towing the boat, Davy. He's way down there tiring himself and tiring himself all the time."

"He's tiring me, too," David said.

"You got a headache?" Eddy asked.

"No."

"Get a cap for him," Roger said.

"I don't want it, Mr. Davis. I'd rather have some water on my head."

Eddy dipped a bucket of sea water and wet the boy's head carefully with his cupped hand, soaking his head and pushing the hair back out of his eyes.

"You say if you get a headache," he told him.

"I'm fine," David said. "You tell me what to do, Mr. Davis."

"See if you can get any line on him," Roger said.

David tried and tried and tried again but he could not raise the fish an inch.

"All right. Save your strength," Roger told him. Then to Eddy, "Soak a cap and put it on him. This is a hell of a hot day with the calm."

Eddy dipped a long-visored cap in the bucket of salt water and put it on Dave's head.

"The salt water gets in my eyes, Mr. Davis. Really. I'm sorry."

"I'll wipe it out with some fresh," Eddy said. "Give me a handkerchief, Roger. You go get some ice water, Andy."

While the boy hung there, his legs braced, his body arched against the strain, the boat kept moving slowly out to sea. To the westward a school of either bonito or albacore were troubling the calm of the surface and terns commenced to come flying, calling to each other as they flew. But the school of fish went down and the terns lit on the calm water to wait for the fish to come up again. Eddy had wiped the boy's face and now was dipping the handkerchief in the glass of ice water and laying it across David's neck. Then he cooled his wrist with it and then, with the handkerchief soaked in ice water again, wrung it out while he pressed it against the back of David's neck.

"You say if you have a headache," Eddy told him. "That ain't quitting. That's just sense. This is a hell of a goddam hot sun when it's a calm."

"I'm all right," David told him. "I hurt bad in the shoulders and the arms is all."

"That's natural," Eddy said. "That'll make a man out of you. What we don't want is for you to get no sunstroke nor bust any gut."

"What will he do now, Mr. Davis?" David asked. His voice sounded dry.

"Maybe just what he's doing. Or he might start to circle. Or he may come up."

"It's a damn shame he sounded so deep at the start so we haven't any line to maneuver him with," Thomas Hudson said to Roger.

"Dave stopped him is the main thing," Roger said. "Pretty soon the fish will change his mind. Then we'll work on him. See if you can get any just once, Dave."

David tried but he could not raise him at all.

"He'll come up," Eddy said. "You'll see. All of a sudden there won't be anything to it, Davy. Want to rinse your mouth out?"

David nodded his head. He had reached the breath-saving stage.

"Spit it out," Eddy said. "Swallow just a little." He turned to Roger. "One hour even," he said. "Is your head all right, Davy?"

The boy nodded.

"What do you think, papa?" young Tom said to his father. "Truly?"

"He looks pretty good to me," his father said. "Eddy wouldn't let anything happen to him."

"No, I guess not," Tom agreed. "I wish I could do something useful. I'm going to get Eddy a drink."

"Get me one, too, please."

"Oh good. I'll make one for Mr. Davis, too."

"I don't think he wants one."

"Well, I'll ask him."

"Try him once more, Davy," Roger said very quietly, and the boy lifted with all his strength, holding the sides of the spool of the reel with his hands.

"You got an inch," Roger said. "Take it in and see if you can get some more."

Now the real fight began. Before David had only been holding him while the fish moved out to sea and the boat moved with him. But now he had to lift, let the rod straighten with the line he had gained, and then lower the rod slowly while he took the line in by reeling.

"Don't try to do it too fast," Roger told him. "Don't rush yourself. Just keep it steady."

The boy was bending forward and pulling up from the soles of his feet, using all the leverage of his body and all of what weight he had on each lift; then reeling fast with his right hand as he lowered.

"David fishes awfully pretty," young Tom said. "He's fished since he was a little boy but I didn't know he could fish this well. He always makes fun of himself because he can't play games. But look at him now."

"The hell with games," Thomas Hudson said. "What did you say, Roger?"

"Go ahead on him just a touch," Roger called up.

"Ahead on him just a touch," Thomas Hudson repeated and on the next lift, as they nudged slowly forward, David recovered more line.

"Don't you like games either, papa?" Tom asked.

"I used to. Very much. But not anymore."

"I like tennis and fencing," Tom said. "The throw-and-catch ball games are the ones I don't like. That's from being brought up in Europe I guess. I'll bet David could be a fine fencer if he wanted to learn because he has so much brains. But he doesn't want to learn. All he wants to do is read and fish and shoot and tie flies. He shoots better than Andy does in the field. He can tie beautiful flies too. Am I bothering you, papa, talking so much?"

"Of course not, Tom."

He was holding to the rail of the flying bridge and looking aft as his father was and his father put one hand on his shoulder. It was salty from the buckets of sea water the boys had thrown over each other on the stern before the fish struck. The salt was very fine and felt faintly sandy under his hand.

"You see I get so nervous watching David I talk to take my mind off it. I'd rather have David catch that fish than anything on earth."

"He's a hell of a fish. Wait till we see him."

"I saw one one time when I was fishing with you years ago. He hit a big mackerel bait with his sword and he jumped and threw the hook. He was enormous and I used to dream about him. I'll go down and make the drinks."

"There's no hurry," his father told him.

Down in the backless fighting chair, set in its swivel base, David braced his feet against the stern and lifted with his arms, back, withers, and thighs; then lowered and reeled and lifted again. Steadily, an inch, two inches, three inches at a time he was getting more and more line on the reel.

"Is your head all right?" Eddy, who was holding the arms of the chair to steady it, asked him.

David nodded. Eddy put his hand on the top of the boy's head and felt his cap.

"Cap's still wet," he said. "You're giving him hell, Davy. Just like a machine."

"It's easier now than holding him," David said, his voice still dry.

"Sure," Eddy told him. "Something gives now. Other way it was just pulling your back out by the roots."

"Don't work him any faster than you can," Roger said. "You're doing wonderfully, Dave."

"Will we gaff him when he comes up this time?" Andrew asked.

"Oh keep your mouth off of him, please," David said.

179

"I wasn't trying to mouth him."

"Oh just shut up, Andy, please. I'm sorry."

Andrew came climbing up topside. He had on one of the long-peaked caps but under it his father could see his eyes were wet and the boy turned his head away because his lips trembled.

"You didn't say anything bad," Thomas Hudson told him.

Andrew spoke with his head turned away. "Now if he loses him he'll think I mouthed him," he said bitterly. "All I wanted to do was help get everything ready."

"It's natural for Dave to be nervous," his father told him. "He's trying to be polite."

"I know it," Andrew said. "He's fighting him just as good as Mr. Davis could. I just felt bad he could think that."

"Lots of people are irritable with a big fish. This is the first one Dave's ever had."

"You're always polite and Mr. Davis is always polite."

"We didn't use to be. When we were learning to fish big fish together we used to be excited and rude and sarcastic. We both used to be terrible."

"Truly?"

"Sure. Truly. We used to suffer and act as though everybody was against us. That's the natural way to be. The other's discipline or good sense when you learn. We started to be polite because we found we couldn't catch big fish being rude and excited. And if we did, it wasn't any fun. We were both really awful, though; excited and sore and mis-understood and it wasn't any fun. So now we always fight them politely. We talked it over and decided we'd be polite no matter what."

"I'll be polite," Andrew said. "But it's hard sometimes with Dave. Papa, do you think he can *really* get him? That it isn't just like a dream or something?"

"Let's not talk about it."

"Have I said something wrong again?"

"No. Only it always seems bad luck to talk that way. We got it from the old fishermen. I don't know what started it."

"I'll be careful."

"Here's your drink, papa," Tom said, handing it up from below. The glass was wrapped in a triple thickness of paper towel with a rubber band around to hold the paper tight against the glass and keep the ice from melting. "I put lime, bitters, and no sugar in it. Is that how you want it? Or can I change it?"

"That's fine. Did you make it with coconut water?"

"Yes, and I made Eddy a whisky. Mr. Davis didn't want anything. Are you staying up there, Andy?"

"No. I'm coming down."

Tom climbed up and Andrew went down.

Looking back over the stern, Thomas Hudson noticed the line starting to slant up in the water.

"Watch it, Roger," he called. "It looks like he's coming up."

"He's coming up!" Eddy yelled. He had seen the slant in the line too. "Watch your wheel."

Thomas Hudson looked down at the spool of the reel to see how much line there was to maneuver with. It was not yet a quarter full and as he watched it started to whiz off and Thomas Hudson started backing, turning sharp toward the slant of the line, well under way as Eddy yelled, "Back on him, Tom. The son of a bitch is coming up. We ain't got no line to turn."

"Keep your rod up," Roger said to David. "Don't let him get it down." Then to Thomas Hudson, "Back on him all you can, Tom. You're going right. Give her all she'll take."

Then, astern of the boat and off to starboard, the calm of the ocean broke open and the great fish rose out of it, rising, shining dark blue and silver, seeming to come endlessly out of the water, unbelievable as his length and bulk rose out of the sea into the air and seemed to hang there until he fell with a splash that drove the water up high and white.

"Oh God," David said. "Did you see him?"

"His sword's as long as I am," Andrew said in awe.

"He's so beautiful," Tom said. "He's much better than the one I had in the dream."

"Keep backing on him," Roger said to Thomas Hudson. Then to David, "Try and get some line out of that belly. He came up from way down and there's a big belly of line and you can get some of it."

Thomas Hudson, backing fast onto the fish, had stopped the line going out and now David was lifting, lowering, and reeling, and the line was coming onto the reel in sweeps as fast as he could turn the reel handle.

"Slow her down," Roger said. "We don't want to get over him."

"Son of a bitch'll weigh a thousand pounds," Eddy said. "Get that easy line in, Davy boy."

The ocean was flat and empty where he had jumped but the circle made where the water had been broken was still widening.

"Did you see the water he threw when he jumped, papa?" young Tom asked his father. "It was like the whole sea bursting open."

"Did you see the way he seemed to climb up and up, Tom? Did you ever see such a blue and that wonderful silver on him?"

"His sword is blue too," young Tom said. "The whole back of it is blue. Will he really weigh a thousand pounds, Eddy?" he called down.

"I think he will. Nobody can say. But he'll weigh something awful."

"Get all the line you can, Davy, now while it's cheap," Roger told him. "You're getting it fine."

The boy was working like a machine again, recovering line from the great bulge of line in the water and the boat was backing so slowly that the movement was barely perceptible.

"What will he do now, papa?" Tom asked his father. Thomas Hudson was watching the slant of the line in the water and thinking it would be safer to go ahead just a little but he knew how Roger had suffered with so much line out. The fish had only needed to make one steady rush to strip all the line from the reel and break off and now Roger was taking chances to get a reserve of line. As Thomas

Hudson watched the line, he saw that David had the reel nearly half full and that he was still gaining.

"What did you say?" Thomas Hudson asked his boy Tom.

"What do you think he'll do now?"

"Wait a minute, Tom," his father said and called down to Roger. "I'm afraid we're going to get over him, kid."

"Then put her ahead easy," Roger said.

"Ahead easy," Thomas Hudson repeated. David stopped getting in so much line but the fish was in a safer position.

Then the line started to go out again and Roger called up, "Throw her out," and Thomas Hudson threw out the clutches and let the motors idle.

"She's out," he said. Roger was bending over David and the boy was braced and holding back on the rod and the line was slipping steadily away.

"Tighten on him a little bit, Davy," Roger said. "We'll make him work for it."

"I don't want him to break," David said. But he tightened the drag.

"He won't break," Roger told him. "Not with that drag."

The line kept going out but the rod was bent heavier and the boy was braced back holding against the pressure with his bare feet against the wood of the stern. Then the line stopped going out.

"Now you can get some," Roger told the boy. "He's circling and this is the in-turn. Get back all you can."

The boy lowered and reeled, then lifted; let the rod straighten; lowered and reeled. He was getting line beautifully again.

"Am I doing all right?" he asked.

"You're doing wonderful," Eddy told him. "He's hooked deep, Davy. I could see when he jumped."

Then, while the boy was lifting, the line started to go out again.

"Hell," David said.

"That's OK," Roger told him. "That's what's supposed to happen. He's on the out-turn now. He circled in toward you and you got line. Now he's taking it back."

Steadily, slowly, with David holding him with all the strain the line would take, the fish took out all the line the boy had just recovered and a little more. Then the boy held him.

"All right. Get to work on him," Roger said quietly. "He widened his circle a little bit but he's on the in-swing now."

Thomas Hudson was using the engines only occasionally now to keep the fish astern. He was trying to do everything for the boy that the boat could do and he was trusting the boy and the fight to Roger. As he saw it there was no other thing to do.

On the next circle the fish gained a little line again. On the circle after that he gained too. But the boy still had almost half the line on the reel. He was still working the fish exactly as he should and delivering each time Roger asked him to do something. But he was getting very tired and the sweat and salt water had made salty blotches on his brown back and shoulders.

"Two hours even," Eddy said to Roger. "How's your head, Davy?"

"All right."

"Not ache?"

The boy shook his head.

"You better drink some water this time," Eddy said.

David nodded and drank when Andrew put the glass to his lips.

"How do you feel, Davy, really?" Roger asked him, bending close over him.

"Fine. All except my back and legs and arms." He shut his eyes for an instant and held to the bucking of the rod as the line went out against the heavy drag.

"I don't want to talk," he said.

"You can get some on him now," Roger told him and the boy went back to work.

"David's a saint and a martyr," Tom said to his father. "Boys don't have brothers like David. Do you mind if I talk, papa? I'm awfully nervous about this."

"Go ahead and talk, Tommy. We're both worried."

"He's always been wonderful, you know," Tom said. "He's not

a damn genius nor an athlete like Andy. He's just wonderful. I know you love him the most and that's right because he's the best of us and I know this must be good for him or you wouldn't let him do it. But it certainly makes me nervous."

Thomas Hudson put an arm around his shoulder and steered, looking astern with only one hand on the wheel.

"The trouble is, Tommy, what it would do to him if we made him give it up. Roger and Eddy know everything about what they're doing and I know they love him and wouldn't have him do what he can't do."

"But there is no limit with him, papa. Truly. He'll always do what he can't do."

"You trust me and I'll trust Roger and Eddy."

"All right. But I'm going to pray for him now."

"You do," said Thomas Hudson. "Why did you say I loved him the best?"

"You ought to."

"I've loved you the longest."

"Let's not think about me nor you. Let's both of us pray for Davy."

"Good," said Thomas Hudson. "Now look. We hooked him right at noon. There's going to be some shade now. I think we've got some already. I'm going to work her around very softly and put Davy in the shade."

Thomas Hudson called down to Roger. "If it's OK with you, Roge, I'd like to work her around slow and put Dave in the shade. I don't think it will make any difference with the fish the way he's circling and we'll be on his real course."

"Fine," Roger said. "I should have thought of it."

"There hasn't been any shade until now," Thomas Hudson said. He worked the boat around so slowly, just swinging her on her stern, that they lost almost no line by the maneuver. David's head and shoulders were now shaded by the aft part of the house. Eddy was wiping the boy's neck and shoulders with a towel and putting alcohol on his back and on the back of his neck.

"How's that, Dave?" young Tom called down to him.

"Wonderful," David said.

"I feel better about him now," young Tom said. "You know at school somebody said David was my half brother, not my real brother, and I told him we didn't have half brothers in our family. I wish I didn't worry so much though, papa."

"You'll get over it."

"In a family like ours somebody has to worry," young Tom said. "But I never worry about you anymore. It's David now. I guess I better make a couple of more drinks. I can pray while I make them. Do you want one, papa?"

"I'd love one."

"Eddy probably needs one pretty badly," the boy said. "It must be nearly three hours. Eddy's only had one drink in three hours. I've certainly been remiss about things. Why do you suppose Mr. Davis shouldn't take one, papa?"

"I didn't think he would take one while David was going through all that."

"Maybe he will now Dave's in the shade. I'll try him now anyway." He went below.

"I don't think so, Tommy," Thomas Hudson heard Roger say.

"You haven't had one all day, Mr. Davis," Tom urged.

"Thanks, Tommy," Roger said. "You drink a bottle of beer for me." Then he called up to the wheel. "Put her ahead a little easy, Tom. He's coming better on this tack."

"Ahead a little easy," Thomas Hudson repeated.

The fish was still circling deep, but in the direction the boat was headed now he was shortening the circle. It was the direction he wanted to move in. Now, too, it was easier to see the slant of the line. It was easier to see its true slant much deeper in the dark water with the sun behind the boat and Thomas Hudson felt safer steering with the fish. He thought how fortunate it was that the day was calm for he knew David could never have taken the punishment that he would have had if he were hooked to such a fish in even a moderate sea. Now that David was in the shade and the sea stayed calm he began to feel better about it all.

"Thanks, Tommy," he heard Eddy say and then the boy climbed up with his paper-wrapped glass and Thomas Hudson tasted, took a swallow and felt the cold that had the sharpness of the lime, the aromatic varnishy taste of the Angostura and the gin stiffening the lightness of the ice-cold coconut water.

"Is it all right, papa?" the boy asked. He had a bottle of beer from the ice box that was perspiring cold drops in the sun.

"It's excellent," his father told him. "You put in plenty of gin too."

"I have to," young Tom said. "Because the ice melts so fast. We ought to have some sort of insulated holders for the glass so the ice wouldn't melt. I'm going to work out something at school. I think I could make them out of cork blocks. Maybe I can make them for you for Christmas."

"Look at Dave now," his father said.

David was working on the fish as though he had just started the fight.

"Look how sort of slab-sided he is," young Tom said. "His chest and his back are all the same. He looks sort of like he was glued together. But he's got the longest arm muscles you could ever see. They're just as long on the back of his arms as on the front. The biceps and the triceps I mean. He's certainly built strangely, papa. He's a strange boy and he's the best damn brother you can have."

Down in the cockpit Eddy had drained his glass and was wiping David's back with a towel again. Then he wiped his chest and his long arms.

"You all right, Davy?"

David nodded.

"Listen," Eddy told him, "I've seen a grown man, strong, shoulders like a bull, yellow-out and quit on half the work you've put in on that fish already."

David kept on working.

"Big man. Your dad and Roger both know him. Trained for it.

Fishing all the time. Hooked the biggest goddam fish a man ever hooked and yellowed-out and quit on him just because he hurt. Fish made him hurt so he quit. You just keep it steady, Davy."

David did not say anything. He was saving his breath and pumping, lowering, raising, and reeling.

"This damn fish is so strong because he's a he," Eddy told him. "If it was a she it would have quit long ago. It would have bust its insides or its heart or burst its roe. In this kind of fish the he is the strongest. In lots of other fish it's the she that is strongest. But not with broadbill. He's awfully strong, Davy. But you'll get him."

The line started to go out again and David shut his eyes a moment, braced his bare feet against the wood, hung back against the rod, and rested.

"That's right, Davy," Eddy said. "Only work when you're working. He's just circling. But the drag makes him work for it and it's tiring him all the time."

Eddy turned his head and looked below and Thomas Hudson knew from the way he squinted his eyes that he was looking at the big brass clock on the cabin wall.

"It's five over three, Roger," he said. "You've been with him three hours and five minutes, Davy old boy."

They were at the point where David should have started to gain line. But instead the line was going out steadily.

"He's sounding again," Roger said. "Watch yourself, Davy. Can you see the line OK, Tom?"

"I can see it OK," Thomas Hudson told him. It was not yet at a very steep slant and he could see it a long way down in the water from the top of the house.

"He may want to go down to die," Thomas Hudson told his oldest boy, speaking very low. "That would ruin Dave."

Young Tom shook his head and bit his lips.

"Hold him all you can, Dave," Thomas Hudson heard Roger say. "Tighten up on him and give it all it will take."

The boy tightened up the drag almost to the breaking point of the rod and line and then hung on, bracing himself to take the punishment the best he could, while the line went out and out and down and down.

"When you stop him this time I think you will have whipped him," Roger told David. "Throw her out, Tom."

"She's cut," Thomas Hudson said. "But I think I could save a little backing."

"OK. Try it."

"Backing now," Thomas Hudson said. They saved a little line by backing but not much, and the line was getting terribly straight up and down. There was less on the reel now than at the worst time before.

"You'll have to get out on the stern, Davy," Roger said. "You'll have to loosen the drag up a little to get the butt out."

David loosened the drag.

"Now get the butt into your butt rest. You hold him around the waist, Eddy."

"Oh God, papa," young Tom said. "He's taking it all right to the bottom now."

David was on his knees on the low stern now, the rod bent so that its tip was underwater, its butt in the leather socket of the butt rest that was strapped around his waist. Andrew was holding on to David's feet and Roger knelt beside him watching the line in the water and the little there was on the reel. He shook his head at Thomas Hudson.

There was not twenty yards more on the reel and David was pulled down with half the rod underwater now. Then there was barely fifteen yards on the reel. Now there was not ten yards. Then the line stopped going out. The boy was still bent far over the stern and most of the rod was in the water. But no line was going out.

"Get him back into the chair, Eddy. Easy. Easy," Roger said. "When you can, I mean. He's stopped him."

Eddy helped David back into the fighting chair, holding him around the waist so that a sudden lurch by the fish would not pull the boy overboard. Eddy eased him into the chair and David got the rod butt into the gimbal socket and braced with his feet and pulled back on the rod. The fish lifted a little.

"Only pull when you are going to get some line," Roger told David. "Let him pull the rest of the time. Try and rest inside the action except when you are working on him."

"You've got him, Davy," Eddy said. "You're getting it on him all the time. Just take it slow and easy and you'll kill him."

Thomas Hudson eased the boat a little forward to put the fish further astern. There was good shadow now over all the stern. The boat was working steadily further out to sea and no wind troubled the surface.

"Papa," young Tom said to his father. "I was looking at his feet when I made the drinks. They're bleeding."

"He's chafed them pulling against the wood."

"Do you think I could put a pillow there? A cushion for him to pull against?"

"Go down and ask Eddy," Thomas Hudson said. "But don't interrupt Dave."

It was well into the fourth hour of the fight now. The boat was still working out to sea and David, with Roger holding the back of his chair now, was raising the fish steadily. David looked stronger now than he had an hour before but Thomas Hudson could see where his heels showed the blood that had run down from the soles of his feet. It looked varnished in the sun.

"How's your feet, Davy?" Eddy asked.

"They don't hurt," David said. "What hurts is my hands and arms and my back."

"I could put a cushion under them."

David shook his head.

"I think they'd stick," he said. "They're sticky. They don't hurt. Really."

Young Tom came up to the top side and said, "He's wearing the bottoms of his feet right off. He's getting his hands bad too. He's had blisters and now they're all open. Gee, papa. I don't know."

"It's the same as if he had to paddle against a stiff current, Tommy. Or if he had to keep going up a mountain or stick with a horse after he was awfully tired."

"I know it. But just watching it and not doing it seems so sort of awful when it's your brother."

"I know it, Tommy. But there is a time boys have to do things if they are ever going to be men. That's where Dave is now."

"I know it. But when I see his feet and his hands I don't know, papa."

"If you had the fish would you want Roger or me to take him away from you?"

"No. I'd want to stay with him till I died. But to see it with Davy is different."

"We have to think about how he feels," his father told him. "And what's important to him."

"I know," young Tom said hopelessly. "But to me it's just Davy. I wish the world wasn't the way it is and that things didn't have to happen to brothers."

"I do too," Thomas Hudson said. "You're an awfully good boy, Tommy. But please know I would have stopped this long ago except that I know that if David catches this fish he'll have something inside him for all his life and it will make everything else easier."

Just then Eddy spoke. He had been looking behind him into the cabin again.

"Four hours even, Roger," he said. "You better take some water, Davy. How do you feel?"

"Fine," David said.

"I know what I'll do that is practical," young Tom said. "I'll make a drink for Eddy. Do you want one, papa?"

"No. I'll skip this one," Thomas Hudson said.

Young Tom went below and Thomas Hudson watched David working slowly, tiredly but steadily; Roger bending over him and speaking to him in a low voice; Eddy out on the stern watching the slant of the line in the water. Thomas Hudson tried to picture how it would be down where the swordfish was swimming. It was dark of course but probably the fish could see as a horse can see. It would be very cold.

He wondered if the fish was alone or if there could be another fish swimming with him. They had seen no other fish but that did not prove this fish was alone. There might be another with him in the dark and the cold.

Thomas Hudson wondered why the fish had stopped when he had gone so deep the last time. Did the fish reach his maximum possible depth the way a plane reached its ceiling? Or had the pulling against the bend of the rod, the heavy drag on the line, and the resistance of its friction in the water discouraged him so that now he swam quietly in the direction he wished to go? Was he only rising a little, steadily, as David lifted on him; rising docilely to ease the unpleasant tension that held him? Thomas Hudson thought that was probably the way it was and that David might have great trouble with him yet if the fish was still strong.

Young Tom had brought Eddy's own bottle to him and Eddy had taken a long pull out of it and then asked Tom to put it in the bait box to keep it cool. "And handy," he added. "If I see Davy fight this fish much longer it will make a damned rummy out of me."

"I'll bring it any time you want it," Andrew said.

"Don't bring it when I want it," Eddy told him. "Bring it when I ask for it."

The oldest boy had come up with Thomas Hudson and together they watched Eddy bend over David and look carefully into his eyes. Roger was holding the chair and watching the line.

"Now listen, Davy," Eddy told the boy, looking close into his face. "Your hands and your feet don't mean a damn thing. They hurt and they look bad but they are all right. That's the way a fisherman's hands and feet are supposed to get and next time they'll be tougher. But is your bloody head all right?"

"Fine," David said.

"Then God bless you and stay with the son of a bitch because we are going to have him up here soon."

"Davy," Roger spoke to the boy. "Do you want me to take him?"

David shook his head.

"It wouldn't be quitting now," Roger said. "It would just make sense. I could take him or your father could take him."

"Am I doing anything wrong?" David asked bitterly.

"No. You're doing perfectly."

"Then why should I quit on him?"

"He's giving you an awful beating, Davy," Roger said. "I don't want him to hurt you."

"He's the one has the hook in his goddam mouth." David's voice was unsteady. "He isn't giving me a beating. I'm giving him a beating. The son of a bitch."

"Say anything you want, Dave," Roger told him.

"The damn son of a bitch. The big son of a bitch."

"He's crying," Andrew, who had come up topside and was standing with young Tom and his father, said. "He's talking that way to get rid of it."

"Shut up, horseman," young Tom said.

"I don't care if he kills me, the big son of a bitch," David said. "Oh hell. I don't hate him. I love him."

"You shut up now," Eddy said to David. "You save your wind."

He looked at Roger and Roger lifted his shoulders to show he did not know.

"If I see you getting excited like that I'll take him away from you," Eddy said.

"I'm always excited," David said. "Just because I never say it nobody knows. I'm no worse now. It's only the talking."

"Well, you shut up now and take it easy," Eddy said. "You stay calm and quiet and we'll go with him forever."

"I'll stay with him," David said. "I'm sorry I called him the

193

names. I don't want to say anything against him. I think he's the finest thing in the world."

"Andy, get me that bottle of pure alcohol," Eddy said. "I'm going to loosen up his arms and shoulders and his legs," he said to Roger. "I don't want to use any more of that ice water for fear I'd cramp him up."

He looked into the cabin and said, "Five and a half even, Roger." He turned to David, "You don't feel too heated up now, do you, Davy?"

The boy shook his head.

"That straight-up-and-down sun in the middle of the day was what I was afraid of," Eddy sid. "Nothing going to happen to you now, Davy. Just take it easy and whip this old fish. We want to whip him before dark."

David nodded.

"Papa, did you ever see a fish fight like this one?" young Tom asked.

"Yes," Thomas Hudson told him.

"Very many?"

"I don't know, Tommy. There are some terrible fish in this Gulf. Then there are huge big fish that are easy to catch."

"Why are some easier?"

"I think because they get old and fat. Some I think are almost old enough to die. Then, of course, some of the biggest jump themselves to death."

There had been no boats in sight for a long time and it was getting late in the afternoon and they were a long way out between the island and the great Isaacs light.

"Try him once more, Davy," Roger said.

The boy bent his back, pulled back against his braced feet, and the rod, instead of staying solid, lifted slowly.

"You've got him coming," Roger said. "Get that line on and try him again."

The boy lifted and again recovered line.

"He's coming up," Roger told David. "Keep on him steady and good."

David went to work like a machine, or like a very tired boy performing as a machine.

"This is the time," Roger said. "He's really coming up. Put her ahead just a touch, Tom. We want to take him to the port side if we can."

"Ahead just a touch," Thomas Hudson said.

"Use your own judgment on it," Roger said. "We want to bring him up easy where Eddy can gaff him and we can get a noose over him. I'll handle the leader. Tommy, you come down here to handle the chair and see the line doesn't foul on the rod when I take the leader. Keep the line clear all the time in case I have to turn him loose. Andy, you help Eddy with anything he asks for and give him the noose and the club when he asks for them."

The fish was coming up steadily now and David was not breaking the rhythm of his pumping.

"Tom, you better come down and take the wheel below," Roger called up.

"I was just coming down," Thomas Hudson told him.

"Sorry," he said. "Davy, remember if he runs and I have to turn him loose keep your rod up and everything clear. Slack off your drag as soon as I take hold of the leader."

"Keep her spooled even," Eddy said. "Don't let her jam up now, Davy."

Thomas Hudson swung down from the flying bridge into the cockpit and took the wheel and the controls there. It was not as easy to see into the water as it was on the flying bridge but it was handier in case of any emergency and communication was easier. It was strange to be on the same level as the action after having looked down on it for so many hours, he thought. It was like moving down from a box seat onto the stage or to the ringside or close against the railing of the track. Everyone looked bigger and closer and they were all taller and not foreshortened.

He could see David's bloody hands and lacquered-looking ooz-ing feet and he saw the welts the harness had made across his back and the almost hopeless expression on his face as he turned his head at the last finish of a pull. He looked in the cabin and the brass clock showed that it was ten minutes to six. The sea looked different to him now that he was so close to it, and looking at it from the shade and from David's bent rod, the white line slanted into the dark water and the rod lowered and rose steadily. Eddy knelt on the stern with the gaff in his sun-spotted freckled hands and looked down into the almost purple water trying to see the fish. Thomas Hudson noticed the rope hitches around the haft of the gaff and the rope made fast to the Samson post in the stern and then he looked again at David's back, his outstretched legs, and his long arms holding the rod.

"Can you see him, Eddy?" Roger asked from where he was hold-ing the chair.

"Not yet. Stay on him, Davy, steady and good."

David kept on his same raising, lowering, and reeling; the reel heavy with line now; bringing in a sweep of line each time he swung it around.

Once the fish held steady for a moment and the rod doubled toward the water and line started to go out.

"No. He can't be," David said.

"He might," Eddy said. "You can't ever know."

But then David lifted slowly, suffering against the weight and, after the first slow lift, the line started to come again as easily and steadily as before.

"He just held for a minute," Eddy said. His old felt hat on the back of his head, he was peering down into the clear, dark purple water.

"There he is," he said.

Thomas Hudson slipped back quickly from the wheel to look over the stern. The fish showed, deep astern, looking tiny and fore-shortened in the depth but in the small time Thomas Hudson looked at him he grew steadily in size. It was not as rapidly as a plane grows as it comes in toward you but it was as steady.

Thomas Hudson put his arm on David's shoulder and went back to the wheel. Then he heard Andrew say, "Oh look at him," and this time he could see him from the wheel deep in the water and well astern, showing brown now and grown greatly in length and bulk.

"Keep her just as she is," Roger said without looking back and Thomas Hudson answered, "Just as she is."

"Oh God look at him," young Tom said.

Now he was really huge, bigger than any swordfish Thomas Hudson had ever seen. All the great length of him was purple blue now instead of brown and he was swimming slowly and steadily in the same direction the boat was going; astern of the boat and on David's right.

"Keep him coming all the time, Davy," Roger said. "He's coming in just right."

"Go ahead just a touch," Roger said, watching the fish.

"Ahead just a touch," Thomas Hudson answered.

"Keep it spooled," Eddy told David. Thomas Hudson could see the swivel of the leader now out of water.

"Ahead just a little more," Roger said.

"Going ahead just a little more," Thomas Hudson repeated. He was watching the fish and easing the stern onto the course that he was swimming. He could see the whole great purple length of him now, the great broad sword forward, the slicing dorsal fin set in his wide shoulders, and his huge tail that drove him almost without a motion.

"Just a touch more ahead," Roger said.

"Going ahead a touch more."

David had the leader within reach now.

"Are you ready for him, Eddy?" Roger asked.

"Sure," Eddy said.

"Watch him, Tom," Roger said and leaned over and took hold of the cable leader.

"Slack off on your drag," he said to David and began slowly raising the fish, holding and lifting on the heavy cable to bring him within reach of the gaff.

The fish was coming up looking as long and as broad as a big log in the water. David was watching him and glancing up at his rod tip to make sure it was not fouled. For the first time in six hours he had no strain on his back and his arms and legs and Thomas Hudson saw the muscles in his legs twitching and quivering. Eddy was bending over the side with the gaff and Roger was lifting slowly and steadily.

"He'd go over a thousand," Eddy said. Then he said, very quiet, "Roger, hook's only holding by a thread."

"Can you reach him?" Roger asked.

"Not yet," Eddy said. "Keep him coming easy, easy."

Roger kept lifting on the wire cable and the great fish rose steadily toward the boat.

"It's been cutting," Eddy said. "It's just holding by nothing."

"Can you reach him now?" Roger asked. His tone had not changed.

"Not quite yet," Eddy said as quietly. Roger was lifting as gently and as softly as he could. Then, from lifting, he straightened, all strain gone, holding the slack leader in his two hands.

"No. No. No. Please God, no," young Tom said.

Eddy lunged down into the water with the gaff and then went overboard to try to get the gaff into the fish if he could reach him.

It was no good. The great fish hung there in the depth of water where he was like a huge dark purple bird and then settled slowly. They all watched him go down, getting smaller and smaller until he was out of sight.

Eddy's hat was floating on the calm sea and he was holding on to the gaff handle. The gaff was on the line that was fast to the Samson post in the stern. Roger put his arms around David and Thomas Hudson could see David's shoulders shaking. But he left David to Roger. "Get the ladder out for Eddy to come aboard," he said to young Tom. "Take Davy's rod, Andy. Unhook it."

198

Roger lifted the boy out of the chair and carried him over to the bunk at the starboard side of the cockpit and laid him down in it. Roger's arms were around David and the boy lay flat on his face on the bunk.

Eddy came on board soaked and dripping, and started to undress. Andrew fished out his hat with the gaff and Thomas Hudson went below to get Eddy a shirt and a pair of dungarees and a shirt and shorts for David. He was surprised that he had no feeling at all except pity and love for David. All other feeling had been drained out of him in the fight.

When he came up David was lying, naked, face-down on the bunk and Roger was rubbing him down with alcohol.

"It hurts across the shoulders and my tail," David said. "Watch out, Mr. Davis, please."

"It's where it's chafed," Eddy told him. "Your father's going to fix your hands and feet with Mercurochrome. That won't hurt."

"Get the shirt on, Davy," Thomas Hudson said. "So you won't get cold. Go get one of the lightest blankets for him, Tom."

Thomas Hudson touched the places where the harness had chafed the boy's back with Mercurochrome and helped him into the shirt.

"I'm all right," David said in a toneless voice. "Can I have a Coke, papa?"

"Sure," Thomas Hudson told him. "Eddy will get you some soup in a little while."

"I'm not hungry," David said. "I couldn't eat yet."

"We'll wait a while," Thomas Hudson said.

"I know how you feel, Dave," Andrew said when he brought the Coke.

"Nobody knows how I feel," David said.

Thomas Hudson gave his oldest boy a compass course to steer back to the island.

"Synchronize your motors at three hundred, Tommy," he said. "We'll be in sight of the light by dark and then I'll give you a correction."

199

"You check me every once in a while, will you please, papa. Do you feel as awful as I do?"

"There's nothing to do about it."

"Eddy certainly tried," young Tom said. "Not everybody would jump in this ocean after a fish."

"Eddy nearly made it," his father told him. "It could have been a hell of a thing with him in the water with a gaff in that fish."

"Eddy would have got out all right," young Tom said. "Are they synchronized all right?"

"Listen for it," his father told him. "Don't just watch the tachometers."

Thomas Hudson went over to the bunk and sat down by David. He was rolled up in the light blanket and Eddy was fixing his hands and Roger his feet.

"Hi, papa," he said and looked at Thomas Hudson and then looked away.

"I'm awfully sorry, Davy," his father said. "You made the best fight on him I ever saw anyone make. Roger or any man ever."

"Thank you very much, papa. Please don't talk about it."

"Can I get you anything, Davy?"

"I'd like another Coke, please," David said.

Thomas Hudson found a cold bottle of Coca-Cola in the ice of the bait box and opened it. He sat by David and the boy drank the Coke with the hand Eddy had fixed.

"I'll have some soup ready right away. It's heating now," Eddy said. "Should I heat some chile, Tom? We've got some conch salad."

"Let's heat some chile," Thomas Hudson said. "We haven't eaten since breakfast. Roger hasn't had a drink all day."

"I had a bottle of beer just now," Roger said.

"Eddy," David said. "What would he really weigh?"

"Over a thousand," Eddy told him.

"Thank you very much for going overboard," David said. "Thank you very much, Eddy."

"Hell," Eddy said. "What else was there to do?"

"Would he really have weighed a thousand, papa?" David asked.

"I'm sure of it," Thomas Hudson answered. "I've never seen a bigger fish, either broadbill or marlin, ever."

The sun had gone down and the boat was driving through the calm sea, the boat alive with the engines, pushing fast through the same water they had moved so slowly through for all those hours.

Andrew was sitting on the edge of the wide bunk now, too.

"Hello, horseman," David said to him.

"If you'd have caught him," Andrew said, "you'd have been probably the most famous young boy in the world."

"I don't want to be famous," David said. "You can be famous."

"We'd have been famous as your brothers," Andrew said. "I mean really."

"I'd have been famous as your friend," Roger told him.

"I'd have been famous because I steered," Thomas Hudson said. "And Eddy because he gaffed him."

"Eddy ought to be famous anyway," Andrew said. "Tommy would be famous because he brought so many drinks. All through the terrific battle Tommy kept them supplied."

"What about the fish? Wouldn't he be famous?" David asked. He was all right now. Or, at least, he was talking all right.

"He'd be the most famous of all," Andrew said. "He'd be immortal."

"I hope nothing happened to him," David said. "I hope he's all right."

"I know he's all right," Roger told him. "The way he was hooked and the way he fought I know he was all right."

"I'll tell you sometime how it was," David said.

"Tell now," Andy urged him.

"I'm tired now and besides it sounds crazy."

"Tell now. Tell a little bit," Andrew said.

"I don't know whether I better. Should I, papa?"

"Go ahead," Thomas Hudson said.

"Well," David said with his eyes tight shut. "In the worst parts, when I was the tiredest I couldn't tell which was him and which was me."

"I understand," Roger said.

"Then I began to love him more than anything on earth."

"You mean really love him?" Andrew asked.

"Yeah. Really love him."

"Gee," said Andrew. "I can't understand that."

"I loved him so much when I saw him coming up that I couldn't stand it," David said, his eyes still shut. "All I wanted was to see him closer."

"I know," Roger said.

"Now I don't give a shit I lost him," David said. "I don't care about records. I just thought I did. I'm glad that he's all right and that I'm all right. We aren't enemies."

"I'm glad you told us," Thomas Hudson said.

"Thank you very much, Mr. Davis, for what you said when I first lost him," David said with his eyes still shut.

Thomas Hudson never knew what it was that Roger had said to him.

from *The Old Man and the Sea*

I could just drift, he thought, and sleep and put a bight of line around my toe to wake me. But today is eighty-five days and I should fish the day well.

Just then, watching his lines, he saw one of the projecting green sticks dip sharply.

"Yes," he said. "Yes," and shipped his oars without bumping the boat. He reached out for the line and held it softly between the thumb and forefinger of his right hand. He felt no strain nor weight and he held the line lightly. Then it came again. This time it was a tentative pull, not solid nor heavy, and he knew exactly what it was. One hundred fathoms down a marlin was eating the sardines that covered the point and the shank of the hook where the hand-forged hook projected from the head of the small tuna.

The old man held the line delicately and softly, with his left hand, unleashed it from the stick. Now he could let it run through his fingers without the fish feeling any tension.

This far out, he must be huge in this month, he thought. Eat them, fish. Eat them. Please eat them. How fresh they are and you down there six hundred feet in that cold water in the dark. Make another turn in the dark and come back and at them.

He felt the light delicate pulling and then a harder pull when a sardine's head must have been more difficult to break from the hook. Then there was nothing.

"Come on," the old man said aloud. "Make another turn. Just smell them. Aren't they lovely? Eat them good now and then there is the tuna. Hard and cold and lovely. Don't be shy, fish. Eat them."

He waited with the line between his thumb and his finger, watching it and the other lines at the same time for the fish might have swum up or down. Then came the same delicate pulling touch again.

"He'll take it," the old man said aloud. "God help him to take it."

He did not take it though. He was gone and the old man felt nothing.

"He can't have gone," he said. "Christ knows he can't have gone. He's making a turn. Maybe he has been hooked before and he remembers something of it."

Then he felt the gentle touch on the line and he was happy.

"It was only his turn," he said. "He'll take it."

He was happy feeling the gentle pulling and then he felt something hard and unbelievably heavy. It was the weight of the fish and he let the line slip down, down, down, unrolling off the first of the two reserve coils. As it went down, slipping lightly through the old man's fingers, he still could feel the great weight, though the pressure of his thumb and finger were almost imperceptible.

"What a fish," he said. "He has it sideways in his mouth now and he is moving off with it."

Then he will turn and swallow it, he thought. He did not say that because he knew that if you said a good thing it might not happen. He knew what a huge fish this was and he thought of him moving away in the darkness with the tuna held crosswise in his mouth. At that moment he felt him stop moving but the weight was still there. Then the weight increased and he gave more line. He tightened the pressure of his thumb and finger for a moment and the weight increased and was going straight down.

"He's taken it," he said. "Now I'll let him eat it well."

He let the line slip through his fingers while he reached down with his left hand and made fast the free end of the two reserve coils to the loop of the two reserve coils of the next line. Now he was ready. He had three forty-fathom coils of line in reserve now, as well as the coil he was using.

"Eat it a little more," he said. "Eat it well."

Eat it so that the point of the hook goes into your heart and kills you, he thought. Come up easy and let me put the harpoon into you. All right. Are you ready? Have you been long enough at table?

"Now!" he said aloud and stuck hard with both hands, gained a yard of line and then struck again and again, swinging with each arm alternately on the cord with all the strength of his arms and the pivoted weight of his body.

Nothing happened. The fish just moved away slowly and the old man could not raise him an inch. His line was strong and made for heavy fish and he felt it against his back until it was so taut that beads of water were jumping from it. Then it began to make a slow hissing sound in the water and he still held it, bracing himself against the thwart and leaning back against the pull. The boat began to move slowly off toward the north-west.

The fish moved steadily and they travelled slowly on the calm water. The other baits were still in the water but there was nothing to be done.

"I wish I had the boy," the old man said aloud. "I'm being towed by a fish and I'm the towing bitt. I could make the line fast. But then he could break it. I must hold him all I can and give him line when he must have it. Thank God he is travelling and not going down."

What I will do if he decides to go down, I don't know. What I'll do if he sounds and dies I don't know. But I'll do something. There are plenty of things I can do.

He held the line against his back and watched its slant in the water and the skiff moving steadily to the north-west.

This will kill him, the old man thought. He can't do this forever. But four hours later the fish was still swimming steadily out to sea, towing the skiff, and the old man was still braced solidly with the line across his back.

"It was noon when I hooked him," he said. "And I have never seen him."

He had pushed his straw hat hard down on his head before he hooked the fish and it was cutting his forehead. He was thirsty too and he got down on his knees and, being careful not to jerk on the line, moved as far into the bow as he could get and reached the water bottle with one hand. He opened it and drank a little. Then he rested against the bow. He rested sitting on the un-stepped mast and sail and tried not to think but only to endure.

Then he looked behind him and saw that no land was visible. That makes no difference, he thought. I can always come in on the glow from Havana. There are two more hours before the sun sets and maybe he will come up before that. If he doesn't maybe he will come up with the moon. If he does not do that maybe he will come up with the sunrise. I have no cramps and I feel strong. It is he that has the hook in his mouth. But what a fish to pull like that. He must have his mouth shut tight on the wire. I wish I could see him. I wish I could see him only once to know what I have against me.

The fish never changed his course nor his direction all that night as far as the man could tell from watching the stars. It was cold after the sun went down and the old man's sweat dried cold on his back and his arms and his old legs. During the day he had taken the sack that covered the bait box and spread it in the sun to dry. After the sun went down he tied it around his neck so that it hung down over his back and he cautiously worked it down under the line that was across his shoulders now. The sack cushioned the line and he had found a way of leaning forward against the bow so that he was almost comfortable. The position actually was only some-what less intolerable, but he thought of it as almost comfortable.

I can do nothing with him and he can do nothing with me, he thought. Not as long as he keeps this up.

Once he stood up and urinated over the side of the skiff and looked at the stars and checked his course. The line showed like a phosphorescent streak in the water straight out from his shoulders. They were moving more slowly now and the glow of Havana was not so strong, so that he knew the current must be carrying them to the eastward. If I lose the glare of Havana we must be going more to the eastward, he thought. For if the fish's course held true I must see it for many more hours. I wonder how the baseball came out in the grand leagues today, he thought. It would be wonderful to do this with a radio. Then he thought, think of it always. Think of what you are doing. You must do nothing stupid.

Then he said aloud, "I wish I had the boy. To help me and to see this."

No one should be alone in their old age, he thought. But it is unavoidable. I must remember to eat the tuna before he spoils in order to keep strong. Remember, no matter how little you want to, that you must eat him in the morning. Remember, he said to himself.

During the night two porpoises came around the boat and he could hear them rolling and blowing. He could tell the difference between the blowing noise the male made and the sighing blow of the female.

"They are good," he said. "They play and make jokes and love one another. They are our brothers like the flying fish."

Then he began to play the great fish that he had hooked. He is wonderful and strange and who knows how old he is, he thought. Never have I had such a strong fish nor one who acted so strangely. Perhaps he is too wise to jump. He could ruin me by jumping or by a wild rush. But perhaps he has been hooked many times before and he knows that this is how he should make his fight. He cannot know that it is only one man against him, nor that it is an old man.

But what a great fish he is and what will he bring in the market if the flesh is good. He took the bait like a male and he pulls like a male and his fight has no panic in it. I wonder if he has any plans or if he is just as desperate as I am?

He remembered the time he had hooked one of a pair of marlin. The male fish always let the female fish feed first and the hooked fish, the female, made a wild, panic-stricken, despairing fight that soon exhausted her, and all the time the male had stayed with her, crossing the line and circling with her on the surface. He had stayed so close that the old man was afraid he would cut the line with his tail which was sharp as a scythe and almost of that size and shape. When the old man had gaffed her and clubbed her, holding the rapier bill with its sandpaper edge and clubbing her across the top of her head until her colour turned to a colour almost like the backing of mirrors, and then, with the boy's aid, hoisted her aboard, the male fish had stayed by the side of the boat. Then, while the old man was clearing the lines and preparing the harpoon, the male fish jumped high into the air beside the boat to see where the female was and then went down deep, his lavender wings, that were his pectoral fins, spread wide and all his wide lavender stripes showing. He was beautiful, the old man remembered, and he had stayed.

That was the saddest thing I ever saw with them, the old man thought. The boy was sad too and we begged her pardon and butchered her promptly

"I wish the boy was here," he said aloud and settled himself against the rounded planks of the bow and felt the strength of the great fish through the line he held across his shoulders moving steadily toward whatever he had chosen.

When once, through my treachery, it had been necessary to him to make a choice, the old man thought.

His choice had been to stay in the deep dark water far out beyond all snares and traps and treacheries. My choice was to go there to find him beyond all people. Beyond all people in the world. Now we are alone together and have been since noon. And no one to help either one of us.

Perhaps I should not have been a fisherman, he thought. But that was the thing that I was born for. I must surely remember to eat the tuna after it gets light.

Some time before daylight something took one of the baits that were behind him. He heard the stick break and the line begin to rush out over the gunwale of the skiff. In the darkness he loosened his sheath knife and taking all the strain of the fish on his left shoulder he leaned back and cut the line against the wood of the gunwale. Then he cut the other line closest to him and in the dark made the loose ends of the reserve coils fast. He worked skillfully with the one hand and put his foot on the coils to hold them as he drew his knots tight. Now he had six reserve coils of line. There were two from each bait he had severed and the two from the bait the fish had taken and they were all connected.

After it is light, he thought, I will work back to the forty-fathom bait and cut it away too and link up the reserve coils. I will have lost two hundred fathoms of good Catalan *cardel* and the hooks and leaders. That can be replaced. But who replaces this fish if I hook some fish and it cuts him off? I don't know what that fish was that took the bait just now. It could have been a marlin or a broadbill or a shark. I never felt him. I had to get rid of him too fast.

Aloud he said, "I wish I had the boy."

But you haven't got the boy, he thought. You have only yourself and you had better work back to the last line now, in the dark or not in the dark, and cut it away and hook up the two reserve coils.

So he did it. It was difficult in the dark and once the fish made a surge that pulled him down on his face and made a cut below his eye. The blood ran down his cheek a little way. But it coagulated and dried before it reached his chin and he worked his way back to the bow and rested against the wood. He adjusted the sack and carefully worked the line so that it came across a new part of his shoulders and, holding it anchored with his shoulders, he carefully felt the pull of the fish and then felt with his hand the progress of the skiff through the water.

I wonder what he made that lurch for, he thought. The wire must have slipped on the great hill of his back. Certainly his back cannot feel as badly as mine does. But he cannot pull this skiff forever, no matter how great he is. Now everything is cleared away that might make trouble and I have a big reserve of line; all that a man can ask.

"Fish," he said softly, aloud, "I'll stay with you until I am dead."

He'll stay with me too, I suppose, the old man thought and he waited for it to be light. It was cold now in the time before daylight and he pushed against the wood to be warm. I can do it as long as he can, he thought. And in the first light the line extended out and down into the water. The boat moved steadily and when the first edge of the sun rose it was on the old man's right shoulder.

"He's headed north," the old man said. The current will have set us far to the eastward, he thought. I wish he would turn with the current. That would show that he was tiring.

When the sun had risen further the old man realized that the fish was not tiring. There was only one favorable sign. The slant of the line showed he was swimming at a lesser depth. That did not necessarily mean that he would jump. But he might.

"God let him jump," the old man said. "I have enough line to handle him."

Maybe if I can increase the tension just a little it will hurt him and he will jump, he thought. Now that it is daylight let him jump so that he'll fill the sacks along his backbone with air and then he cannot go deep to die.

He tried to increase the tension, but the line had been taut up to the very edge of the breaking point since he had hooked the fish and he felt the harshness as he leaned back to pull and knew he could put no more strain on it. I must not jerk it ever, he thought. Each jerk widens the cut the hook makes and then when he does jump he might throw it. Anyway I feel better with the sun and for once I do not have to look into it.

There was yellow weed on the line but the old man knew that only made an added drag and he was pleased. It was the yellow Gulf weed that had made so much phosphorescence in the night.

"Fish," he said, "I love you and respect you very much. But I will kill you dead before this day ends."

Let us hope so, he thought.

A small bird came toward the skiff from the north. He was a warbler and flying very low over the water. The old man could see that he was very tired.

The bird made the stern of the boat and rested there. Then he flew around the old man's head and rested on the line where he was more comfortable.

"How old are you?" the old man asked the bird. "Is this your first trip?"

The bird looked at him when he spoke. He was too tired even to examine the line and he teetered on it as his delicate feet gripped it fast.

"It's steady," the old man told him. "It's too steady. You shouldn't be that tired after a windless night. What are birds coming to?"

The hawks, he thought, that come out to sea to meet them. But he said nothing of this to the bird who could not understand him anyway and who would learn about the hawks soon enough.

"Take a good rest, small bird," he said. "Then go in and take your chance like any man or bird or fish."

It encouraged him to talk because his back had stiffened in the night and it hurt truly now.

"Stay at my house if you like, bird," he said. "I am sorry I cannot hoist the sail and take you in with the small breeze that is rising. But I am with a friend."

Just then the fish gave a sudden lurch that pulled the old man down onto the bow and would have pulled him overboard if he had not braced himself and given some line.

The bird had flown up when the line jerked and the old man had not even seen him go. He felt the line carefully with his right hand and noticed his hand was bleeding.

"Something hurt him then," he said aloud and pulled back on the line to see if he could turn the fish. But when he was touching the breaking point he held steady and settled back against the strain of the line.

"You're feeling it now, fish," he said. "And so, God knows, am I."

He looked around for the bird now because he would have liked him for company. The bird was gone.

You did not stay long, the man thought. But it is rougher where you are going until you make the shore. How did I let the fish cut me with that one quick pull he made? I must be getting very stupid. Or perhaps I was looking at the small bird and thinking of him. Now I will pay attention to my work and then I must eat the tuna so that I will not have a failure of strength.

"I wish the boy were here and that I had some salt," he said aloud.

Shifting the weight of the line to his left shoulder and kneeling carefully he washed his hand in the ocean and held it there, submerged, for more than a minute watching the blood trail away and the steady movement of the water against his hand as the boat moved.

"He has slowed much," he said.

The old man would have liked to keep his hand in the salt water longer but he was afraid of another sudden lurch by the fish and he stood up and braced himself and held his hand up against the sun. It was only a line burn that had cut his flesh. But it was in the working part of his hand. He knew he would need his hands before this was over and he did not like to be cut before it started.

"Now," he said, when his hand had dried, "I must eat the small tuna. I can reach him with the gaff and eat him here in comfort."

He knelt down and found the tuna under the stern with the gaff and drew it toward him keeping it clear of the coiled lines.

Holding the line with his left shoulder again, and bracing on his left hand and arm, he took the tuna off the gaff hook and put the gaff back in place. He put one knee on the fish and cut strips of dark red meat longitudinally from the back of the head to the tail. They were wedge-shaped strips and he cut them from next to the back bone down to the edge of the belly. When he had cut six strips he spread them out on the wood of the bow, wiped his knife on his trousers, and lifted the carcass of the bonito by the tail and dropped it overboard.

"I don't think I can eat an entire one," he said and drew his knife across one of the strips. He could feel the steady hard pull of the line and his left hand was cramped. It drew up tight on the heavy cord and he looked at it in disgust.

"What kind of a hand is that," he said. "Cramp then if you want. Make yourself into a claw. It will do you no good."

Come on, he thought and looked down into the dark water at the slant of the line. Eat it now and it will strengthen the hand. It is not the hand's fault and you have been many hours with the fish. But you can stay with him forever. Eat the bonito now.

He picked up a piece and put it in his mouth and chewed it slowly. It was not unpleasant.

Chew it well, he thought, and get all the juices. It would not be bad to eat with a little lime or with lemon or with salt.

"How do you feel, hand?" he asked the cramped hand that was almost as stiff as rigor mortis. "I'll eat some more for you."

He ate the other part of the piece that he had cut in two. He chewed it carefully and then spat out the skin.

"How does it go, hand? Or is it too early to know?"

He took another full piece and chewed it.

"It is a strong full-blooded fish," he thought. "I was lucky to get him instead of dolphin. Dolphin is too sweet. This is hardly sweet at all and all the strength is still in it."

There is no sense in being anything but practical though, he thought. I wish I had some salt. And I do not know whether the sun will rot or dry what is left, so I had better eat it all although I am not hungry. The fish is calm and steady. I will eat it all and then I will be ready.

"Be patient, hand," he said. "I do this for you."

I wish I could feed the fish, he thought. He is my brother. But I must kill him and keep strong to do it. Slowly and conscientiously he ate all of the wedge-shaped strips of fish.

He straightened up, wiping his hand on his trousers.

"Now," he said. "You can let the cord go, hand, and I will handle him with the right arm alone until you stop that nonsense." He put his left foot on the heavy line that the left hand had held and lay back against the pull against his back.

"God help me to have the cramp go," he said. "Because I do not know what the fish is going to do."

But he seems calm, he thought, and following his plan. But what is his plan, he thought. And what is mine? Mine I must improvise to his because of his great size. If he will jump I can kill him. But he stays down forever. Then I will stay down with him forever.

He rubbed the cramped hand against his trousers and tried to gentle the fingers. But it would not open. Maybe it will open with the sun, he thought. Maybe it will open when the strong raw tuna is digested. If I have to have it, I will open it, cost whatever it costs. But I do not want to open it now by force. Let it open by itself and come back of its own accord. After all I abused it much in the night when it was necessary to free and untie the various lines.

He looked across the sea and knew how alone he was now. But he could see the prisms in the deep dark water and the line stretching ahead and the strange undulation of the calm. The clouds were building up now for the trade wind and he looked ahead and saw a flight of wild ducks etching themselves against the sky over the water, then blurring, then etching again and he knew no man was ever alone on the sea.

He thought of how some men feared being out of sight of land in a small boat and knew they were right in the months of sudden bad weather. But now they were in hurricane months and, when there are no hurricanes, the weather of hurricane months is the best of all the year.

If there is a hurricane you always see the signs of it in the sky for days ahead, if you are at sea. They do not see it ashore because they do not know what to look for, he thought. The land must make a difference too, in the shape of the clouds. But we have no hurricane coming now.

He looked at the sky and saw the white cumulus built like friendly piles of ice cream and high above were the thin feathers of the cirrus against the high September sky.

"Light *brisa*," he said. "Better weather for me than for you, fish."

His left hand was still cramped, but he was unknotting it slowly.

I hate a cramp, he thought. It is a treachery of one's own body. It is humiliating before others to have a diarrhoea from ptomaine poisoning or to vomit from it. But a cramp, he thought of it as a *calambre*, humiliates oneself especially when one is alone.

If the boy were here he could rub it for me and loosen it down from the forearm, he thought. But it will loosen up.

Then, with his right hand he felt the difference in the pull of the line before he saw the slant change in the water. Then, as he leaned against the line and slapped his left hand hard and fast against his thigh he saw the line slanting slowly upward.

"He's coming up," he said. "Come on hand. Please come on."

The line rose slowly and steadily and then the surface of the ocean bulged ahead of the boat and the fish came out. He came out unendingly and water poured from his sides. He was bright in the sun and his head and back were dark purple and in the sun the stripes on his sides showed wide and a light lavender. His sword was as long as a baseball bat and tapered like a rapier and he rose his full length from the water and then re-entered it, smoothly, like a diver and the old man saw the great scythe-blade of his tail go under and the line commenced to race out.

215

"He is two feet longer than the skiff," the old man said. The line was going out fast but steadily and the fish was not panicked. The old man was trying with both hands to keep the line just inside of breaking strength. He knew that if he could not slow the fish with a steady pressure the fish could take out all the line and break it.

He is a great fish and I must convince him, he thought. I must never let him learn his strength nor what he could do if he made his run. If I were him I would put in everything now and go until something broke. But, thank God, they are not as intelligent as we who kill them; although they are more noble and more able.

The old man had seen many great fish. He had seen many that weighed more than a thousand pounds and he had caught two of that size in his life, but never alone. Now alone, and out of sight of land, he was fast to the biggest fish that he had ever seen and bigger than he had ever heard of, and his left hand was still as tight as the gripped claws of an eagle.

It will uncramp though, he thought. Surely it will uncramp to help my right hand. There are three things that are brothers: the fish and my two hands. It must uncramp. It is unworthy of it to be cramped. The fish had slowed again and was going at his usual pace.

I wonder why he jumped, the old man thought. He jumped almost as though to show me how big he was. I know now, anyway, he thought. I wish I could show him what sort of man I am. But then he would see the cramped hand. Let him think I am more man than I am and I will be so. I wish I was the fish, he thought, with everything he has against only my will and my intelligence.

He settled comfortably against the wood and took his suffering as it came and the fish swam steadily and the boat moved slowly through the dark water. There was a small sea rising with the wind coming up from the east and at noon the old man's left hand was uncramped.

"Bad news for you, fish," he said and shifted the line over the sacks that covered his shoulders.

He was comfortable but suffering, although he did not admit the suffering at all.

"I am not religious," he said. "But I will say ten Our Fathers and ten Hail Marys that I should catch this fish, and I promise to make a pilgrimage to the Virgin of Cobre if I catch him. That is a promise."

He commenced to say his prayers mechanically. Sometimes he would be so tired that he could not remember the prayer and then he would say them fast so that they would come automatically. Hail Marys are easier to say than Our Fathers, he thought.

"Hail Mary full of Grace the Lord is with thee. Blessed art thou among women and blessed is the fruit of thy womb, Jesus. Holy Mary, Mother of God, pray for us sinners now and at the hour of our death. Amen." Then he added, "Blessed Virgin, pray for the death of this fish. Wonderful though he is."

With his prayers said, and feeling much better, but suffering exactly as much, and perhaps a little more, he leaned against the wood of the bow and began, mechanically, to work the fingers of his left hand.

The sun was hot now although the breeze was rising gently.

"I had better re-bait that little line out over the stern," he said. "If the fish decides to stay another night I will need to eat again and the water is low in the bottle. I don't think I can get anything but a dolphin here. But if I eat him fresh enough he won't be bad. I wish a flying fish would come on board tonight. But I have no light to attract them. A flying fish is excellent to eat raw and I would not have to cut him up. I must have all my strength now. Christ, I did not know he was so big."

"I'll kill him though," he said. "In all his greatness and his glory."

Although it is unjust, he thought. But I will show him what a man can do and what a man endures.

"I told the boy I was a strange old man," he said. "Now is when I must prove it."

The thousand times that he had proved it meant nothing. Now he was proving it again. Each time was a new time and he never thought about the past when he was doing it.

I wish he'd sleep and I could sleep and dream about the lions, he thought. Why are the lions the main thing that is left? Don't think, old man, he said to himself. Rest gently now against the wood and think of nothing. He is working. Work as little as you can.

It was getting into the afternoon and the boat still moved slowly and steadily. But there was an added drag now from the easterly breeze and the old man rode gently with the small sea and the hurt of the cord across his back came to him easily and smoothly.

Once in the afternoon the line started to rise again. But the fish only continued to swim at a slightly higher level. The sun was on the old man's left arm and shoulder and on his back. So he knew the fish had turned east of north.

Now that he had seen him once, he could picture the fish swimming in the water with his purple pectoral fins set wide as wings and the great erect tail slicing through the dark. I wonder how much he sees at that depth, the old man thought. His eye is huge and a horse, with much less eye, can see in the dark. Once I could see quite well in the dark. Not in the absolute dark. But almost as a cat sees.

The sun and his steady movement of his fingers had uncramped his left hand now completely and he began to shift more of the strain to it and he shrugged the muscles of his back to shift the hurt of the cord a little.

"If you're not tired, fish," he said aloud, "you must be very strange."

He felt very tired now and he knew the night would come soon and he tried to think of other things. He thought of the Big Leagues, to him they were the *Gran Ligas*, and he knew that the Yankees of New York were playing the *Tigres* of Detroit.

This is the second day now that I do not know the result of the *juegos*, he thought. But I must have confidence and I must be worthy of the great DiMaggio who does all things perfectly even with the pain of the bone spur in his heel. What is a bone spur? he asked himself. *Un espuela de hueso.* We do not have them. Can it be as painful as the spur of a fighting cock in one's heel? I do not think I could endure that or the loss of the eye and of both eyes and continue to fight as the fighting cocks do. Man is not much beside the great birds and beasts. Still I would rather be that beast down there in the darkness of the sea.

"Unless sharks come," he said aloud. "If sharks come, God pity him and me."

Do you believe the great DiMaggio would stay with a fish as long as I will stay with this one? he thought. I am sure he would and more since he is young and strong. Also his father was a fisherman. But would the bone spur hurt him too much?

"I do not know," he said aloud. "I never had a bone spur."

As the sun set he remembered, to give himself more confidence, the time in the tavern at Casablanca when he had played the hand game with the great negro from Cienfuegos who was the strongest man on the docks. They had gone one day and one night with their elbows on a chalk line on the table and their forearms straight up and their hands gripped tight. Each one was trying to force the other's hand down onto the table. There was much betting and people went in and out of the room under the kerosene lights and he had looked at the arm and hand of the negro and at the negro's face. They changed the referees every four hours after the first eight so that the referees could sleep. Blood came out from under the fingernails of both his and the negro's hands and they looked each other in the eye and at their hands and forearms and the bettors went in and out of the room and sat on high chairs against the wall and watched. The walls were painted bright blue and were of wood and the lamps threw their shadows against them. The negro's shadow was huge and it moved on the wall as the breeze moved the lamps.

The odds would change back and forth all night and they fed the negro rum and lighted cigarettes for him. Then the negro, after the rum, would try for a tremendous effort and once he had the old man, who was not an old man then but was Santiago *El Campeón*, nearly three inches off balance. But the old man had raised his hand up to dead even again. He was sure then that he had the negro, who was a fine man and a great athlete, beaten. And at daylight when the bettors were asking that it be called a draw and the referee was shaking his head, he had unleashed his effort and forced the hand of the negro down and down until it rested on the wood. The match had started on a Sunday morning and ended on a Monday morning. Many of the bettors had asked for a draw because they had to go to work on the docks loading sacks of sugar or at the Havana Coal Company. Otherwise everyone would have wanted it to go to a finish. But he had finished it anyway and before anyone had to go to work.

For a long time after that everyone had called him The Champion and there had been a return match in the spring. But not much money was bet and he had won it quite easily since he had broken the confidence of the negro from Cienfuegos in the first match. After that he had a few matches and then no more. He decided that he could beat anyone if he wanted to badly enough and he decided that it was bad for his right hand for fishing. He had tried a few practice matches with his left hand. But his left hand had always been a traitor and would not do what he called on it to do and he did not trust it.

The sun will bake it out well now, he thought. It should not cramp on me again unless it gets too cold in the night. I wonder what this night will bring.

An airplane passed overhead on its course to Miami and he watched its shadow scaring up the schools of flying fish.

"With so much flying fish there should be dolphin," he said, and leaned back on the line to see if it was possible to gain any on his fish. But he could not and it stayed at the hardness and waterdrop shivering that preceded breaking. The boat moved ahead slowly and he watched the airplane until he could no longer see it.

It must be very strange in an airplane, he thought. I wonder what the sea looks like from that height? They should be able to see the fish well if they do not fly too high. I would like to fly very slowly at two hundred fathoms high and see the fish from above. In the turtle boats I was in the cross-trees of the mast-head and even at that height I saw much. The dolphin look greener from there and you can see their stripes and their purple spots and you can see all of the schools they swim. Why is it that all the fast-moving fish of the dark current have purple backs and usually purple stripes or spots? The dolphin looks green of course because he is really golden. But when he comes to feed, truly hungry, purple stripes show on his sides as on a marlin. Can it be anger, or the greater speed he makes that brings them out?

Just before it was dark, as they passed a great island of Sargasso weed that heaved and swung in the light sea as though the ocean were making love with something under a yellow blanket, his small line was taken by a dolphin. He saw it first when it jumped in the air, true gold in the last of the sun and bending and flapping wildly in the air. It jumped again and again in the acrobatics of its fear and he worked his way back to the stern and crouching and holding the big line with his right hand and arm, he pulled the dolphin in with his left hand, step-ping on the gained line each time with his bare left foot. When the fish was at the stern, plunging and cutting from side to side in despera-tion, the old man leaned over the stern and lifted the burnished gold fish with its purple spots over the stern. Its jaws were working convul-sively in quick bites against the hook and it pounded the bottom of the skiff with its long flat body, its tail and its head until he clubbed it across the shining golden head until it shivered and was still.

The old man unhooked the fish, re-baited the line with another sardine and tossed it over. Then he worked his way slowly back to the bow. He washed his left hand and wiped it on his trousers. Then he shifted the heavy line from his right hand to his left and washed his right hand in the sea while he watched the sun go into the ocean and the slant of the big cord.

"He hasn't changed at all," he said. But watching the movement of the water against his hand he noted that it was perceptibly slower.

"I'll lash the two oars together across the stern and that will slow him in the night," he said. "He's good for the night and so am I."

It would be better to gut the dolphin a little later to save the blood in the meat, he thought. I can do that a little later and lash the oars to make a drag at the same time. I had better keep the fish quiet now and not disturb him too much at sunset. The setting of the sun is a difficult time for all fish.

He let his hand dry in the air then grasped the line with it and eased himself as much as he could and allowed himself to be pulled forward against the wood so that the boat took the strain as much, or more, than he did.

I'm learning how to do it, he thought. This part of it anyway. Then too, remember he hasn't eaten since he took the bait and he is huge and needs much food. I have eaten the whole bonito. Tomorrow I will eat the dolphin. He called it *dorado*. Perhaps I should eat some of it when I clean it. It will be harder to eat than the bonito. But, then, nothing is easy.

"How do you feel, fish?" he asked aloud. "I feel good and my left hand is better and I have food for a night and a day. Pull the boat, fish."

He did not truly feel good because the pain from the cord across his back had almost passed pain and gone into a dullness that he mistrusted. But I have had worse things than that, he thought. My hand is only cut a little and the cramp is gone from the other. My legs are all right. Also now I have gained on him in the question of sustenance.

It was dark now as it becomes dark quickly after the sun sets in September. He lay against the worn wood of the bow and rested all that he could. The first stars were out. He did not know the name of Rigel but he saw it and knew soon they would all be out and he would have all his distant friends.

"The fish is my friend too," he said aloud. "I have never seen or heard of such a fish. But I must kill him. I am glad we do not have to try to kill the stars."

Imagine if each day a man must try to kill the moon, he thought. The moon runs away. But imagine if a man each day should have to try to kill the sun? We were born lucky, he thought.

Then he was sorry for the great fish that had nothing to eat and his determination to kill him never relaxed in his sorrow for him. How many people will he feed, he thought. But are they worthy to eat him? No, of course not. There is no one worthy of eating him from the manner of his behaviour and his great dignity.

I do not understand these things, he thought. But it is good that we do not have to try to kill the sun or the moon or the stars. It is enough to live on the sea and kill our true brothers.

Now, he thought, I must think about the drag. It has its perils and its merits. I may lose so much line that I will lose him, if he makes his effort and the drag made by the oars is in place and the boat loses all her lightness. Her lightness prolongs both our suffering but it is my safety since he has great speed that he has never yet employed. No matter what passes I must gut the dolphin so he does not spoil and eat some of him to be strong.

Now I will rest an hour more and feel that he is solid and steady before I move back to the stern to do the work and make the decision. In the meantime I can see how he acts and if he shows any changes. The oars are a good trick; but it has reached the time to play for safety. He is much fish still and I saw that the hook was in the corner of his mouth and he has kept his mouth tight shut. The punishment of the hook is nothing. The punishment of hunger, and that he is against something that he does not comprehend, is everything. Rest now, old man, and let him work until your next duty comes.

He rested for what he believed to be two hours. The moon did not rise now until late and he had no way of judging the time. Nor was he really resting except comparatively. He was still bearing the pull of the fish across his shoulders but he placed his left hand on the gunwale of the bow and confided more and more of the resistance to the fish to the skiff itself.

How simple it would be if I could make the line fast, he thought. But with one small lurch he could break it. I must cushion the pull of the line with my body and at all times be ready to give line with both hands.

"But you have not slept yet, old man," he said aloud. "It is half a day and a night and now another day and you have not slept. You must devise a way so that you sleep a little if he is quiet and steady. If you do not sleep you might become unclear in the head."

I'm clear enough in the head, he thought. Too clear. I am as clear as the stars that are my brothers. Still I must sleep. They sleep and the moon and the sun sleep and even the ocean sleeps sometimes on certain days when there is no current and a flat calm.

But remember to sleep, he thought. Make yourself do it and devise some simple and sure way about the lines. Now go back and prepare the dolphin. It is too dangerous to rig the oars as a drag if you must sleep.

I could go without sleeping, he told himself. But it would be too dangerous.

He started to work his way back to the stern on his hands and knees, being careful not to jerk against the fish. He may be half asleep himself, he thought. But I do not want him to rest. He must pull until he dies.

Back in the stern he turned so that his left hand held the strain of the line across his shoulders and drew his knife from its sheath with his right hand. The stars were bright now and he saw the dolphin clearly and he pushed the blade of his knife into his head and drew him out from under the stern. He put one of his feet on the fish and slit him quickly from the vent up to the tip of his lower jaw. Then he put his knife down and gutted him with his right hand, scooping him clean and pulling the gills clear. He felt the maw heavy and slippery in his hands and he slit it open. There were two flying fish inside. They were fresh and hard and he laid them side by side and dropped the guts and the gills over the stern. They sank leaving a trail of phosphorescence in the water. The dolphin was cold and a leprous gray-white now in the starlight and the old man skinned one side of him while he held his right foot on the fish's head. Then he turned him over and skinned the other side and cut each side off from the head down to the tail.

He slid the carcass overboard and looked to see if there was any swirl in the water. But there was only the light of its slow descent. He turned then and placed the two flying fish inside the two fillets of fish and putting his knife back in its sheath, he worked his way slowly back to the bow. His back was bent with the weight of the line across it and he carried the fish in his right hand.

Back in the bow he laid the two fillets of fish out on the wood with the flying fish beside them. After that he settled the line across his shoulders in a new place and held it again with his left hand resting on the gunwale. Then he leaned over the side and washed the flying fish in the water, noting the speed of the water against his hand. His hand was phosphorescent from skinning the fish and he watched the flow of the water against it. The flow was less strong and as he rubbed the side of his hand against the planking of the skiff, particles of phosphorus floated off and drifted slowly astern.

"He is tiring or he is resting," the old man said. "Now let me get through the eating of this dolphin and get some rest and a little sleep."

Under the stars and with the night colder all the time he ate half of one of the dolphin fillets and one of the flying fish, gutted and with its head cut off.

"What an excellent fish dolphin is to eat cooked," he said. "And what a miserable fish raw. I will never go in a boat again without salt or limes."

If I had brains I would have splashed water on the bow all day and drying, it would have made salt, he thought. But then I did not hook the dolphin until almost sunset. Still it was a lack of preparation. But I have chewed it all well and I am not nauseated.

The sky was clouding over the east and one after another the stars he knew were gone. It looked now as though he were moving into a great canyon of clouds and the wind had dropped.

"There will be bad weather in three or four days," he said. "But not tonight and not tomorrow. Rig now to get some sleep, old man, while the fish is calm and steady."

He held the line tight in his right hand and then pushed his thigh against his right hand as he leaned all his weight against the wood of the bow. Then he passed the line a little lower on his shoulders and braced his left hand on it.

My right hand can hold it as long as it is braced, he thought. If it relaxes in sleep my left hand will wake me as the line goes out. It is hard on the right hand. But he is used to punishment. Even if I sleep twenty minutes or a half an hour it is good. He lay forward cramping himself against the line with all of his body, putting all his weight onto his right hand, and he was asleep.

He did not dream of the lions but instead of a vast school of porpoises that stretched for eight or ten miles and it was in the time of their mating and they would leap high into the air and return into the same hole they had made in the water when they leaped.

Then he dreamed that he was in the village on his bed and there was a norther and he was very cold and his right arm was asleep because his head had rested on it instead of a pillow.

After that he began to dream of the long yellow beach and he saw the first of the lions come down onto it in the early dark and then the other lions came and he rested his chin on the wood of the bows where the ship lay anchored with the evening off-shore breeze and he waited to see if there would be more lions and he was happy.

The moon had been up for a long time but he slept on and the fish pulled on steadily and the boat moved into the tunnel of clouds.

He woke with the jerk of his right fist coming up against his face and the line burning out through his right hand. He had no feeling of his left hand but he braked all he could with his right and the line rushed out. Finally his left hand found the line and he leaned back against the line and now it burned his back and his left hand, and his left hand was taking all the strain and cutting badly. He looked back at the coils of line and they were feeding smoothly. Just then the fish jumped making a great bursting of the ocean and then a heavy fall. Then he jumped again and again and the boat was going fast although line was still racing out and the old man was raising the strain to breaking point and raising it to breaking point again and again. He had been pulled down tight onto the bow and his face was in the cut slice of dolphin and he could not move.

This is what we waited for, he thought. So now let us take it.

Make him pay for the line, he thought. Make him pay for it.

He could not see the fish's jumps but only heard the breaking of the ocean and the heavy splash as he fell. The speed of the line was cutting his hands badly but he had always known this would happen and he tried to keep the cutting across the calloused parts and not let the line slip into the palm nor cut the fingers.

If the boy was here he would wet the coils of line, he thought. Yes. If the boy were here. If the boy were here.

The line went out and out and out but it was slowing now and he was making the fish earn each inch of it. Now he got his head up from the wood and out of the slice of fish that his cheek had crushed. Then he was on his knees and then he rose slowly to his feet. He was ceding line but more slowly all the time. He worked back to where he could feel with his foot the coils of line that he could not see. There was plenty of line still and now the fish had to pull the friction of all that new line through the water.

Yes, he thought. And now he has jumped more than a dozen times and filled the sacks along his back with air and he cannot go down deep to die where I cannot bring him up. He will start circling soon and then I must work on him. I wonder what started him so suddenly? Could it have been hunger that made him desperate, or was he frightened by something in the night? Maybe he suddenly felt fear. But he was such a calm, strong fish and he seemed so fearless and so confident. It is strange.

"You better be fearless and confident yourself, old man," he said. "You're holding him again but you cannot get line. But soon he has to circle."

The old man held him with his left hand and his shoulders now and stooped down and scooped up water in his right hand to get the crushed dolphin flesh off of his face. He was afraid that it might nauseate him and he would vomit and lose his strength. When his face was cleaned he washed his right hand in the water over the side and then let it stay in the salt water while he watched the first light come before the sunrise. He's headed almost east, he thought. That means he is tired and going with the current. Soon he will have to circle. Then our true work begins.

After he judged that his right hand had been in the water long enough he took it out and looked at it.

"It is not bad," he said. "And pain does not matter to a man."

He took hold of the line carefully so that it did not fit into any of the fresh line cuts and shifted his weight so that he could put his left hand into the sea on the other side of the skiff.

"You did not do so badly for something worthless," he said to his left hand. "But there was a moment when I could not find you."

Why was I not born with two good hands? he thought. Perhaps it was my fault in not training that one properly. But God knows he has had enough chances to learn. He did not do so badly in the night, though, and he has only cramped once. If he cramps again let the line cut him off.

When he thought that he knew that he was not being clear-headed and he thought he should chew some more of the dolphin. But I can't, he told himself. It is better to be light-headed than to lose your strength from nausea. And I know I cannot keep it if I eat it since my face was in it. I will keep it for an emergency until it goes bad. But it is too late to try for strength now through nourishment. You're stupid, he told himself. Eat the other flying fish.

It was there, cleaned and ready, and he picked it up with his left hand and ate it chewing the bones carefully and eating all of it down to the tail.

It has more nourishment than almost any fish, he thought. At least the kind of strength that I need. Now I have done what I can, he thought. Let him begin to circle and let the fight come.

The sun was rising for the third time since he had put to sea when the fish started to circle.

He could not see by the slant of the line that the fish was circling. It was too early for that. He just felt a faint slackening of the pressure of the line and he commenced to pull on it gently with his right hand. It tightened, as always, but just when he reached the point where it would break, line began to come in. He slipped his shoulders and head from under the line and began to pull in line steadily and gently. He used both of his hands in a swinging motion and tried to do the pulling as much as he could with his body and his legs. His old legs and shoulders pivoted with the swinging of the pulling.

"It is a very big circle," he said. "But he is circling."

Then the line would not come in any more and he held it until he saw the drops jumping from it in the sun. Then it started out and the old man knelt down and let it go grudgingly back into the dark water.

"He is making the far part of his circle now," he said. I must hold all I can, he thought. The strain will shorten his circle each time. Perhaps in an hour I will see him. Now I must convince him and then I must kill him.

But the fish kept on circling slowly and the old man was wet with sweat and tired deep into his bones two hours later. But the circles were much shorter now and from the way the line slanted he could tell the fish had risen steadily while he swam.

For an hour the old man had been seeing black spots before his eyes and the sweat salted his eyes and salted the cut over his eye and on his forehead. He was not afraid of the black spots. They were normal at the tension that he was pulling on the line. Twice, though, he had felt faint and dizzy and that had worried him.

"I could not fail myself and die on a fish like this," he said. "Now that I have him coming so beautifully, God help me endure. I'll say a hundred Our Fathers and a hundred Hail Marys. But I cannot say them now."

Consider them said, he thought. I'll say them later.

Just then he felt a sudden banging and jerking on the line he held with his two hands. It was sharp and hard-feeling and heavy.

He is hitting the wire leader with his spear, he thought. That was bound to come. He had to do that. It may make him jump though and I would rather he stayed circling now. The jumps were necessary for him to take air. But after that each one can widen the opening of the hook wound and he can throw the hook.

"Don't jump, fish," he said. "Don't jump."

The fish hit the wire several times more and each time he shook his head the old man gave up a little line.

I must hold his pain where it is, he thought. Mine does not matter. I can control mine. But his pain could drive him mad.

After a while the fish stopped beating at the wire and started circling slowly again. The old man was gaining line steadily now. But he felt faint again. He lifted some sea water with his left hand and put it on his head. Then he put more on and rubbed the back of his neck.

"I have no cramps," he said. "He'll be up soon and I can last. You have to last. Don't even speak of it."

He kneeled against the bow and, for a moment, slipped the line over his back again. I'll rest now while he goes out on the circle and then stand up and work on him when he comes in he decided.

It was a great temptation to rest in the bow and let the fish make one circle by himself without recovering any line. But when the strain showed the fish had turned to come toward the boat, the old man rose to his feet and started the pivoting and the weaving pulling that brought in all the line he gained.

I'm tireder than I have ever been, he thought, and now the

trade wind is rising. But that will be good to take him in with. I need that badly.

"I'll rest on the next turn as he goes out," he said. "I feel much better. Then in two or three turns more I will have him."

His straw hat was far on the back of his head and he sank down into the bow with the pull of the line as he felt the fish turn.

You work now, fish, he thought. I'll take you at the turn.

The sea had risen considerably. But it was a fair-weather breeze and he had to have it to get home.

"I'll just steer south and west," he said. "A man is never lost at sea and it is a long island."

It was on the third turn that he saw the fish first.

He saw him first as a dark shadow that took so long to pass under the boat that he could not believe its length.

"No," he said. "He can't be that big."

But he was that big and at the end of this circle he came to the surface only thirty yards away and the man saw his tail out of water. It was higher than a big scythe blade and a very pale lavender above the dark blue water. It raked back and as the fish swam just below the surface the old man could see his huge bulk and the purple stripes that banded him. His dorsal fin was down and his huge pectorals were spread wide.

On this circle the old man could see the fish's eye and the two gray sucking fish that swam around him. Sometimes they attached themselves to him. Sometimes they darted off. Sometimes they would swim easily in his shadow. They were each over three feet long and when they swam fast they lashed their whole bodies like eels.

The old man was sweating now but from something else besides the sun. On each calm placid turn the fish made he was gaining line and he was sure that in two turns more he would have a chance to get the harpoon in.

But I must get him close, close, close, he thought. I mustn't try for the head. I must get the heart.

"Be calm and strong, old man," he said.

On the next circle the fish's back was out but he was a little too far from the boat. On the next circle he was still too far away but he was higher out of water and the old man was sure that by gaining some more line he could have him alongside.

He had rigged his harpoon long before and its coil of light rope was in a round basket and the end was made fast to the bitt in the bow.

The fish was coming in on his circle now calm and beautiful looking and only his great tail moving. The old man pulled on him all that he could to bring him closer. For just a moment the fish turned a little on his side. Then he straightened himself and began another circle.

"I moved him," the old man said, "I moved him then."

He felt faint again now but he held on the great fish all the strain that he could. I moved him, he thought. Maybe this time I can get him over. Pull, hands, he thought. Hold up, legs. Last for me, head. Last for me. You never went. This time I'll pull him over.

But when he put all of his effort on, starting it well out before the fish came alongside and pulling with all his strength, the fish pulled part way over and then righted himself and swam away.

"Fish," the old man said. "Fish, you are going to have to die anyway. Do you have to kill me too?"

That way nothing is accomplished, he thought. His mouth was too dry to speak but he could not reach for the water now. I must get him alongside this time, he thought. I am not good for many more turns. Yes you are, he told himself. You're good forever.

On the next turn, he nearly had him. But again the fish righted himself and swam slowly away.

You are killing me, fish, the old man thought. But you have a right to. Never have I seen a greater, or more beautiful, or a calmer or more noble thing than you, brother. Come on and kill me. I do not care who kills who.

Now you are getting confused in the head, he thought. You

must keep your head clear. Keep your head clear and know how to suffer like a man. Or a fish, he thought.

"Clear up head," he said in a voice he could hardly hear. "Clear up."

Twice more it was the same on the turns.

I do not know, the old man thought. He had been on the point of feeling himself go each time. I do not know. But I will try it once more.

He tried it once more and he felt himself going when he turned the fish. The fish righted himself and swam off again slowly with the great tail weaving in the air.

I'll try it again, the old man promised, although his hands were mushy now and he could only see well in flashes.

He tried it again and it was the same. So he thought, and he felt himself going before he started; I will try it once again.

He took all his pain and what was left of his strength and his long gone pride and he put it against the fish's agony and the fish came over onto his side and swam gently on his side, his bill almost touching the planking of the skiff and started to pass the boat, long, deep, wide, silver and barred with purple and interminable in the water.

The old man dropped the line and put his foot on it and lifted the harpoon as high as he could and drove it down with all his strength, and more strength he had just summoned, into the fish's side just behind the great chest fin that rose high in the air to the altitude of the man's chest. He felt the iron go in and he leaned on it and drove it further and then pushed all his weight after it.

Then the fish came alive, with his death in him, and rose high out of the water showing all his great length and width and all his power and his beauty. He seemed to hang in the air above the old man in the skiff. Then he fell in the water with a crash that sent spray over the old man and over all of the skiff.

The old man felt faint and sick and he could not see well. But he cleared the harpoon line and let it run slowly through his raw hands and, when he could see, he saw the fish was on his back with his silver belly up. The shaft of the harpoon was projecting at an angle from the fish's shoulder and the sea was discolouring with the red of the blood from his heart. First it was dark as a shoal in the blue water that was more than a mile deep. Then it spread like a cloud. The fish was silvery and still and floated with the waves.

The old man looked carefully in the glimpse of vision that he had. Then he took two turns of the harpoon line around the bitt in the bow and laid his head on his hands.

"Keep my head clear," he said against the wood of the bow. "I am a tired old man. But I have killed this fish which is my brother and now I must do the slave work."

Now I must prepare the nooses and the rope to lash him alongside, he thought. Even if we were two and swamped her to load him and bailed her out, this skiff would never hold him. I must prepare everything, then bring him in and lash him well and step the mast and set sail for home.

He started to pull the fish in to have him alongside so that he could pass a line through his gills and out his mouth and make his head fast alongside the bow. I want to see him, he thought, and to touch and to feel him. He is my fortune, he thought. But that is not why I wish to feel him. I think I felt his heart, he thought. When I pushed on the harpoon shaft the second time. Bring him in now and make him fast and get the noose around his tail and another around his middle to bind him to the skiff.

"Get to work, old man," he said. He took a very small drink of the water. "There is very much slave work to be done now that the fight is over."

He looked up at the sky and then out to his fish. He looked at the sun carefully. It is not much more than noon, he thought. And the trade wind is rising. The lines all mean nothing now. The boy and I will splice them when we are home.

"Come on, fish," he sid. But the fish did not come. Instead he lay there wallowing now in the seas and the old man pulled the skiff up onto him.

When he was even with him and had the fish's head against the bow he could not believe his size. But he untied the harpoon rope from the bitt, passed it through the fish's gills and out his jaws, made a turn around his sword then passed the rope through the other gill, made another turn around the bill and knotted the double rope and made it fast to the bitt in the bow. He cut the rope then and went astern to noose the tail. The fish had turned silver from his original purple and silver, and the stripes showed the same pale violet colour as his tail. They were wider than a man's hand with his fingers spread and the fish's eye looked as detached as the mirrors in a periscope or as a saint in a procession.

"It was the only way to kill him," the old man said. He was feeling better since the water and he knew he would not go away and his head was clear. He's over fifteen hundred pounds the way he is, he thought. Maybe much more. If he dresses out two-thirds of that at thirty cents a pound?

"I need a pencil for that," he said. "My head is not that clear. But I think the great DiMaggio would be proud of me today. I had no bone spurs. But the hands and the back hurt truly." I wonder what a bone spur is, he thought. Maybe we have them without knowing of it.

He made the fish fast to bow and stern and to the middle thwart. He was so big it was like lashing a much bigger skiff alongside. He cut a piece of line and tied the fish's lower jaw against his bill so his mouth would not open and they would sail as cleanly as possible. Then he stepped the mast and, with the stick that was his gaff and with his boom rigged, the patched sail drew, the boat began to move, and half lying in the stern he sailed south-west.

He did not need a compass to tell him where south-west was. He only needed the feel of the trade wind and the drawing of the sail. I better put a small line out with a spoon on it and try and get something to eat and drink for the moisture. But he could not find a spoon and his sardines were rotten. So he hooked a patch of yellow Gulf weed with the gaff as they passed and shook it so that the small shrimps that were in it fell onto the planking of the skiff. There were more than a dozen of them and they jumped and kicked like sand fleas. The old man pinched their heads off with his thumb and forefinger and ate them chewing up the shells and the tails. They were very tiny but he knew they were nourishing and they tasted good.

The old man still had two drinks of water in the bottle and he used half of one after he had eaten the shrimps. The skiff was sailing well considering the handicaps and he steered with the tiller under his arm. He could see the fish and he had only to look at his hands and feel his back against the stern to know that this had truly happened and was not a dream. At one time when he was feeling so badly toward the end, he had thought perhaps it was a dream. Then when he had seen the fish come out of the water and hang motionless in the sky before he fell, he was sure there was some great strangeness and he could not believe it. Then he could not see well, although now he saw as well as ever.

Now he knew there was the fish and his hands and back were no dream. The hands cure quickly, he thought. I bled them clean and the salt water will heal them. The dark water of the true gulf is the greatest healer that there is. All I must do is keep the head clear. The hands have done their work and we sail well. With his mouth shut and his tail straight up and down we sail like brothers. Then his head started to become a little unclear and he thought, is he bringing me in or am I bringing him in? If I were towing him behind there would be no question. Nor if the fish were in the skiff, with all dignity gone, there would be no question either. But they were sailing together lashed side by side and the old man thought, let him bring me in if it pleases him. I am only better than him through trickery and he meant me no harm.

They sailed well and the old man soaked his hands in the salt water and tried to keep his head clear. There were high cumulus clouds and enough cirrus above them so that the old man knew the breeze would last all night. The old man looked at the fish constantly to make sure it was true. It was an hour before the first shark hit him.

Selected Bibliography

Works by Ernest Hemingway

There is still an astonishing trove of unpublished writing by Hemingway at the Hemingway Archives at the John F. Kennedy Library in Boston; some of it is about fishing—including hundreds of pages of diary and day-log material, a number of stories and articles in various stages of completion, and some nonfiction (such as an aborted attempt to do a collection of "sportsman's sketches," inspired by Ivan Turgenev).

By-Line: Ernest Hemingway. Selected Articles and Dispatches of Four Decades. William White, ed. New York. Charles Scribner's Sons, 1961.

The Complete Stories of Ernest Hemingway. New York. Charles Scribner's Sons, 1987.

"Cuban Fishing." In *Game Fish of the World.* Brian Vesey, Fitzgerald, and Francesca LaMonte, eds. New York. Harper & Brothers, 1949.

Ernest Hemingway: Selected Letters, 1917–1961. Carlos Baker, ed. New York. Charles Scribner's Sons, 1981.

There are thousands of references to fishing in the published letters. Some speak of the origins and development of works such as "Big Two-Hearted River," *The Old Man and the Sea,* and other important fiction, along with comments on the relationship he found between his love of fishing and his much greater commitment to writing; others speak baldly of his fishing life. Some of the more interesting passages may be found in letters to: Howell Jenkins (7/26/19); Howell Jenkins (9/15/19); William B. Smith Jr. (4/28/21); Gertrude Stein (8/15/24); Howell Jenkins (11/9/24); Robert McAlmon (11/15/24); Dr. C. E. Hemingway (3/20/25); Dr. C. E. Hemingway (8/20/25); Maxwell Perkins (5/31/30); Henry Strater (9/10/30); John Dos Passos (5/30/32); Janet Flanner (4/8/33); Arnold Gingrich (5/24/33); Arnold Gingrich (5/25/33); Maxwell Perkins (7/26/33); Arnold Gingrich (7/15/34); Arnold Gingrich (6/4/35); Maxwell Perkins (7/11/36); Marjorie Kinnan Rawlings (8/16/36); Maxwell Perkins (2/7/39); Thomas Shevlin (4/4/39); Lillian Ross (7/2/48); Harvey Breit (6/21/52); Bernard Berenson (9/13/52); Philip Percival (9/4/55); Alfred Rice (1/24/56); Wallace Meyer (4/2/56); Gianfranco Ivancich (5/25/56); Charles Scribner Jr.

> *The Garden of Eden.* New York. Charles Scribner's Sons, 1986.
>
> Introduction to *Atlantic Game Fishing.* S. Kip Farrington Jr. New York. Kennedy Bros., Inc., 1937.
>
> *Islands in the Stream.* New York. Charles Scribner's Sons, 1970.
>
> "Marlin Off Cuba." In *American Big Game Fishing.* Eugene V. Connett, ed. New York. The Derrydale Press, 1935.
>
> *A Moveable Feast.* New York. Charles Scribner's Sons, 1964.
>
> *The Nick Adams Stories.* New York. Charles Scribner's Sons, 1972.
>
> *The Old Man and the Sea.* New York. Charles Scribner's Sons, 1952.
>
> Preface to *Salt Water Fishing.* Van Campen Heilner. New York. Alfred A. Knopf, 1953.
>
> *The Sun Also Rises.* New York. Charles Scribner's Sons, 1926.

A Very Brief List of Works About Ernest Hemingway

(Especially his life as a fisherman)

Just about everyone and his grandmother has commented on EH—and there are literally hundreds of essays, articles, and books on his fishing life alone. The ones listed below are a few that I found particularly interesting.

Selected Bibliography

Baker, Carlos. *Ernest Hemingway: A Life Story.* New York. Charles Scribner's Sons, 1969. Still the best place to start for fullness and breadth—with much of EH's fishing life given a sensible position. Some material has been discredited or updated.

Baker, Sheridan. "Hemingway's Two-Hearted River." In *Michigan Alumnus Quarterly*, Vol. LXV, No. 14 (February 28, 1959). A superb essay on this story—and the first to identify the river as the Fox.

Brian, Denis. *The True Gen: An Intimate Portrait of Hemingway by Those Who Knew Him.* New York. Grove Press, 1988. Fascinating, often contradictory glimpses of EH from a variety of vantage points.

Farrington, S. Kip, Jr. *Fishing with Hemingway and Glassell.* New York. David McKay Company, 1971. A pedestrian book but with the perspective of one major big-game fisherman observing and commenting on another.

Finney, Ben. *Feet First.* New York. Crown Publishers, 1971. Some anecdotal looks at Hemingway by a close friend.

Gingrich, Arnold. *The Well-Tempered Angler.* New York. Alfred A. Knopf, 1965. The chapter "Horsing Them in with Hemingway" is a pithy and first-hand look at EH as a fisherman by the publisher of *Esquire* magazine—and a passionate fly fisher.

Hemingway, Jack. *Misadventures of a Fly Fisherman.* Dallas. Taylor Publishing, 1986. A very interesting account of the fishing life of EH's oldest son—with excellent insights into his father's methods and proclivities on the water.

Hotchner, A. E. *Papa Hemingway.* New York. Random House, 1966. The popular and enthusiastic memoir of one of EH's most important late friendships.

Johnson, Donald S. "Hemingway: A Trout Fisher's Apprenticeship." In *The American Fly Fisher*, Vol. 15, No. 1 (Summer 1989). This issue also contains "Hike to Walloon Lake: A Diary, June 10–21, 1916," the diary Hemingway kept, with thoughtful commentary by Johnson. This issue of the official publication of the American Museum of Fly Fishing, Manchester, Vermont, is exceptionally valuable. I am not aware of any other publication of the early diary.

Palin, Michael. *Michael Palin's Hemingway Adventure.* New York. St. Martin's Press, 1999. Fun and occasionally very insightful on matters piscatorial.

Reiger, George. *Profiles in Saltwater Angling.* Englewood Cliffs, NJ. Prentice Hall, Inc., 1973. The chapter "The Literary Naturalist" is one of the few works to focus on EH's deep, expert, and abiding interest in natural history as well as sport.

Reynolds, Michael. *Hemingway: The Paris Years*. New York. W. W. Norton & Co., 1989. I'm a bit less persuaded than many others that he is fully inside EH's head, but there's much valuable assimilation of scattered details here on all aspects of EH's life, including his writing about fishing.